Praise for *The Joshua Files*

"A gripping survival story . . . a fantasy of
pyramids, caves and tunnels"
Daily Telegraph

"Fast-paced and exciting, this is one for fans of
Alex Rider and Young Bond"
Bookseller

"A splendid adventure story of UFOs, ancient Mayan
documents and a lost city"
Mail on Sunday

"It's the Mexican and Mayan flavourings that give
Harris's adventure yarn that bit of extra bite as she weaves
a satisfyingly twisty plot around the science fiction
staples of UFOs and time travel"
Financial Times

Also by M.G. Harris

The Joshua Files
Invisible City
Ice Shock
Zero Moment

THE JOSHUA FILES

DaRK PaRaLLeL

M. G. HARRIS

■SCHOLASTIC

For Raph and Ali, who are all too close to growing up.

First published in the UK in 2011 by Scholastic Children's Books.
This edition published by Scholastic Children's Books, 2011.
An imprint of Scholastic Ltd
Euston House, 24 Eversholt Street
London, NW1 1DB, UK
Registered office: Westfield Road, Southam, Warwickshire, CV47 0RA
SCHOLASTIC and associated logos are trademarks and/or registered
trademarks of Scholastic Inc.

Text copyright © M. G. Harris, 2011
The right of M. G. Harris to be identified as the
author of this work has been asserted by her.

ISBN 978 1407 12443 8

Printed in the UK by CPI Bookmarque, Croydon, Surrey
Papers used by Scholastic Children's Books are
made from wood grown in sustainable forests.

1 3 5 7 9 10 8 6 4 2

www.scholastic.co.uk/zone

He believed in an infinite series of times, in a growing, dizzying net of divergent, convergent and parallel times.

From *The Garden of Forking Paths* by Jorge Luis Borges

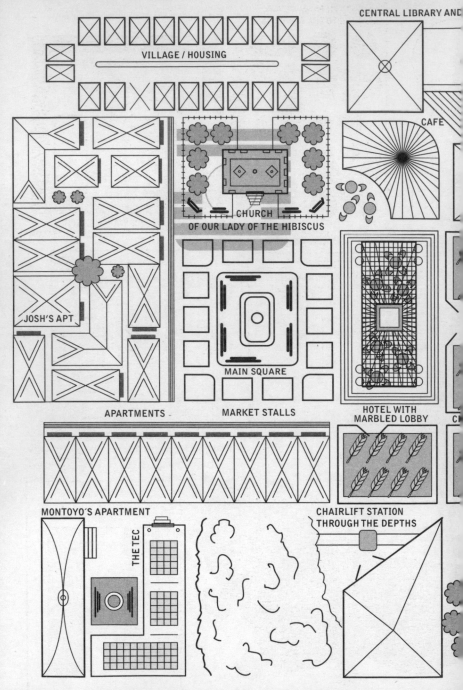

Map design by Megan Evans from Birmingham, winner of the *Joshua Files* "Design a Map" competition

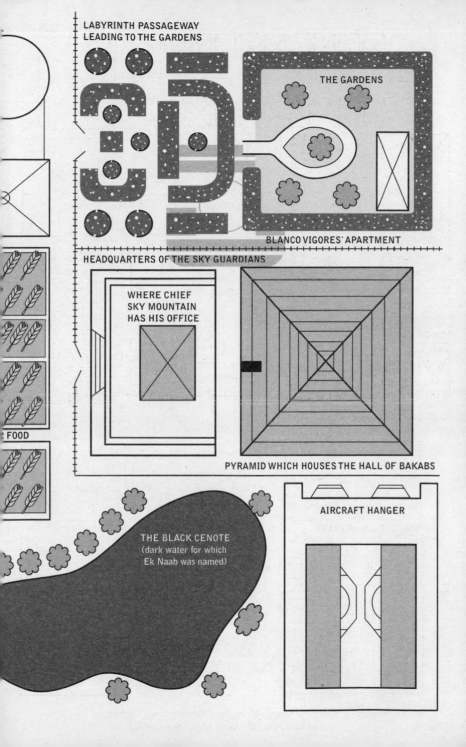

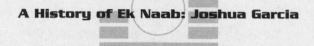

A History of Ek Naab: Joshua Garcia

Josh – what do you think of this draft? It's for the latest update to the History of Ek Naab. Time we had an entry about you! Carlos Montoyo

"Josh" (born 7 August 1996) is the son of Eleanor and Professor Andres Garcia. He is the grandson of Ek Naab resident Aureliano Witz Garcia, who was Bakab of Ix, protector of the Ix Codex, which is one of the four Books of Itzamna.

Like his father, Josh grew up knowing nothing of their connection to Ek Naab, nor of the Ix Codex, which contains vital information to prevent an ancient prophecy of catastrophe in 2012.

When Andres was reported to have died in an air crash in the jungle of Campeche, Josh began to investigate. His search for the truth led him to discover that his father had been looking for a lost book of the ancient Maya, the Ix Codex. The search led Josh to Ek Naab, but tragically cost the life of Josh's half-sister, Camila Pastor. She died in a car crash as the two were pursued by the Sect of Huracan.

This was the first action that brought the Sect to our attention in Ek Naab. We've long known of their existence as a death cult. However, the modern Sect seems to have become focused on 2012. They aim to take power where governments fall after an apocalypse.

In Ek Naab, Josh was installed as the Bakab of Ix. He resumed the search for the Ix Codex, missing since the seventh century. (See also **Ix Codex and 2012**.)

Josh discovered that his grandfather, Aureliano, had located the Ix Codex in England, in the house of a famous Mayan archaeologist, Sir J Eric Thompson. Returning from England with the Ix Codex, Aureliano suffered an asthma attack and ejected from his aircraft, landing near the town of Catemaco. The crashed remains of his Muwan Mark I were found in the Orizaba mountain range.

Aureliano died before medication could be sought. Tragically, a local boy was exposed to the toxic bio-defences of the Ix Codex. The boy died, and the people of Catemaco buried the book. A *brujo* (local witch or shaman) cast an incantation to lure Aureliano's relatives to Catemaco, so that they might be rid of the "cursed" book.

Josh's search for the Ix Codex led him to Catemaco, where he recovered the book and returned it to Ek Naab.

This remarkable feat was somewhat overshadowed by an incident some months later. Josh learned that his missing father had been seen visiting the house of J Eric Thompson.

Josh broke into the house and removed Thompson's transcriptions of the first pages of the Ix Codex.

But Josh was unaware that a close friend was a secret agent of the Sect of Huracan. Josh was betrayed; he and the pages fell into the hands of the Sect. Josh barely escaped with his life, and was rescued by his cousin, pilot Benicio Zak, who flew Josh to Ek Naab.

Josh and Ixchel Maria Chi Stephens, his betrothed, set off on an unauthorized investigation of a sighting of the Sect at the ruined Mayan city of Becan. They discovered a buried Revival Chamber of the ancient Erinsi, the long-extinct, mysterious "people of memory" whose writings Itzamna transcribed in his four books. The Sect had been trying to activate the Erinsi's underground Revival Chamber, using information from the stolen pages of the Ix Codex. They failed, but vowed to try again after they perfected the Crystal Key.

Josh and Ixchel followed a series of encrypted messages that Josh received on postcards. They led Josh to an American woman living in Mexico, Susannah St John. In 1962 Susannah had befriended a certain "Arcadio Garcia", who left her a letter to pass on to Joshua Garcia – in 2010. Josh followed instructions in the letter to ascend Mount Orizaba. There Josh found his father, Andres, who had been missing for several months and presumed dead.

Tragedy struck when an avalanche hit. Andres plunged to his death, sacrificing himself to save his son.

The ruling Executive of Ek Naab now felt that Josh was at risk from capture by the Sect. However, against the advice of the Executive, Josh returned to Oxford.

When Josh and others travelled to Brazil to represent England in the world capoeira championships, the Sect of Huracan struck again. Josh's mother and Ixchel were kidnapped. The Sect demanded Josh in return.

A rescue mission was mounted from Ek Naab. It failed. Josh was captured. The Sect took Josh to their headquarters in Switzerland, where he was subjected to genetic experiments. The Sect intends to steal all four Books of Itzamna, but their members only include descendants of the Bakabs of Ix. Members of the Sect therefore cannot survive the bio-defences of the other three books. The Sect's genetic procedures on Josh were designed to introduce cross-immunity to all four bio-defence toxins. With Ixchel's help, Josh escaped and both were recovered by Benicio.

The experiments seem to have succeeded; Josh is our first "total" Bakab, potentially a guardian to all four Books of Itzamna. A side effect of the genetic changes means that his eyes (previously brown) are now blue.

Josh's mother, Eleanor, agreed that she and Josh should leave Oxford and take their place among us as we strive to solve the 2012 Problem.

Josh and Eleanor Garcia share an apartment in Ek Naab. Josh is now a student at the Tec Preparatory School. His interests include capoeira, music and blogging. His blog is called **myinvisiblecity.com** – after Josh's own prosaic name for our "invisible" community of Ek Naab.

Not bad. A few gaps, though... Like, you forgot to mention that my mate from Oxford, Tyler Marks, was also kidnapped in Brazil!

Also, nothing about how <u>my dad</u> gave me the Bracelet of Itzamna, and how it's a <u>time-travel device</u>. Or that I fixed it – I guess we're still keeping that a secret between you and me?

Oh – no mention that Arcadio is a time traveller? That we don't understand how Arcadio fits into the whole Itzamna mystery?

In fact, we don't even know – who is Arcadio?

BLOG ENTRY: IN A FOREIGN PLACE

Something was bothering me, but I couldn't think what.

I'd get this vibe. I might be standing in the lane, looking down towards the plaza while market stalls are still being set out. Staring at the flowers that crawl out of balconies, scatter like Christmas decorations over the streets. Or maybe I'd look up towards the blurry sky – the wire-mesh ceiling of an underground, "invisible" city.

Ek Naab.

I'd watch the people wandering by. I've lived in the city for three months, so they didn't bother to look twice at me. Instead I finally saw their normal, everyday faces. The way they moved sluggishly, as if through smoke.

It's the *air*. In the city. *It doesn't move.*

Finally, I understood.

There's no weather in Ek Naab. No rain, no wind. I can barely remember what it feels like to close my eyes against a breeze.

Then this morning I woke up with a memory of England. I remembered a cold day in Oxford, a day full of harsh, icy wind. I was playing football in the park with some friends. Tyler, Emmy; they were there. I was in goal, as always. Getting cold, really cold, from the wind.

Not a particularly memorable day. But for some reason it is all I can think about. I can even feel the ache of cold in my ears. Thought I'd forgotten what that felt like, living in a windless city. But no. A flash of memory and there it is again. Amazing.

Why can't I shake the memory? It's an ordinary day of a life I've left behind. I miss my friends a bit, just like you'd expect. . . It really shouldn't be that big of a deal.

Comment (1) from Saint_Emmy

Yo, Joshy, JOSH? What's this, what's this? Thought you said you were going to close your blog down. After the shenanigans with the postcards from Mexico and all. What about all your *sekrits*, huh? What a drama queen. Sometimes, you know, I think that if I hadn't seen you all beat up that morning on Port Meadow, I wouldn't have believed anything you told me.

You're so lame, it kills me. Course you miss me! Go on, admit it.

You don't reply to texts, you don't go on Facebook. It's the twenty-first century. You gotta INTER-ACT.

Reply from Josh

Hey! I didn't expect to see any comments here, Emmy – if you really are Emmy, that is, and not someone, oh, I don't know, from the Sect or the National Reconnaissance Office spying on me. AGAIN.

Comment (2) from Saint_Emmy

National Reconnaissance Office?! Just for fun, I looked them up.

You're either mental or you think I'm Miss Gullible if you think I believe the NRO ever spied on you.

There's my good ol' paranoid Josh. Course it's really Emmy. This isn't like that time with Mikey's sister turning out to be your blog stalker, TopShopPrincess, and not that girl you fancied – what was her name, Ollie?

I was in the mood to read your blog and it turns out my password still works. You're the one who said you were gonna close it down. Don't get weird with me.

I wish you were still in Oxford. I miss you. (There I've said it.) School is such a nightmare now you have no idea. Coursework, exams, gah. It never ends. Then I get to thinking of you swanning around in Mexico, in some fancy international school going to the beach at weekends.

You've been thinking about me too. Dreaming about me, even!

So why don't you write, hey? It's possible to be friends with someone on the other side of the world now, didn't you know?

I'm still mad at you for just going off to Mexico, by the way, and no farewell party or anything.

Ohhhh, Josh. It's been a long time since we played footy in the park. Those days, they're gone.

Reply from Josh

This is pretty strange, Emmy. I know for a fact I didn't tell you about this blog. And you didn't see me all beat up on Port Meadow. Did you? Unless my memory is playing tricks.

I'm gonna take a little while to think this over. Don't get mad if I don't respond for a bit.

Comment (3) from Saint_Emmy

Whatever, dude. You sound a bit out of it. Btw, you're not the only one whose memory is getting dodgy. I don't remember any Tyler playing footy with us. Do you mean Tyler Marks from your capoeira?

"Another day in the upside-down world of Josh Garcia?" a voice says, very casual.

I'm standing on my hands on the edge of the cavernous sinkhole in the middle of Ek Naab. A face comes into my field of view.

Benicio.

I lower myself as slowly as possible. So slowly that it hurts. Total control at the edge of the abyss.

Benicio looks me up and down for a second. He seems vaguely embarrassed.

"Am I disturbing you?"

You know you are.

I was trying to figure out how come Emmy knows things she shouldn't, couldn't know. Until he broke my concentration. Yet I pause, shake my head, wipe hands on my vest. "Nope."

He flashes that bashful grin, the one that girls love so

much, the grin that makes me want to punch him in the face.

"Seems like it's some kinda meditation for you, Josh. A ritual, you know? Every morning, standing on your hands at the edge of the *cenote*. Daring yourself to fall in?"

I take a breath. "It's just a capoeira exercise. Best done every day." Our eyes meet. "I could teach you."

Oh yeah. I'd love to see what you're made of, cousin.

Benicio grins yet again. Does he want to DIE? *"No manches, guey,"* he drawls, with a little jab at my shoulder. *Stop messing, dude.* "I've seen you in action, man. You'd kill me."

I look down so he won't see the glint in my eye. I'm as tall as Benicio now, but my arms and shoulders are bigger than his. Skinny student. Nerdy geek-boy.

"You could always work out," I suggest. I hope he doesn't. How can Ixchel like him that way? He's skin and bone.

Benicio nods. "I should. Some of the guys have been talking about that. Ever since you got here, and all the girls started admiring the muscled look."

I suppress a smile. *Not quite all of the girls.* "Yeah, well. It takes work."

"Sure, I know it. Well, here I guess we've been a little obsessed by our studies. But since the whole Ix Codex thing . . . and you moving to Ek Naab . . . well . . . the mood has changed."

12

Something jars for a second. Why mention the Ix Codex? Seems funny to bring up the book that details a plan to save the world from disaster in 2012 in a conversation about impressing girls. I brush it off, for now.

"Now you want to train?" I say. "Learn capoeira?"

He nods again. "All of us in Ek Naab, we hit the books pretty hard," he says. "And for what?" He sighs deeply. "Maybe we should have some fun now, while we still can. Concentrate on the physical, not the intellectual."

While we still can? He's really not making sense now.

But before I can ask Benicio what he's talking about, Ixchel arrives. She's wearing a short, black-and-white tartan skirt. They've become insanely fashionable in Ek Naab, ever since my mum brought a few over from Oxford. It makes Ixchel look like a cute girl from a manga comic. Fantastic.

Every sense in my body turns its focus on her. I'm like a sunflower rotating towards the sun.

It's the only way I can survive. OK, she's with him; she's chosen the scrawny, brainy fly-boy. So I'm left only with impossible dreams, dreams that I can't bear to give up.

One day Ixchel will be with me.

That's what I've decided. No idea when or how but . . . one day. In the meantime I take every opportunity to breathe her in. The way she looks, her voice, the way she smells. If I ever get a chance to touch her, I remember that especially.

Like some freakish stalker. Obsessed. I gave up trying to

13

fight it about a month ago, when I realized that over two months had gone by during which my every waking moment was filled with thoughts of Ixchel.

I thought I'd been obsessed before. About my dad's disappearance, about travelling back in time to change things.

By comparison, they were just hobbies.

Is it like this for everyone? Because I feel as if I've gone insane. I don't even want to get better.

Is she thinking about me? She has to be. There's something between us, I know I'm not imagining it. But for some reason . . . she's with Benicio.

Jeez. It *can't* be like this for everyone else. We'd all be walking around like dozy zombies if this were normal. Is it something the Sect has done to me, when they genetically engineered something into me? I can't stop wondering.

What's me, what's normal, and what have they changed?

"Hey, Ixchel," Benicio says before I can speak. He gives her an affectionate smile, obviously appealing for her attention. Ixchel swings away slightly, looking at me.

"So this is where you hang out in the mornings?"

"Yeah, that's right. It's today's big news story."

Ixchel pulls a face. "You don't have to get sarcastic."

"I'm not being sarcastic," I growl. "British understatement. We're famous for it, right, Benicio?"

14

"Well, it's a nice country," Benicio admits. "But I never really got that whole Britishness thing."

You liked it at the time, I want to say. *You liked all the attention from those Oxford University students, too.* But I don't; instead, I bite my lip.

"I just saw Carlos Montoyo," Ixchel says, smiling first at me, then Benicio. "He was looking for you at your apartment, Josh. He wants you to go see him right away."

"Better hop to it, buddy," Benicio grins. "Be a good boy now."

I wrench my attention away from Ixchel. (I wasn't actually looking at her, of course, but I've learned how to look without staring. It's kind of the same way you look-but-don't-look at the sun.)

"A 'good boy'? Huh. Funny, coming from you."

"Don't you know what Montoyo wants? Maybe you saw it in a dream."

I can sense myself bristling. "Leave it out."

"Hey!" Benicio shrugs. "You're the one who talks to the dead. Maybe they told you what Montoyo wants? Like when your dead sister came to you in a dream and showed you the secret hideout of the Sect of Huracan at Lake Bacalar. . . Who am I to argue with your mystical powers?"

I summon all my self-control and force a grin. "Can't blame you."

Only Ixchel remains serious. "What amazes me," she says,

15

"is that you still question it. After everything that's happened! You must have something weird going on with your mind, Josh. Some kind of extrasensory power."

I turn to Ixchel. In a low voice I say, "That must be it."

Extrasensory power, hey? I love you. Read my mind, Ixchel. Did you hear that?

I watch closely, but she doesn't react. Of course not.

Benicio smiles, trying to flirt with Ixchel again. It turns my stomach, so I start to walk.

"I'm gonna go and . . . write my blog," I tell them.

"Oh, you're still doing that?" Ixchel sounds interested. Benicio chuckles.

"Blog Boy! I love how there's someone here who's a bigger geek than me."

"That's right," I say, turning to face him. "A bigger geek, bigger and stronger than you, probably almost as good as Tyler at capoeira by now and after two weeks of lessons, already better at handling a motorbike than you. Just wait until I start taking flying lessons, Benicio. You might not be the pilot supremo for ever."

Benicio erupts into peals of laughter. "Better at handling a motorbike? *Caramba*, Josh. Now that is funny."

"I'm better," I say quietly. "And you've seen me ride, so you know it. Want me to prove it?"

My cousin just shakes his head, grinning in amazement. "Prove it? Sure, sure! Why not?"

I don't move. "OK. Where. When?"

"*Pues ahorita, guey, ahorita!* 'Right away' sounds like a good time to me."

I'm a little surprised that he's calling my bluff, but I don't show it. "OK," I repeat. "Let me get my bike gear."

"What about Montoyo?" he says. There's an edge of challenge to his tone.

"Montoyo can wait."

"Oooff." Benicio claps, twice, pretending to be impressed. "Tough guy."

If Ixchel wasn't here, I'd probably thump him right now. But she is, so I just stand there with thunder in my eyes.

"I'll pick you up at your place, cousin," Benicio says with a smirk. He turns away, then stops. "Oh, and by the way, who is that other guy you were talking about, Josh? Who's 'Tyler'?"

Benicio's teasing about Tyler is obviously designed to annoy me. It's like he enjoys reminding me that I don't have any new friend in Ek Naab who's as good as Tyler.

It'll be a pleasure to show him up in front of Ixchel.

I try not to think about Ixchel's reaction to my motorbike challenge. I wasn't really focusing on her during that exchange, but now that I cast my mind back, I can't avoid the memory of her look of astonishment. She didn't *seem* impressed, now I think about it. Mainly stunned, actually.

I grab my new leather jacket and motorbike helmet. I'm gonna be wearing motorbike gear and riding a bike in front of Ixchel. How can that be anything but cool?

Life in Ek Naab might be weird, and it seems sometimes that I can do nothing but stand by and watch myself become a scary stalker-guy around Ixchel, but still. . .

Some of the new stuff I've been doing, learning to drive a car, a motorbike, all this new gear . . . it's pretty great.

Benicio picks me up outside, just as he promised. He's gone for the casual look. He's in blue jeans, cowboy boots and a blue checked shirt with the wristbands turned up once. Suddenly I feel like a little kid getting all dressed up. But it's too late to go back and change now – I'd look like an indecisive, anxious idiot.

My cousin will always have four years on me. I wish I could get used to that. Wish I could stop comparing myself to him.

It's kind of impossible, though. Ixchel likes *him*, not me. And when I'm not busy hating Benicio . . . well, I like him too. He's a cool guy. Funny, because that's why I hate him.

I follow Benicio to the grandest building in Ek Naab, the one that fronts as a deluxe eco-hotel. The elevator in the ornate marble-lined lobby takes us up to the surface level. I've heard that there's a false display that is programmed into all the elevators so that it can look to outsiders as if the lowest floor is S – the *sotano* (basement). When in fact there are three storeys below – into the underground city of Ek Naab. It's "just in case" anyone from the outside world ever has to visit. In which case they'd be shown the exemplary eco-resort with its solar-heated swimming pools and the outdoor blue *cenote*, the lush tropical gardens, the surrounding farms on which all food served in the resort is grown, the pretty white Spanish-style church with its orange grove and the cemetery in which they bury everyone who's ever lived in Ek Naab. My dad, too.

Privately, though, I've heard it muttered that if the Mexican government were to realize there's anything more than fruit-growing and eco-tourism going on in Ek Naab . . . things could get very serious.

Ek Naab's location is utterly secret. It has to be. They guard the secret knowledge of the Erinsi – the "People of Memory". A civilization so ancient that there's almost no record of their existence. A civilization with knowledge of time travel, sophisticated bioengineering and anti-gravity propulsion.

But most of all – the last Earth civilization to be finished off by the galactic superwave. Their computer technology was wrecked overnight by the superwave's electromagnetic energy. Their civilization collapsed. Who knows when it happened to the Erinsi – but they knew when the superwave would be around again: 22 December, AD 2012.

A Mayan god (or was he really a time traveller?) called Itzamna copied the ancient Erinsi writings into the four Books of Itzamna. The books – or codices – have been guarded in Ek Naab since Itzamna's time, around 350 BC. One of the four books – the Ix Codex – went missing for centuries when it was stolen by a king of the Mayan Snake Kingdom, a place we know nowadays as Calakmul. That was back in AD 653.

The men in my family – the Bakabs of Ix – have been hunting for the Ix Codex ever since. We're the only ones who can touch it and survive the blast of bio-toxin that hits

20

anyone within a five-metre radius of the book's deadly cover. A gene protects us, just as a gene protects every Bakab – the ones who protect the other Books of Itzamna: the Kan, Cuauc and Muluc codices. A bit before my fourteenth birthday, I found the codex buried near the crater lake of Catemaco, in the Mexican state of Veracruz.

Itzamna named his four sons – the Bakabs – with the names of the four corners of the Mayan universe. But I reckon Itzamna wasn't even a Mayan. Were the Bakabs really his sons? Lately, I've been wondering.

The people of Ek Naab are definitely descended from Itzamna, as well as from those Bakabs. And from a bunch of other folk who managed to get into the Cult of Itzamna and live in the hidden community of Ek Naab – which means *dark water*. Including quite a few Spanish and other visitors who discovered the secret city over the years. The famous American explorer who discovered the Mayan ruins, John Lloyd Stephens, for one. I'm descended from John Lloyd Stephens too, as it turns out. On my great-grandmother's side.

It's a small place, Ek Naab. Small and windless.
Stifling.

We stroll through the gardens and pass gardeners trimming the bougainvillea. When I came to live here with my mother I wondered about two things: how come such a small place had so many smart people? I mean, Ixchel finished high school at fourteen! The ancient languages stuff she's studying now is university level. That's not even unusual here. Benicio is a pilot and an aeronautical engineer. He's only just turned eighteen.

The other thing I wondered was – what do you do if you're not smart enough for that? What if you're happy to be a gardener or a cook?

Well, it seems that gardeners and cooks and cleaners and doctors and aeronautical engineers all get paid more or less the same. Housing is all provided by the city; most people live in similar small apartments. You can get any food or clothes you need in the daily market. There's a kind of money, but it only works in Ek Naab.

Call me old-fashioned, but I don't like it. It's creepy having so many people know who you are and know your business. Carlos Montoyo getting together with my mother, for example. The news of that spread across Ek Naab within one day. Lorena, the chief scientist, saw the way Montoyo held my mother's hand when she was giving us the results of my genetic tests. The next day, everyone knew about what Lorena had seen.

"It's so nice for Carlos," people tell me. They actually stop me in the street to say it.

"Excuse me," I want to say, "but I don't care about Carlos Montoyo's love life. I wish my mother would have respected my dad's memory for a bit longer. A couple of years, at least!"

I don't, of course. Instead I give them this weak smile and nod and try to remember who they are: second cousin, third cousin once removed?

Everyone's interested in Carlos Montoyo. He's the richest guy in Ek Naab – but not with money.

The real privileges of Ek Naab are this: access to secrets and access to the outside world.

Carlos Montoyo isn't the mayor of Ek Naab – that's Chief Sky Mountain. Montoyo's apartment is nothing special. It's the same as the one I share with my mother: two small bedrooms, a lounge and a kitchen. But in terms of secrets and access to the outside world, Montoyo is top dog. Partly because his job allows him to spend much of his time posing as a lecturer at Yucatan University in Merida. I've heard rumours that his apartment in Merida is pretty palatial.

Benicio is one of the Sky Guardians, the Muwan pilots who patrol the airspace near Ek Naab. The way I see it, though, Benicio is more like Montoyo's personal gopher, his fixer.

Benicio hasn't said a word to me since we set off. I'm lost in my own thoughts, so I scarcely notice. But as we pass the open-air blue *cenote*, he sighs. Then he turns to me with a tough-guy glance.

"You've guessed about me and Ixchel, haven't you?"

I stare ahead and keep moving. I realize that I need to come up with a speedy, breezy reply if I'm going to be able to seem convincingly unbothered.

I open my mouth but nothing comes out.

Benicio continues to stare at me for a few seconds. "All right," he says in a low voice. "I knew it."

I find my voice. "You knew what?"

"You're angry with me. Because she's your intended."

"You know as well as me, mate," I tell him, "that Ixchel and me have never agreed to that arranged marriage thing."

If Benicio has anything to add on the matter, the way I closed down the discussion seems to stop him.

We arrive at the garage where all the road vehicles in Ek Naab are stored. Most of them are pickup trucks designed to be used on the ranches. There are about eight motorbikes. Benicio's is the Harley. Gently, he prises it free of the stand and pushes it out. Then he points at a second bike, the 250cc Honda that I've been learning to drive.

"What, and you get the Harley?" I say, annoyed.

"You don't know how to handle the Harley. The Honda can go fast enough. We're racing in a banana plantation, Josh. Bananas! Not exactly the highway to Cancun."

"Just as well," I mutter, grabbing hold of the Honda by the handlebars. "Tyler would never believe I was riding a Harley in the outside world, anyway."

Benicio eases his head into a Shoei motorcycle helmet. "You keep mentioning this guy Tyler," he observes. "Why?"

There's no time to answer Benicio's question and it doesn't seem like he even really wants an answer, because he's on the bike and revving up the engine two seconds later. I'm left wondering what's going on, but I have to get moving fast to follow him to the banana plantation.

That's the second time he's seemed surprised to hear me talking about Tyler. The first time, I thought he was being intentionally annoying. Just now, he looked totally serious. Benicio not knowing who Tyler is . . . that felt real.

But how? It doesn't make sense.

All in all, things have been very strange in Ek Naab lately.

First there's the way that people keep having parties. When Mum and I arrived three months ago and had our house-warming party, I'm pretty sure that people commented on how nice it was finally to go to a party and hang out. Like it was an unusual thing.

Since then, though, I swear, there's a thing every week.

These teens from Ek Naab could even teach my friends in Oxford a thing or two about how to party. They may study hard during the day but from what I've seen, lately they seem to have gone off the rails a bit at the weekends.

Loud music, drinking, girls and boys getting together. It's like being back in Oxford sometimes. Was it like this when I arrived in Ek Naab? Somehow I had the impression things were pretty quiet here. But no. I've not been short of offers, either. It's just that I'm not interested in anyone except Ixchel and . . . I'm not sure about how the jealousy thing is supposed to work? Tyler's theory is that girls like you more if they see you with another girl.

What if they don't, though? Seems a risky strategy to me. Not to say a bit mean. I wouldn't like it if a girl used me like that, to make another boy jealous.

But Tyler is a big fan of the jealousy trick. He advised me to use it to get Ixchel interested. He said that right here in Ek Naab, actually. The very night of our house-warming party.

How come Benicio can't remember him? *That's just madness, man* (as Tyler would say).

It's not the only strange thing Benicio has said. What did he mean, mentioning the Ix Codex earlier today? As if it had changed things for the *worse* in Ek Naab. That's not what happened at all. Finding the Ix Codex put the whole mission of Ek Naab back on track. With the information in that book, they can use the Revival Chambers and save the world from the 2012 galactic superwave problem.

Not that anyone has ever told me the 2012 plan, of course. I'm not even allowed to know what's in the Ix Codex, or how they'll use that ancient knowledge to stop the effects of a gigantic electromagnetic pulse that's coming along with the superwave. It'll zap all the computer hard drives and electronic systems and put the world back a hundred years as far as technology goes. To them, I'm just the Bakab kid who retrieved the Ix Codex. But it seemed like things were under control. That slowly they were working their way through the Ix Codex and getting the information they needed.

It seems odd that they don't include me on the whole plan for 2012. In just over a year I'll be sixteen, able to take my place as a Bakab on the ruling Executive. If Montoyo ever lets that happen! I wouldn't put it past him to change the rules so that I have to be eighteen. That way he gets two more years as my proxy on the Executive. Basically, running the whole show.

Another thing that freaks me out is the way Emmy just popped up, commenting on a blog that I was sure was private. Knowing things she couldn't know, like that Simon Madison left me beaten up on Port Meadow, the night I discovered that Ollie and Madison were working together, for the Sect.

Emmy did *not* see me "all beat up". After I got away from

27

Madison I spent the night frozen in some crummy coal shed. Then at dawn, Benicio picked me up, plucked me right out of there, flew us straight to Ek Naab.

Emmy didn't get a look in. So what is she going on about?

I'm paranoid enough as it is, being the focus of all this attention in Ek Naab, worrying about what the Sect of Huracan have done to my genes. (Apart from turning my eyes blue.)

I guess I can sort it out later. For now, I decide to concentrate on the task at hand.

A motorbike race. What was I thinking? I've never raced a bike in my life.

The banana plantations lie to the north of the citrus groves, about a kilometre away. There's a wide, dusty avenue between the two, about three kilometres long. At the end it bends to the right, forms a perimeter to the banana trees. Smaller dust tracks criss-cross the banana plantation, and the fruit pickers drive their pickups down tracks as wide as two-carriageway roads, loading up with stacks of green bananas.

I've never met anyone in Ek Naab who picks fruit, and the other day I found out why. They're all Mexican locals, from outside the city. "Think how suspicious it would be to the people who live in Mexico around Ek Naab, if they didn't know anyone who worked on these plantations," Montoyo told me. "So we employ outsiders. They come in, they pick fruit and coffee. That way we seem no different to any other big farming company."

"You're rich, powerful landowners," I'd commented, but he didn't take it the way I meant, which was ironically.

He just nodded and muttered, "Something like that."

As Benicio and I ride our bikes slowly to the starting point, I think about Ek Naab and its weird relationship with Mexico. It doesn't seem to feel like it's part of the country, or part of anywhere.

If the Big Secret Plan doesn't work out at the end of 2012, would they really care what was going on in the rest of the world?

I have to start thinking about stuff like this. I'm going to be sixteen in a bit over a year, and then I'll have to make decisions. The outside world most definitely does matter to *me*. It's where I plan to spend the rest of my life.

When we get to the starting line, Ixchel is already there. This time I succeed in not staring at her. In fact, I hardly give her a glance. Instead I make out I'm doing a careful check of my bike, the fit of helmet, my gloves and leather jacket. It's sizzling hot even in the shade; the air is almost choking with dust. Under the jacket, my sleeveless T-shirt is already soaked with sweat. I don't care, though; this is a chance to wear the whole motorbike outfit in front of Ixchel. No way I'm missing out.

I cast a quick glance over at Ixchel. My blood begins to boil when I see Benicio's hand rest lazily on her waist, see him giving her a light kiss on the lips. I guess he thinks it's OK, now that I "officially" know about them. I can hear Ixchel speaking to him quietly in Spanish. "Are you sure I can't talk you out of this, pet? You don't need to impress me."

"Hey, don't lay it on me!" he replies with a wide grin, holding up his hands. "It's your *fiancé* over there who insisted!"

He says *fiancé* with a really snide, sarcastic air.

"You're a lousy liar," I interrupt, not even bothering to disguise my anger. "I said I was better at handling a bike than you, and that's a fact. You're the one who wants me to prove it."

"Listen, *guey*, around here a boast like that means something. It's gonna cost you. You get what I'm saying?"

I'd rather hit him. Right now it's hard to restrain the urge to do exactly that.

"You're a great fly-boy, Benicio, I'm not arguing with that. But a motorbike is all about balance, and mine is better. It's simple enough."

Benicio laughs. He turns his attention back to Ixchel. "The kid's grown some stones since he got here, you gotta admit it. But it takes more than talk."

I rev up the engine and lower my visor. "Then why don't you stop talking?"

"OK, OK. Once around the outer perimeter. You'll be OK, dude – just follow my dust."

Benicio takes a red bandana out of his jacket pocket, kisses it once and hands it to Ixchel. She gives him a wry grin, then looks over at me. I could swear her eyes soften, just slightly. I make my face very hard then, gaze back at her with a flat expression.

Benicio winks at Ixchel, then leans forward. He lowers the visor on his helmet. "Just don't crash into the bananas, cousin. So, are you ready?"

In reply, I rev the engine a couple more times. Ixchel stands in the alley between us, lifts the red bandana high, her arm pointing at the sky. There's a rapid motion; she whips her arm downwards; the red cloth flashes in the air. I release the throttle and brakes; the bike pulls hard beneath me, wheels spinning. Benicio pulls away even faster. Within a second he's a whole length ahead. Swiftly, I catch him. He pulls away again. I check my speedometer. We're both hitting sixty. He pulls further away. But he's too fast, by my estimation. At this speed he'll have to decelerate too hard to make the first bend.

Just as I expected, Benicio has to brake hard as we approach the bend. The bike tilts, wobbles slightly, but amazingly, he stays in control. I slow down more gradually, but manage to maintain a higher average speed. By the time we pull out of the turn he's only ahead by half a length. He turns his head very slightly, flashes me a grin and then speeds off in a cloud of dust.

OK, maybe I was wrong about who is better on a motorbike. I didn't count on Benicio turning into a speed-and-danger freak.

The second turn isn't as sharp; it's the fuzzy end of the plantation where they haven't bothered to delineate the edge quite so well. We both make the turn with a hard lean to the left, hardly dropping any speed. For a fraction of a second, my knee scrapes the ground. A surge of adrenaline bursts through me.

That was close. Another centimetre and I'd have lost control.

The third, final, turn looms. My face and hands are still hot from my brush with disaster. I can feel sweat pouring, not trickling, down my back.

And Benicio is still ahead, by a length.

Without thinking, I twist the throttle and accelerate. In the next second I'm level with Benicio, the front wheels of our bikes seemingly clamped together by an invisible thread.

He hesitates. I sense it, for just a beat.

Then he pulls ahead. I don't even have time to think about whether to follow him when he throws his bike into the final turn.

It's as though I see a snapshot of the whole event in an instant. Benicio's dramatic lean, the bike tilting almost

horizontal, the wobble, the fatal wobble. The bike and
Benicio hang in space, almost parallel with the ground, boy
and machine suspended in a cloud of warm dust.

Then chaos hits.

The bike careers off course; I hear Benicio's muffled yell,
the high-pitched grind of brakes, the smell of scorched
rubber and hot, metallic sparks. The machine spins a couple
of times, scrapes along for about twenty metres with Benicio
trapped underneath. Finally it smacks into a banana palm and
comes crashing to a halt.

I start slowing down the instant it all begins. I'm already
leaping off my bike and dashing to Benicio's side before his
machine has stopped. I'm dimly aware of Ixchel rushing
alongside me too. When we reach Benicio he's groaning
loudly, very much conscious and in pain.

"Get it off me, get me out. . ." he moans. There's blood
all over his left side. Heart slamming with anxiety, I lift the
bike off him. The wheels are still spinning.

I'm about to undo his helmet when Ixchel grabs my arm
angrily.

"Do you know what you're doing?" she yells.

"So he can breathe!"

"You don't move someone in a road accident! Not unless
you know what you're doing!"

"He needs to breathe! He's gonna get all overheated in
there!"

Benicio's moans are turning into sobs. He's trying – unsuccessfully – to bury them. There's a spectacular amount of blood on his arm. Gingerly, I lift the sleeve of his T-shirt to see the damage. One quick glimpse is enough. The bone is broken, and there's a sharp tip of white bone poking through a bleeding, fleshy wound. I drop the fabric quickly, before Ixchel can see.

"What did you see?"

"Oh . . . he's broken the arm," I say, all light, casual.

Benicio isn't looking at his arm; he's actually doing his best not to look. I guess he has some idea of how bad it is.

"How do you know it's broken?"

Ixchel leans in closer to Benicio. Gently, I restrain her. "Don't. Just call for help. Please, Ixchel. He needs to get to hospital."

"A proper hospital? Or the surgery in Ek Naab?"

"I'm not an expert," I begin.

Ixchel fixes me with a hard, very pointed glare.

"Oh, you're not an expert? Well, Josh, I wish you'd thought of that a few minutes ago. . ."

I stared at her, baffled.

"Huh . . . what?"

She turns her back on me then, makes soothing sounds over Benicio. His eyes have closed, his face contorted in a silent grimace of pain.

"Ixchel, I think I dropped something before I fell. My bandana. Can you go see?"

She looks a little puzzled, but this isn't a time to argue with Benicio, I guess. A second later I'm alone with him.

"Hey, man, I'm sorry it turned out this way. You're faster, OK? You'd have won."

Benicio laughs, chokes a bit, then finishes the laugh. "It wasn't about speed, it was about who handles the machine better. I guess you proved your point. At least, I did."

"No, no, it was a freak accident. Listen now, you've got to stay calm in front of Ixchel. She'll be worried."

"Yeah." He nods, pensive. "But not so worried as if things had turned out another way. . ."

"Huh? What other way?"

Benicio closes his eyes. "Get lost, Josh."

Within thirty minutes the emergency jeep from the
underground city arrives. Two young women dressed in blue
jumpsuits put Benicio on a stretcher and carry him into the
back. When I try to climb in along with Ixchel, she pushes me
back.

"There's no room for you," she says. I can't tell if she
means literally no room in the jeep – or that she doesn't want
me there. Either way, her manner is pretty cold. I step down.

"I'll get the bikes back to the city," I say, in the briskest,
most businesslike voice I can manage.

"Yeah, yeah," Ixchel says. She's already turned away. I
watch them leave, then pick up Benicio's Harley. It's not
damaged, as far as I can tell. Just a few scratches. Just to be
on the safe side, I ride it back very slowly. Even though I'm
tempted to give the machine a quick speed test, I don't. The
memory of Benicio's broken arm is kind of off-putting. After
replacing the Harley, I go back for the Honda. It's a long,

sweaty walk, with a blazing-hot leather jacket slung over my shoulder.

By the time I'm done with the errands it's mid-morning. I swing by the surgery, which is on the campus of the Tec. Benicio's being operated on, they tell me. Having his arm pieced together with some titanium screws and the wound getting all stitched up. Ixchel has already left, they tell me. They don't know where she went.

There's not much I can do while I'm waiting for Benicio to get out of his operation, so I head down to the blue *cenote*, strip down to my shorts and dive in. After about fifteen minutes I hear a voice calling to me from the water's edge. There's the usual tingle of excitement, the anticipation of seeing Ixchel alone. Especially after what Benicio said to me before he told me to "get lost".

I climb out at the ladder trying to look casual, dripping with water, trying not to wonder how it is that Ixchel looks more gorgeous each time I see her.

"So. Um. Ixchel. Are you, like . . .?"

She looks up.

". . . mad at me?"

Without warning, Ixchel lunges out with both hands, shoves me so hard in the chest that I stumble backwards.

"You IDIOT!"

Before I can recover my balance, she pushes me again. I'm dangerously close to the *cenote*'s edge.

"What were you *thinking*?"

I can see that she's going for me again, so I lean forward and try, gently, to restrain Ixchel's wrists. "Hey! Please don't do that again, I don't want to fall in."

"You're an idiot! How could you encourage him like that?"

Encourage him? It was Benicio's idea! And Ixchel seemed keen enough on the contest – at the beginning. But I don't want to rub salt into the wound.

"I know." It's hard to stop at that, but somehow I do.

"What made you go along with a stunt like that, anyhow?"

"Guess I wasn't thinking," I say, still holding her hands in mine. It feels nice.

"Let go of me," she says with a sigh. "I won't push you any more."

"Promise?"

But she throws me such a look then that I let go right away. There's a long, very uncomfortable silence. She won't look at me. Eventually, still gazing into the *cenote*, she murmurs, "This is why I don't want to be with you."

Well, that just about takes my breath away.

"You . . . don't want to be with me. . ." I echo, hardly believing my ears. "And this is why?"

"You and your incredibly dangerous life. You think I want that? Someone who's going to end up dead? I thought Benicio had more sense, but . . . obviously he's as crazy as you."

"He may be crazier."

"Oh, stop it."

You like that I'm a bit crazy, I want to tell her. *That's what you look for in a guy.* I'd do anything to have the guts to be able to say it aloud but I can't, I can't, I can't. . .

With difficulty she says, "My father went through hell when my mother died. You know that? I don't want that. To be with someone only to lose them."

Slowly, incredibly, I start to understand what she's saying. "You don't want to be with me . . . because you're afraid of what will happen to me?"

"One day," she pronounces, angrily, "you'll forget me. You'll be gone."

"What are you talking about?"

"You . . . Arcadio . . . Susannah St John. Your adventures with time travel. Love affairs in the past."

"Huh . . . what?!"

"Your future," Ixchel states firmly. "*Yours!* Time travelling and who-knows-what? Where am I in all of that, Josh? *Nowhere.*"

"The Arcadio thing? You're so sure I'm Arcadio?"

"Of course! Ever since we met Susannah St John in Tlacotalpan. I felt it right away. Something about her, something between the two of you. Like she knew you already. How?"

It's true; I remember how oddly Ixchel had behaved

around Susannah. It seems incredible to me now, that Ixchel was already thinking about me back then. I'm sure it took me much longer to realize what was starting between us.

"Look. Montoyo has *actually met* Arcadio," I say, trying to stall her. "Years ago. And even Montoyo's not sure that I'm Arcadio. That he's me. You know, whatever."

"Montoyo?" Ixchel says, incredulous. "Since when is he reliable? Susannah St John believes that you are Arcadio, I *know* it. And she was *in love* with him! It was disgusting to watch her around you, you know that? She looked at you like you were her beloved son. Only that's not what she's thinking really, is it? AT ALL!"

Tears are brimming in Ixchel's eyes now. Desperately, I search for the right words, but I can't find them. And she keeps going. "I know you're mad about me and Benicio. And maybe you even want you and me to go ahead with the arranged marriage," she says, choking on her sobs. "You don't need to say anything, it's kind of obvious. But I don't want to be the girl you forgot."

Jeez. How did we go from arguing about Benicio to *this*? It's a mess. I can feel my own eyes welling up now.

"It's even worse. . ." Ixchel says, holding her fingers to her cheeks, brushing away the tears. "Because now you've infected Benicio with these stupid ideas. He wants to be just as reckless as you, showing off. He was *so* nice to me when

40

we were growing up. The best friend I had. Always looked out for me."

"Oh yeah," I say bitterly, sniffing. "Benicio sure had plans for you. . ."

"Shut up about Benicio!" she snaps.

But can I let it go? No. "If you liked Benicio all along," I continue angrily, "then why didn't you say? Back in Veracruz last year. I asked you if there was a boy in Ek Naab that you liked and you said no. You could have told me then and I'd never have. . ."

Never have got my hopes up. Never have let myself fall for her. I can't say any of that though; it's way too soppy.

"You . . . are just so stupid. . ." Ixchel says, staring at me. "When are you gonna grow up?"

That really stings. I feel my face flush red with anger. "Stick to your *grown-up* boyfriend then," I tell her. "See if I care."

"You know what, I think I will," she replies. We exchange one final look of pure resentment and then she turns and walks away.

Everyone in Ek Naab knows that Ixchel and I are supposedly betrothed. And everyone probably knows that Ixchel is going out with Benicio. On my way back to the straw hut to get dressed, a couple of older guys, students at the Tec in their early twenties, pat me on the shoulder.

"Love is a minefield, my friend," says one, chuckling. "But don't give up!"

41

I shake them off, scowling.

We've both ended up in tears and I don't even understand what just happened. I head back to the apartment. I'm going to call Tyler. He's the one guy I know I can talk to about this.

The phone in our apartment has been routed to give us
access to call outside Ek Naab without the call being traced.
Even so, I won't risk being overheard, or being questioned
about where I've been by my mother and Montoyo. So I call
Tyler from one of the outside phones. His mother answers,
asks who I am and then fetches him.

"Hallo?"

"Tyler, mate, it's me, Josh."

There's a lengthy pause, then a sort of gasp of recognition.
"Oh yeah! Josh Garcia, yeah? How've you been?"

"Not good, not good. It's all going off with Benicio and Ixchel.
Like you said it would. She knows I like her, Ty! She's known all
along, doesn't even seem to care! Gave me all this about how
she prefers Benicio to me cos unlike me, he's not a raving
psycho always getting into trouble, but now maybe he's turning
into another danger-freak. . ." I take a deep breath and sigh.

I stop then, waiting almost breathless for his reply. Until

that moment I haven't realized how badly I need to talk about this. How much I've missed Tyler's listening . . . even if he rarely has much to say.

Tyler seems to be having difficulty coming up with a response. No surprise there. It's complicated.

Finally he says, "This is Josh Garcia, yeah? From the capoeira group, right?"

My face feels suddenly clammy. "Yeah . . . yeah, of course, who else?"

"Josh Garcia, who moved away to Mexico with his mum, that Josh?"

I fall silent. If it wasn't for the odd things that Emmy and Benicio have said, I'd be laughing now. Instead, though, a numb sensation creeps through me.

"Yes, Tyler, it's me."

"Mate . . . did you call the right number? I'm Tyler Marks, yeah? Did you mean to call some other Tyler?"

The numb sensation turns into cringing, horrible embarrassment. I can hear in his voice that he's not joking. Suddenly I want to end this conversation without looking like a jerk.

"Did you say 'Tyler Marks'?"

"Yep."

Heart sinking, I say, "Wait . . . you're right. I was meant to be calling another Tyler. Your name is right next to his on my phone."

Tyler laughs. "Jokes, man, that's happened to me too. Anyway, hope everything's cool with you in Mexico."

"Yeah," I tell him, feeling the spread of a blush. "It's all fine."

"Capoeira?"

"No classes, but I practise on my own."

"Yeah, well. Don't give it up, man. If I remember right, you was startin' to get good."

I can hardly bring myself to speak. "Thanks. Well. Better go."

He chuckles. "OK! And good luck with the girl and being a psycho and all that. . ."

As I replace the phone, my hand trembles. He doesn't know me. Tyler. It's unimaginable.

I'm so messed up.

Those strange comments about Tyler make sense now, Emmy's and Benicio's. They acted like they didn't remember him. I thought it was a joke, a mistake, anything.

But what if there's something wrong with my memory? If I hadn't been genetically altered by the Sect, I'd totally assume there was something wrong with them, not me.

If only.

I can think of just one person who can help me now – Lorena, the Chief Scientist of Ek Naab. She's also a doctor and the *atanzahab* – the matchmaker who recommended that Ixchel be betrothed to me. Lorena did that without even meeting me. Smart lady.

I hurry over to the Tec and argue with the receptionist to let me through to her office. What with Ek Naab being so miserably tiny, though, of course the story has got out about how I blagged my way into Lorena's labs a few months ago.

I was looking for the Crystal Key, so that I could repair the Bracelet of Itzamna and travel back in time to save my father. But Lorena discovered me before I could find the Key. She doesn't even know that I finally did fix the Bracelet. Or that I travelled back in time but couldn't change what happened with my dad. He still ended up on the slopes of Mount Orizaba, his memory lost, and he still ended up dying in the ice crevasse. Saving my life.

In fact, as I wait for Lorena to come to the lobby, I have to remind myself that Montoyo and Ixchel don't know exactly what happened when I used the Bracelet. All I admitted is that I used it to go back in time by ten minutes. I never mentioned the stuff about my dad.

Tyler guessed that I hadn't told the full details. The Tyler who remembered being my friend, anyway. That's how I remember things.

"I think I'm losing my mind," I tell Lorena, the second she closes her office door behind us.

A wry grin flickers at the edge of her mouth. Her serious brown eyes twinkle for a second, but she remains calm. "I suspect not."

46

"Can you do a brain scan or something?"

"To see if you're losing your mind? Possibly. It depends how you're losing it."

"Do a brain scan," I say firmly. "Please."

With a pencil, Lorena taps the desk between us. "Josh, talk to me. What's wrong?"

"Remember a few months ago, when my mum and Ixchel were kidnapped in Brazil?"

She nods, blinking slowly. "Naturally."

"I came here to your labs. You found me in your cold room."

She smiles at the memory. "Yes."

"Who was with me?"

"No one."

"You don't remember a guy called Tyler?"

"Tyler?" Lorena frowns. "No. You were alone."

"And you . . . you told me all this stuff, remember that? About Montoyo."

"I did?"

"Yeah, and about the five Revival Chambers, and the Crystal Key. . ."

"The *five* Revival Chambers?"

I pause, glancing up at her. "Yes. The one here in Mexico, in the Depths near Becan. Then you said there were four other chambers."

Lorena frowns, gazing deeply at me from over her

black-rimmed glasses. "Josh . . . we just know about one Revival Chamber. The one that you and Ixchel found."

"But they're written about in the Ix Codex. . ."

Lorena sits back, now totally bewildered. "Josh . . . the Ix Codex is mostly blank."

"Mostly blank?" I can't do anything but echo.

"Apart from the first few pages." Lorena nods vigorously. "It's as if the book was torn into pieces and the first few pages grafted on to a blank manuscript. A fake, made to look like the genuine article by someone who got their hands on the first few pages of the real thing." She looks at me curiously. "But everybody knows this. We've known since you returned the codex from Catemaco."

I sit in silence for a few moments, aware of a deepening ache in my lower spine and wrists, and a slight numbness. This is getting to me now, this junk with my memory. It's totally messed up. After the day I've had, it's enough. If there's a conspiracy to play a practical joke on me, I swear, heads will roll. But lurking at the back of my mind there's a sick, sick fear. I hardly dare admit it to myself, let alone Lorena.

What if there is something seriously wrong with me?

"Then you'd better do that brain scan," I tell her, part angry, part flippant. "Cos that's not how I remember things."

BLOG ENTRY: JUST BECAUSE YOU THINK YOU'RE PARANOID DOESN'T MEAN THEY AREN'T REALLY OUT TO GET YOU

What started out as a secret diary might now be my only way to record my memories. . .

From the minute I opened my eyes this morning, I had the feeling it was going to be a weird day. That memory where I was playing football with Tyler. Remembering what it's like to feel an icy wind. Emmy's bizarre comments on my blog, her knowing things I don't remember telling her, things I know she didn't see.

Strange days.

Blanco Vigores once told me: *Ignore nothing.*

Even dreams. They're like messages from the subconscious.

It's like that with me – except the ability to speak to my own subconscious seems to be a bit more developed. Sometimes it seems I can even speak to other people's subconscious minds. It's freaky.

It must be something to do with being a Bakab. I was born with the Ix gene – It makes me immune to the toxin that protects the Ix Codex. Thanks to whatever genetic experiments the Sect did to me in Switzerland, I've now got immunity to the other three types of biotoxin – I have the genes of Bakabs Muluc, Cauac and Kan. I can handle any of the four codices.

Do the genetic changes stop there, though? The Sect changed my eye colour from brown to blue. It's the main reason why even I have started to wonder if I'm Arcadio, the blue-eyed time traveller who left me a letter written in the 1960s.

There were things in that letter that only I could know. So am I going to become Arcadio and start travelling in time? Is he my future son? Or someone else who knows me?

It never occurred to me that Ixchel was worrying about this Arcadio thing. Maybe that's why she seemed upset when my eyes turned blue. Ixchel thinks I have some kind of psychic powers as well. She believes that I'm going to grow up and become this time traveller. To forget all about her, leave her.

My dad lost his memory using the Bracelet of Itzamna. Arcadio lost his memory too, almost certainly. He walked around with a tattoo on his arm; a secret code. A code that led to the formula for the Crystal Key, just in case the Bracelet ever malfunctioned again.

A man in danger of amnesia needs to get used to leaving himself notes, clues to his own identity. What better than a tattoo?

I've already used the Bracelet to time travel. Twice. But it's not me with the amnesia. I remember being friends with Tyler – and no one else does.

Could the Sect have implanted false memories? I don't remember my head being hooked up to any kind of equipment when they experimented on me.

But then if my memory has been tampered with, I wouldn't remember anything suspicious, would I?

It's not good, being unable to trust your own memory, your own feelings. Not good at all.

What I remember – it feels cast-iron, definite, real.

I'm sitting with my laptop at one of the café tables around the market square. In the early evening, it's the noisiest place in Ek Naab, with enough going on that I reckon I won't stand out. When I finish writing the blog I take a sip from a glass of mango and papaya juice. From across the stalls I hear my name being called. I glance up, peering through the heaps of roasted coffee beans, dried-and-toasted grasshoppers covered in chilli and lime, yellow guanabanas, limes and avocados.

It's Montoyo. His gaze is fixed on me and he looks determined, his mouth a hard line in his craggy face. Immediately, I feel nervous. Montoyo's left me alone, more or less, for the past few months, wants me to be a "good boy" from now on. He took the Bracelet of Itzamna away from me, he convinced my mother to move us to Ek Naab, made her fall for him. Montoyo has all the influence over Mum that he needs.

All so that I'll stay right where he can keep an eye on me. So that he can control me.

His control must be slipping, though, if even Benicio is flipping out a bit – reliable ol' Benicio, who used to be errand boy.

I wonder about my cousin then. I think about what he must be going through at that hospital. At least by now he should be over the worst.

Closing up the laptop, I look up at Montoyo. He can probably tell that I'm tense. So is he.

"Where've you been, Josh? I told Ixchel this morning that I was looking for you!"

That's right . . . she did say that. Then we sort of got distracted with the motorbike contest.

I take a deep sigh and tell Montoyo about my contest with Benicio. But I don't get far before he interrupts.

"Josh, you and your cousin need to find a way to get along. If you want Ixchel to change her mind, better to keep that between you and her. Fighting with Benicio won't help." Montoyo seems irritated. "There's something else I need to talk to you about. Something that is for your ears only."

I sit up, curious. I thought he'd be more annoyed, but it's nothing to him, nothing. Instead it seems Montoyo is much keener to tell me what's on his own mind. Sitting opposite me, elbows propped against my laptop, he says very quietly,

"Listen closely. We have a big problem. Blanco Vigores has gone."

The comment takes me by surprise. It's more or less normal for the old blind man to go off on his own once in a while, that's what I've always been told.

I shrug. "So. . .?"

"When you came back from Switzerland with Ixchel, I told you Vigores had gone to visit some people in the outside world, yes?"

I nod. "I remember, yeah." I'd seen Vigores only days before he left, just before the dream-visitation with my sister. He said things that lingered in my memory for a long time afterwards. The old guy has a way of putting things in words that really get under my skin.

"Vigores called in a few times at the beginning of the month. He was in Mexico City. Then New York. The last time he called was over two months ago. I've kept this quiet, Josh, but I began an investigation. About six weeks ago."

"Six weeks?" It starts to hit me that there is something serious going on.

"I've been working with private investigators in the USA. The leads all go cold. One morning around two months ago he left his hotel room in Manhattan, took a taxi to the Yale Club of New York. . ."

"And then?"

Montoyo shakes his head. "That's it. The porter signed him in, but no member's name was attached, which is unusual. He hasn't been seen since."

I stare at him, thrilled by the idea that occurs right then. "I bet it's Marius Martineau – the leader of the Sect of Huracan."

Grimly, he smiles. "My thoughts precisely. Martineau works for Yale University – the Peabody Museum."

"You think Blanco's gone to meet Martineau?"

Montoyo expression darkens. "I'm afraid it's worse, much worse." He leans forward, conspiratorial, practically whispers in my ear. "Josh . . . we have to face the possibility that Vigores has joined our enemies in the Sect. "

"But why? What's in it for him?"

Montoyo shrugs, considering. "Vigores behaves in ways that have always mystified me. I have often sensed that he has a higher master than Ek Naab. His origins here are mysterious – I've told you that. For one thing – he doesn't seem to age."

I start. "What are you talking about? He's, like, really old!"

"And always has been! I don't remember him as anything other than a balding, blind old man. Even allowing for my own youthful impressions of an older, balding man. . ." Montoyo takes a breath. "Haven't you heard what people say about that place where he lives?"

"The Garden?" Vigores had secretly taken me there himself, the first time we met. It's a labyrinth that runs even deeper than the cavernous Ek Naab. A place of strange forces, I suspect; miraculous powers that can make flowers grow without light. "I've heard people say it's a bit strange down there."

"A little 'strange', yes," Montoyo says. "The kind of place where miracles might happen, yes? The kind of place you might find a fountain of youth."

"What, seriously?" I say, astonished.

"It's a very old legend in Mexico. The Spanish explorer Ponce de Leon sought the fount. . ."

I interrupt. "Did Ponce de Leon come to Ek Naab too?"

Montoyo smiles slightly. "No . . . not him. I'm merely illustrating the way a rumour begins, a legend. Vigores has become a legend to us in Ek Naab. His very existence is wrapped in rumours and stories. About where he disappears to. About his friends in the outside world. But very few people know about Vigores and the Bracelet of Itzamna."

Vigores told me, the last time we spoke, that it was he who found the Bracelet of Itzamna. As a young man exploring in the Mayan ruins at Izapa, he'd come across the Bracelet – broken – lacking the Crystal Key. He'd used the Bracelet too – very dangerous indeed without the controlling crystal. Yet he'd lived to tell the tale.

I look into Montoyo's eyes then, hunting out his real intention. "Why are you telling me?"

"Vigores . . . he knows real secrets. Information we wouldn't want the Sect to have."

"Well, yeah, I know! Like – the entire contents of the Ix Codex, for one."

Montoyo looks puzzled, thrown off course. "Naturally, but we know already that the Sect knows as much about the Ix Codex as we do. . ."

I gape. "Uh . . . how? We had the whole Ix Codex . . . the Sect never saw it. . ."

"They saw the same fragment that we have, the opening, which J Eric Thompson translated. . ."

Carefully I say, "And that's all *we* have. . .?"

Montoyo's eyes narrow. "That's all we have . . . of course! Are you telling me that you've forgotten what happened when you brought back the codex?"

Bizarre. It's the same story as Lorena's. . .

"Yeah," I tell him. Might as well go all out now. "Cos that's not how I remember what happened with the Ix Codex. Or quite a lot of things." I sigh, looking away. "You might as well know. There's something bizarre about my memory. I've been to see Lorena; she's done a brain scan but there's nothing wrong that she can see."

Montoyo touches my arm. "But your memories . . . are different?" He sounds incredulous.

"Yes."

There's anxiety in the clouding of his eyes, the set of his mouth. "You're sure?"

I nod. "All day. For days now, in fact. People and events. Like, a guy I was friends with in Oxford, Tyler. He even got kidnapped along with my mum and Ixchel in Brazil. But now . . . no one here remembers him. You don't either. I can see it in your face. So I called him, in Oxford. Tyler doesn't remember being friends with me."

Montoyo nods once, as though he needs to confirm what he can't believe.

Miserably I say, "I'm losing it, aren't I? Whatever the Sect did to me in Switzerland, that genetic engineering . . . it's messing with my mind."

Montoyo looks around us. He stands up. "Let's take a walk."

When we reach the edge of the *cenote*, Montoyo stops and leans over, staring into the still black water. He's silent for so long that I wonder what's going on. Then he straightens up.

"There are many differences between you and the rest of us, Josh. Your Bakab genes set you apart, yes, it's true. But there's something else, something which maybe you have overlooked."

I look blank. "What?"

"*You*, Josh, you have used the Bracelet of Itzamna to travel through time."

"So. . .?"

"Once you've used the Bracelet, your timeline is set. Your memories are protected, somehow, from the changes around you."

"How?"

Montoyo shakes his head. "I don't know. I'd imagine it's to do with the gravitic forces that propel you through space-time."

I'm silent, thinking. "You think my memories could be different because I've used the Bracelet. . .?"

"You've used the Bracelet . . . so you remember how things *were*."

"Before. . .?"

Montoyo bends his head and murmurs, "Before they changed."

The implications of what Montoyo is suggesting start to hit me.

"Things . . . have changed. . .?"

He waves his hands in the air, drawing a circle around us. "Things, yes. The world I live in, me and everyone else. To observe the circle it is first necessary to stand *outside* the circle. And that's you, Josh – outside the circle. Only you can see that things have changed. Your timeline remains consistent. You've time travelled, Josh; you've found a way to exist outside of time."

I'm open-mouthed, clenching and unclenching my hands, trying to grasp what he's saying.

I repeat, "Things have *changed*?"

Something was bothering me, but I couldn't think what...

If the whole of history has changed . . . and I'm the only one who can remember how things used to be . . . wow.

Talk about a fish out of water.

Montoyo nods, watching me. "Things may have changed . . . yes. I believe so."

I'm silent for a long time, thinking about how this makes sense of so much of the utterly baffling day I've been having. Emmy – she remembered things differently because they actually happened differently. She knew about the postcards. She saw me after the fight with Madison. I told her about my blog. But of course, without Tyler being my friend, things would have been different. Emmy must have done things that I remember Tyler doing.

It's harsh to think I never even made friends with a guy I think of almost like family.

But that is as nothing compared to what has happened with the Ix Codex. No codex means no solution to the 2012 problem.

No wonder people in Ek Naab are quietly panicking. No wonder some of them want to go worldwide on the 2012 problem. The enormity of it all takes several minutes to sink in. Montoyo says nothing, just letting me absorb it. I can't help wondering whether he's had his own suspicions that something is wrong. Or that he knows something that he isn't telling me.

Finally I say, "Who changed things?"

"That's the question, isn't it, Josh, my time-travelling friend? Or perhaps I should address you as Arcadio?"

Not Montoyo too. . .? I'm about to object when I notice the slight twinkle in his eye. He's joking.

"Arcadio?"

"We know that Arcadio has the Bracelet; we know he's a time traveller. What we don't know is . . . where he is."

Or who he is.

"You think Arcadio did something," I ask. "You think he changed something in the past?"

"I think a *time traveller* changed something – Arcadio or someone else – whilst using the Bracelet of Itzamna." He fixes me with a stern look. "I've half expected something like this. I've been watching for the signs. Ever since you fixed the Bracelet and travelled in time."

I roll my eyes. "Oh, so it's my fault?"

"Not directly. There are other players involved, that has been clear to me for a while. I think Vigores may know who Arcadio is and where to find him. Vigores disappearing, your memories being altered . . . without a doubt, they are connected."

"How?" I ask, bewildered. "How can you possibly know?"

"Well. . ." Montoyo raises an eyebrow. "Maybe I should show you this. I found it in a search of Vigores's apartments."

He passes me an unmarked envelope of thick, high-quality white paper. I get a flash of recognition – I think immediately of the letter Arcadio left to me, and had Susannah St John hold for him. Without a word I take the envelope and slide the contents out: three sheaves of paper, covered in handwritten, blue ink; neat writing and illustrations that I recognize as symbols from the Bracelet of Itzamna.

"'*Instructions for operation of the Erinsi time-jump device.*'" When I see the title, I glance up at Montoyo. "Who wrote this. . .? Arcadio? Blanco Vigores?"

"You missed someone," Montoyo remarks. "What about Itzamna himself?"

Montoyo's revelations sweeps everything from my mind: the weirdness of Emmy, Tyler not knowing me, Ixchel's admission, everything.

All I can think about right now is the mystery in front of us both.

Could it really be that someone has time travelled, used the Bracelet and changed the past so that somehow, the Ix Codex has been ripped apart at some point in time, most of it lost for ever?

It would explain so much – the weird mood of everyone in Ek Naab, Benicio's strange comments about how everyone in Ek Naab had wasted their time studying when they should have been having fun. Plus, of course, the fact that Tyler didn't remember me.

The people of Ek Naab here and now do seem to have given up. Without the Ix Codex, the 2012 superwave can't be stopped. On 22 December 2012 an electromagnetic pulse is going to blast through the atmosphere and erase all the computers in the world. All the technology we depend on to keep things running smoothly will be disrupted. Civilization will come to a standstill. All over the world, there'll be panic and craziness. Everything will fall apart.

The letter I'm holding is a series of instructions for how to select the time, date and location on the Bracelet of Itzamna. It looks complicated, but I reckon if I had the Bracelet I'd be able to work it out. But Montoyo made me give him the Bracelet three months ago – afraid that I'd use it to try to change my own past.

Of course, Montoyo doesn't know that I'd already had a go at that.

I tried to change things and it made no difference. My dad still died in that ice crevasse, saving me. I've lost the will to try it again. Dad was determined to make the same choice, every time. He would always end up putting his life down for me, I'm convinced of that. It's time to leave the past alone and move on.

Exactly what I tried to do.

"At least I don't have to be suspicious of you, Josh," Montoyo says wryly. "I've kept a close eye on the Bracelet."

Ignoring his implication, I ask, "Whose handwriting is this?"

"Does it look like Arcadio's?"

I shake my head, thinking of Arcadio's letter. It's in my room, still blood-spattered from the time Madison shot me in the leg. "I've never seen this handwriting," I say. "The paper doesn't look very old. My guess is that it's Vigores. He's the only person to have read the Ix Codex and also used the Bracelet of Itzamna."

Montoyo comments, "Apart from Itzamna himself."

I tap the pages. "But the paper. It's pretty new. Like the kind you buy in fancy stationery shops. If Itzamna is a time traveller then he's from the future, yeah? Or the past. Either way you'd expect him to use different paper."

No – it's becoming clear to me. Vigores always knew more than he let on about the Bracelet. He found it, he'd used it in its broken state and realized how dangerous that could be – a one-way teleport ride into space. He'd decoded the Ix Codex and now he knew how to use the Bracelet. He'd even given it to my dad, hoping that my dad would fix it.

Vigores had his own reasons for wanting the Bracelet. Could Montoyo be right – had he planned to hand the information over to the Sect? And if so – why now? Vigores has been in Ek Naab for ages; he could have done something like this years ago.

Except . . . I put the two things together.

What would be the use of that information – unless you also had the Bracelet of Itzamna?

I glance at Montoyo. He's watching me with an expectant

grin. With a start, I realize that he's actually looking at me proudly.

"Could there be . . . a second Bracelet?"

His grin broadens. "I knew you'd see it. Yes! The only explanation. A second Bracelet, in the possession of Marius Martineau and the Sect. They had access to the Revival Chamber for many days before you discovered it. Who knows what artefacts they discovered there?"

"Why would Vigores help them? It doesn't seem like him."

Montoyo grimaces. "It doesn't. I'm not suggesting that he went willingly."

"If the Sect has people inside Ek Naab . . . maybe they tricked him."

He's thoughtful. "The Sect has made this move for a reason. I'm certain it's the Bracelet of Itzamna."

"If they have a second Bracelet . . . and they know how to make the Crystal Key, of course, since I actually nicked one from their own labs . . . and now they have the instructions of how to use it from Vigores . . . then . . . then. . ." I stare at Montoyo. "It's true. They could travel into the past. Nick the codex, rip it apart."

Montoyo nods. "Precisely. They'd have to go to a place and time in history where they knew the codex to exist."

"That would have to be Thompson's house – that archaeologist in Saffron Walden. The place where my granddad found the codex. Or even Catemaco, with the *brujos*, where I found the codex."

Again he nods. "There is a third possibility – ancient Calakmul. AD 653. In the time of Yuknoom the Great, Ruler of the Snake Kingdom."

"Huh? But how would the Sect know about that? We only know because of the Calakmul letter. No one from the Sect ever saw the whole letter except. . ."

I exhale, slowly. Of course. That traitorous cow, Ollie. She was with us when Camila and I read out the whole letter, left by my grandfather Aureliano, found by my dad and then divided into two parts: one for my sister, one for me. Ollie knows what's in the Calakmul letter. The Sect know everything.

"So . . . what are we gonna do? Visit each point in history?"

"*We* are going to do nothing, my friend. This time you'll be staying at home. I'll be the one to take the risks."

It looks like he's serious.

Montoyo continues, "Your mother would never forgive me if I put you in danger again. Even if it was an attempt to save the whole of civilization. . ." he says, with a slight grin.

"Of course not," I say accusingly. "You've got her under your thumb, yeah? She doesn't care about anything but staying here with you and being happy."

Montoyo's eyes flash with danger for a second. "You

underestimate your mother. Her concern for you is natural."

"It's a stupid plan anyway," I tell him. Even as the words leave my mouth I'm surprised at how annoyed I feel that he's doing this without me. Even though I should probably be relieved.

What's happening to me? Have I turned into some kind of adrenaline junkie?

I pursue my argument. "There's no way to know where and when they've gone. Thompson's place, Catemaco; the codex was in those places for ages. We don't know *when* it arrived in either place. How can you be sure to arrive in time to stop the Sect changing things?"

Montoyo's eyes glimmer with a light of excitement that I've never seen before. "It's not the first place I'll try. For the Sect it makes sense to go back as early as possible, precisely so that their intervention has maximum devastation. To damage the codex during its time at Calakmul . . . that would be very difficult for anyone to reverse."

I pause. "So you're really gonna do this, yeah? You're gonna time travel to ancient Calakmul?"

Slowly, he nods. "I think I have to."

I'm finding it hard to believe we're actually discussing this. "To AD 653?"

"The Golden Age of Classic Maya," Montoyo murmurs. "Amazing, yes?"

"How . . . how will you get by? Talking and stuff. The ancient Maya . . . they're pretty fierce, aren't they? Human sacrifice and all that?"

"Yucatec is close enough to the language of Classic Maya. I'll be able to understand, to make myself understood. As for the human sacrifice. . ." Montoyo shrugs. "It wasn't as common as you might think. Religious holidays and special occasions, that kind of time."

I look doubtfully at the instructions. Is he really going to go ahead with this?

"So, Josh . . . will you help me?"

"You need my help?"

"I need a witness. Someone to explain everything to in case . . . to your mother, you know, should things not turn out for the best."

We look at each other. I can see he means it; he really does care about my mother. Meanwhile I'm more relieved by the second that Montoyo isn't asking me to do this.

Ancient Calakmul – that is several steps too far for me. I'd be way, way out of my depth.

"OK," I say, nodding. "I'll help. Where's the Bracelet?"

"It's at my apartment."

I stand up. "All right. Let's go."

Montoyo seems hesitant; unusual for him. He casts around a bit, as if he's looking for something or someone. After a moment, his attention rests back on me. "I have some matters to take care of," he says. "It's not a trivial thing, to venture forth into the seventh century. . ." He almost forces a chuckle and then eyes me sharply. "What would you do?"

The question throws me. I'm not used to Montoyo asking for my advice. Part of me wonders if this isn't some ploy to bond with me as a stepfather type. He's been doing things like that lately, inviting me to listen to music with him, showing an interest in my hobbies.

I hate it. I don't want to be reminded that he's my mum's boyfriend.

"I'd load myself up with some weaponry. Seventh-century Mayans were pretty hardcore."

"Really?" He seems bemused. "I thought you didn't like to shoot people."

I shrug. "Yeah, but . . . you, you're OK with it. Aren't you?"

Montoyo's smile is totally mirthless. In a low voice he says, "Is that what you think of me, Josh?" His eyes are clouded, his expression heavy.

I've no idea how to respond.

He claps me on the back. "Go home, eat something, and see your mother, your friends. I'll meet you in my apartment in two hours."

Without another glance, Montoyo leaves.

Montoyo's instructions leave me feeling disoriented. Plus, I'm tired and hungry, not to mention annoyed. It's all too much to think about. I just want my bed and a big juicy sandwich.

In our cosy second floor apartment, Mum's cooking chicken tacos. The smell of frying tortillas drenches my senses as I walk through the door: maize dough crisping up in sizzling corn oil. I can't sit down fast enough – I heap shredded chicken, refried beans, green tomato salsa, sour cream and crumbly white cheese on to a couple of hot, crunchy tortillas. Mum watches me shovel down the first taco, a smile on her face. She pours me a glass of iced *agua de limón* – limeade.

"Carlos won't be coming round tonight," she tells me softly. "He just called. So it's just you and me."

I swallow a huge mouthful of taco and watch my mother closely. She gives no sign of knowing what Montoyo's up to. I feel guilty then, because I know that Mum loves Montoyo. It's obvious – I don't know when I've seen her so happy. All day long she walks around in a blissful daze. It's like she's drugged. When they're together . . . yuck, I don't want to think about it. *So* gross. That's not even the worst part. What drives me really crazy is watching them build this new domestic routine together when he's over at our house. Sometimes he even cooks us all breakfast and I have to sit and eat it, looking grateful, as if I should be happy to watch some bloke take my dad's place.

Still . . . as grim as it is to watch, I can't say it hasn't made her happy. No wonder they say people who take drugs look "loved-up" – my mum looks like she's been drugged.

She's lucky.

But now Montoyo's about to risk all of that. He's about to put himself in terrible danger. Walking into ancient Calakmul with no plan except to stop whoever interfered with the Ix Codex in the past? Even I'm not mental enough to do something like that.

I eat my second taco in silence, thinking. Is there any other way around this? Why does this Ix Codex business keep falling on to my family and the people I care about?

"Ixchel popped round, by the way."

Before I can stop myself, I'm perking up. "She did?"

Mum covers a smile with her hand. "Yes, Josh. She sounded rather mournful. Have you two sweethearts had a tiff?"

71

Hotly I say, "We're not 'sweethearts'. Who said we were?"

She pauses. "You've looked like . . . well, forgive me, but like a lovelorn teenager, ever since she turned up in Brazil."

Mum's words almost physically sting. Furious, I take a long drink of cold limeade, unable to answer. Maybe something will come to me. It's pointless, though. If I deny it I just know I'm going to go red.

In fact, as my mother watches me, I realize that I'm blushing anyway.

"Rather not talk about it," I say without expression. I push myself away from the table. "I'm going to bed."

I flop down on to my bed without turning on the lights, and think over what Ixchel said today. I replay every single thing over and over, remembering her expression as she said it.

She never said she didn't like me.

She never actually said anything that might mean she didn't fancy me. Obviously she's worked out that I like her . . . but then all of Ek Naab seems to be on to that one. From what I saw, she doesn't seem to mind. Maybe she even enjoys it?

When she said *I don't want to be the girl you forgot*, she was actually sobbing.

I made her cry. *Again*. Reluctantly, I let myself remember that moment on the beach in Brazil after the capoeira tournament, when I said something mean to Ixchel, and she began to cry.

Why does this keep happening? I don't mean to upset Ixchel; it's the last thing on earth I want to do. Is there no way to keep this stuff under control?

Being in love is a nightmare. It's *torture*. She said some horrible things to me today and for a while I was angry. Anger felt better than being pathetic and miserable. But now I can't even stay angry with her for a few hours.

I'm starting to wish that I hadn't rushed out of the kitchen without eating another taco. They were so great, two wasn't enough. Lying on my bed isn't really helping me to straighten anything out in my mind, and my stomach keeps complaining, telling me to go back to the kitchen, mumble something apologetic to Mum and get another couple of tacos.

So, I do. Luckily for me, Mum seems to have worked out that I'm upset and has decided not to press it any harder. She lets me eat the rest of my supper silently while she tidies up. She passes me a bowl of vanilla ice cream with sliced bananas and lemon jelly.

If anything happens to Montoyo, I decide, I'll take care of Mum. I'll have to. She's really hit it off with him, but I can't see her getting on with any of the other blokes in Ek Naab. Most of them are married, but also, they're not like Montoyo. He's lived in the outside world, for one thing, not just Ek

Naab. It would just be too different with any of the others. Mum likes Montoyo because he's so confident – he seems to know about everything and everywhere. My dad was like that too.

I check my watch. Almost time to meet Montoyo.

"I'm going out for a bit, Mum. That all right?"

She turns to me with a smile. "Of course, love. That's fine. Don't stay out too late."

I grin. "I won't. I'm tired . . . I. . ." I stop myself then, before I let anything slip out to prompt questions that lead to the motorbike race or Benicio.

"I want to get a good night's sleep," I say, compromising. At least that much is true.

But Mum isn't quite ready to stop talking. "You're a good lad, you know, Josh. I'm always proud of you. Even though God knows, you make me worried sick. . ."

"Don't worry any more, Mum," I tell her. "We're here now. I'm safe."

Mum rolls her eyes. "Ah well, you will say that. Then you're off somewhere and I've no idea what's going on."

I nod once, gulping. "Yeah. I know. Sorry about that."

"Go on with you," she says, waving a tea towel. "Go and see that girl of yours. See if you can't put her straight on a few things."

For once, I don't argue.

The night air in Ek Naab is warm and fragrant, mingled

smells of cooking and the sweetly fermenting juices of the market's tropical fruit. I step outside, wondering when – if ever – I'll feel the cold again, never mind the wind. I wander down the lane of our apartment block, heading away from the *zocalo*, through the dimly lit labyrinthine network of alleys towards Montoyo's place.

Two doorways down from our apartment block's entrance, I almost have a heart attack when Ixchel steps out in front of me.

"Jeez! What are you doing?"

Ixchel fidgets. Amazingly, she seems flustered, embarrassed. "I was waiting . . . waiting until. . ." She looks up then, eyes pleading. "I was trying to get the courage to come and speak to you." Then, nervously, she touches a hand to mine.

There's nothing I'd like more than to continue this, but I'm already running late for Montoyo.

"Ixchel . . . I can't talk right now. . ."

She withdraws her hand, puzzled. "What. . .?"

"I have to be somewhere," I say. "I'm sorry . . . really am . . . I have to go."

Ixchel is stunned. "You're still angry?"

"No, no way, it's nothing like that. I just . . . have to go." I give her a final, apologetic look and tear myself away, trying to ignore the astonished look on her face.

Even as I walk away, I wonder if I'm making a huge

mistake. But what else could I do? I speed up, jogging. I couldn't mention Montoyo and his plans, of course, and I couldn't let her keep talking. There was no way a conversation about Ixchel, me and Benicio was going to be brief.

A few minutes later, I'm climbing the stairs to Montoyo's apartment. I'm going to have a lot of explaining to do tomorrow. But tomorrow is another day. In fact, if Montoyo gets the job done, tomorrow is *another history*.

Maybe none of what happened today will ever have happened. Maybe I'll get that second chance with Ixchel.

9

The door to Montoyo's apartment is unlocked, so I step
inside. He's sitting on the black leather and metal sofa in his
minimally furnished, white living room. He's listening to slow,
moody piano music that I don't recognize. A mournful bass
line thumps along with the melody. Instead of looking up
when I walk in, Montoyo simply points to the CD in his hand.
It's black and white, a photo of a bearded guy at the piano.

"Your father, Josh. Was he an admirer of Jan Johansson?
Jazz Pa Ryska, for example?"

"Never heard of him," I say.

Montoyo seems disappointed. "A pity. I felt sure his music
would have formed part of your father's collection." He
hunches his shoulders and cricks his neck as if to relieve
tension. He breathes out slowly and stands up. "I always
hoped that you and I would get on better, Josh, partly
because of my tremendous regard, my respect, for your
father."

I shrug. What does he expect me to say?

"This mission is risky, very risky," Montoyo says in a quiet voice, suddenly serious. "I want you to know that I'm aware of that." He looks me in the eyes. "Also that I understand that this may be the last time we see each other."

I gulp slightly. "OK. I get it. I think. . ."

There's a slight smile at the edge of his lips. "What I'm trying to tell you, Josh, is . . . that certain things need to be said."

"OK," I say, nodding, not a clue what he's on about. "Fair enough."

"All right?" He seems to be checking with me again, seeing if it's OK to proceed. "So, I'll go first, if that's acceptable."

He seems to want me to nod again, so I do.

"I love your mother," he says softly, no hint of hesitation. "Of everything that's happened since you first arrived in Ek Naab, it's the most incredible and unpredicted thing for me. To be happy again in this way, to find someone like Eleanor. . ." He chuckles, looks at me inquiringly. "You understand, don't you, what I'm saying?"

"You're obsessed with my mum," I reply in a monotone. "I get it."

"You're not happy with the development," he says. "That's regrettable. Naturally, I understand. However, making you happy isn't my job. You and I, we are men of action, men of will."

"Whatever that means," I mutter.

Montoyo laughs. "You know well enough. What I'm trying to say here is that although I love Eleanor and want to make her happy, there are higher duties that bind me. They always have. Ultimately, I'm a servant of this city and our mission."

"I'll look after my mother," I tell him. "If you don't come back. I promise."

He smiles, chuckles. "I believe you. If the situation were reversed, Josh, I'd make you the same promise."

I nod once. "Good."

"So." Montoyo pushes up his black silk shirtsleeve to reveal the Bracelet of Itzamna on his forearm. He picks up the three sheets of handwritten instructions that he found in Vigores's place. Our eyes rest on the Bracelet. "Shall we begin?

"Wait," I tell him. "What about the weapons and stuff?"

"Oh yes – guns, ammunition, that sort of thing?"

"Right. You can't go without *anything*."

"What do you think will happen if I'm caught in the Mayan past with such objects?"

I snort. "Nothing, that's just the point; no one will dare to come near you."

"All right, let's imagine for the sake of argument that I'm threatened, so I shoot a number of Mayan warriors, yes?"

"I guess. . ."

"And then what? I keep going until the ammunition is exhausted and I'm surrounded by a pile of dead warriors. Then?"

"I guess that wouldn't be ideal. . ."

Emphatically, he shakes his head. "Not at all! To a seventh-century Mayan I'd be a highly suspicious, murderous stranger with apparently demonic powers. If they didn't serve up my still-beating heart to their god Kukulkan by the end of the same day I would be fortunate. And when archaeologists discover Calakmul, what would they make of the discovery of a twenty-first-century weapon?"

"Good point," I say. "So . . . you're going as you are?"

"I think so," he says, nodding. "I think it's safest. To present no threat. To win their curiosity, then their trust. In a situation such as this, knowledge and cunning should win the day."

Let's hope so.

Montoyo picks up a small pair of reading glasses from a leather string around his neck and perches them on his nose. From his right shirt pocket he pulls a folded piece of paper and begins to read.

"**K'inich K'ane Ajk of Cancuen writes to Lord Yuknoom Ch'een of Calakmul**

I am your servant

From Chechan Naab he emerged, from the Great Temple of the Cross

The Bakab was defeated

This sacred Book of Ix speaks of the end of days

13.0.0.0.0 it is written in the Sacred Books of Itzamna

The Black Road will open the Heart of Sky

It will be destroyed

Healer of Worlds will be born.

In the Moon it walks

In their Holy City of Ek Naab they wait

They are still. They wait."

He looks up at me then, expectant. "It's the Calakmul letter," I say, shrugging.

Montoyo smiles. "You remember."

"I deciphered it," I remind him. "At least, I deciphered the first half. My sister, Camila, deciphered the second half. Yeah, I remember it pretty well."

"The date, too, did you remember that?"

I glance again at the paper between his fingers. It's a photocopy of the two fragments of the manuscript that my dad left with me and Camila. Under the images of the Mayan glyphs is a handwritten translation. Not my writing, but as far as I can remember, it's the same translation.

Pointing to the top of Montoyo's paper, where the initial signature glyph, the ISIG, appears, I tell him, "It's here. January AD 653."

"To be precise, the eighth of January," Montoyo says. "The date that the Traitor Bakab – *K'inich K'ane Ajk* – wrote to Yuknoom Ch'een of the Snake Kingdom – Calakmul – telling him about the Books of Itzamna and the 2012 prophecy."

"Right, so that's the date when the Traitor Bakab guy stole the Ix Codex?"

Montoyo pushes the glasses further up the bridge of his nose. "No, there's a great deal more information to be extracted here, if we study it carefully. To begin with, K'inich K'ane Ajk is a historical figure – he's known to the world of Mayan studies."

I stare at Montoyo, impressed. "He is?"

"There's a panel at Cancuen, the Mayan city that your father was studying just before he found Ek Naab. K'inich K'ane Ajk's name appears in that panel. He's clearly a person of importance, and related to Calakmul. He may even have been installed as a ruler of Cancuen three years later, when Calakmul, the Snake Kingdom, was about to make war on the kingdom of Tikal. Tikal was a great rival of Calakmul back then. In Ek Naab we know K'inich K'ane Ajk as the Traitor Bakab, Josh. But he rose to become a man of influence. A reward for bringing the Snake Kingdom's ruler a holy book, perhaps?"

"But Blanco Vigores told me that the Traitor Bakab was killed," I say wonderingly. "Tortured to death at the orders of the king of Calakmul."

Montoyo looks baffled. "Vigores told you that?"

I hesitate, think back to the first night I met Vigores and he'd taken me into the labyrinth of tunnels near his home. "Yeah, I'm pretty sure he said the Traitor Bakab was killed."

"I'd like to know how Vigores knows that," he says thoughtfully. "It's certainly not in any writings I've seen."

For a few minutes I'm silent, thinking it through. "I guess . . . at least we know that the Ix Codex was in Calakmul for three years, from 653 to 656. Then . . . it might have gone to Cancuen with the Traitor Bakab. The king of Calakmul can't have killed him before 656."

Montoyo nods. "I'm going to set the Bracelet of Itzamna to return me to Calakmul in March of AD 653. That gives time for the Traitor Bakab to have arrived at Calakmul with the Ix Codex. He should still be in favour with the king."

I join Montoyo in examining the Bracelet on his arm. The matt metallic sheen is just as I remember it; strange, Sumerian-like cuneiform symbols are cut into the coppery surface, the slightly offset depression in which sits the tiny Crystal Key, an artificially produced protein crystal. With a sense of bafflement, I recall Lorena's words to me about the last of the genetic changes the Sect of Huracan made inside me.

The Key is produced in my own blood. Just as Arcadio predicted in his coded postcard message to me: WHAT.KEY.HOLDS.BLOOD.

I don't understand how the Bracelet of Itzamna works, except that the Key seems to activate the time circuit of the

Bracelet. If the Crystal Key were to burn out again, as it had before, the Bracelet of Itzamna would lose its ability to transport in time, but not in space. It would be a teleporter. Even then, I wouldn't know how to control it.

I have to face the fact that Ixchel might be right about me becoming Arcadio. If I can produce the Key, I'm a natural to be a time traveller. Maybe the only person who can use the Bracelet of Itzamna without risking being lost in time.

Thinking like this just makes me feel even more uneasy at helping Montoyo to zap himself into the Mayan past.

If the Crystal Key burns out, he's toast. Stuck in the past with no way back.

Montoyo touches the Bracelet lightly with a forefinger. "According to the instructions, we need to activate this symbol, then this one. . ."

In silence he taps the Bracelet several more times, changing the symbols that are displayed. When he stops, we stare at the Bracelet. Nothing happens.

"Hmmm."

I ask, "Can you feel anything?"

Montoyo looks blank. "For example?"

I remember when I used the Bracelet, in fact even just when I wore it, I would feel this ripple of energy, a sort of electricity that coursed into me from the device. Or maybe it was the other way around? Truthfully, I could never be sure.

"Like electricity," I suggest. "Like the Bracelet is coated

with that furry metal. What's it called again? Iron filings. You get these little pinpricks of electricity all along its surface."

Montoyo shakes his head. "No . . . I haven't felt that. But you did?"

"Yeah."

He ponders, "Perhaps only a Bakab can change the settings. Perhaps the Bracelet is reacting with some biochemical agent on the surface of your skin."

It's possible, I guess. Would explain the way the Bracelet always seemed to respond to me.

"Why don't you change the settings, Josh? Then before we activate the time crystal, we'll switch it back on to me?"

Montoyo unfastens the catch, slips the Bracelet off his hand. He takes my left hand and slides the device on to my wrist. We look at each other expectantly.

A sharp intake of breath from behind us startles both me and Montoyo. Standing in the open doorway is Ixchel. She's staring at us, pale and drawn. I have no idea how long she's been there. Awkwardly, Montoyo drops his hand from the Bracelet. He strides over towards Ixchel.

"You need to leave, Ixchel. This is a confidential matter."

He places a hand on her arm, as if to shepherd her out of the apartment. Still gazing at me in disbelief, Ixchel steps away from Montoyo, shrinking from his touch.

"Stay away from me."

You could hear a pin drop. Ixchel breaks the silence.

"What's going on here? Josh?" She looks at me, imploringly. "Please tell me you aren't going to use the Bracelet."

"There's this thing. . ." I mumble. "It's not me, anyway . . . Carlos is gonna."

"Leave," Montoyo tells her. "Now."

Ixchel plants her feet firmly, hands by her side. "No." Her eyes lock on to mine. "Josh. Take it off."

Chaos breaks out. To my amazement, Ixchel and Montoyo both lunge at me. Montoyo goes for the Bracelet. Instinctively, I pull away. When his hand moves, I see something that makes my skin crawl.

The Bracelet of Itzamna has come alive. The metallic parts are sliding over each other, creeping like the body of a snake. The outer casing ripples away to reveal another set of symbols underneath. The symbols are moving, changing with a steady rhythm that I've seen before.

The countdown.

"How can I stop it? There's a way to stop it during the countdown . . . how?!"

The last word comes out like a desperate plea. But Montoyo only steps back, gazing solemnly into my eyes. "The Ix Codex must remain in Calakmul," he says, pronouncing the words the way he might give a death sentence.

With rising panic, Ixchel glances from Montoyo to me. Next thing I know, she throws herself on top of me, screaming, "Josh! No!"

There's a dazzling flash. Then it's as though the image of Montoyo's apartment is ripped away from my retina. Windows, walls, paintings, lights are replaced with pitch black. The air is different too; it feels warm, heavy, damp.

It takes a while for me to work out that the sounds I'm hearing are the terrified yells from Ixchel and me. We clutch each other, hanging on for support as we both fall to the ground.

"Oh God," I manage to say. It takes a few seconds for it to sink in. But with each second of realization, I feel terror mounting. "No," I mutter, panting with dread. "No. God, not this. Please!"

In the darkness, Ixchel clings to me even more tightly. I can feel her breath against my neck. When she speaks, I can hear the fear in her voice. "What's happened, Josh? Where are we?"

Seventh-century Calakmul. . .?

I can't say it aloud, can barely even think it. I'm so panicked that it takes me several minutes to remember how to breathe properly.

When I do, I remember something. The Bracelet of Itzamna has a safety setting.

Wherever we are, we can go back.

Ixchel's breathing doesn't calm down; if anything, she becomes more hysterical. Even though we're surrounded by impenetrable darkness, one thing becomes obvious to us both.

We're in the middle of the jungle. The stifling heat, a sickly aroma of foliage, the faint scent of animals, the uninterrupted racket, clicks and buzzing of insects; the smells and sounds are unmistakable. For a moment it's as though I'm right back in the thicket of Campeche next to Highway 186, where I first met Ixchel.

I'm in the dark – again. Terrified – again. This time, Ixchel is too.

I don't want to push Ixchel away, but in her panic she's gripping me so tightly that I can hardly speak. There's a choking sound from her throat; she shoves me aside and retches violently on to the ground behind me. Her body continues to spasm for minutes after she's emptied the contents of her stomach. When she's done she begins to tremble. I take her by the shoulders as gently as possible, and when I'm sure she's not going to resist, I draw her to me.

"We're in the jungle," I whisper against her forehead. "Near Calakmul. In AD 653. So please, Ixchel. Shhh."

I hear the question in her voice. "The Bracelet did this? Oh, it feels horrible, Josh. How could you stand it?"

"What felt horrible?"

"The transporting. Like being sucked into a void. Like being swallowed whole and spat out. *Really* horrible."

Ixchel's description doesn't sound anything like what it feels like to me. "Maybe it's because you weren't actually wearing the Bracelet?"

She's shivering now, in spite of the night's heat. She pulls me closer. I don't resist.

"We can get back," I murmur. I'd like to stroke her hair but I don't dare. "It's going to be OK. The Bracelet has a safety setting. I can take us back to where we came from, just ten minutes before we left."

Ixchel seems confused. "So we'll suddenly appear in front of ourselves?"

"We'll materialize in Montoyo's apartment, ten minutes before we left."

"Were you there? When you arrived at Montoyo's tonight – did you see yourself already there?"

I consider what she's suggesting. "You mean – if we do

89

this, then we've *already done it*? And we'd have been in Montoyo's already?"

"Yes. I'm just trying to understand how this time travel thing works."

"Hmmm. Maybe we were hiding?"

"OK, good idea. Let's remember to hide."

Her comments make me nervous. It's true that I hadn't seen any sign of Future Me and Future Ixchel in Montoyo's apartment. Montoyo himself, though . . . how could he have missed us? I can't work it out right now; it's all so confusing and I really can't think straight.

With the darkness hiding our faces, it's possible for Ixchel and me to be less awkward around each other. Even so, now that we're having a proper conversation, Ixchel seems suddenly shy about being in a clinch with me. Still talking, she edges away.

"OK, Ixchel. Ready to go? I think you need to be holding on to me. You know, properly," I say, stammering slightly. "Like last time."

She pulls away completely. I can't tell if she's angry, but it seems like she might be. "Can . . . can we just wait a minute or two? Please. I can't go through that again just now."

"You want to stay in this forest? Listen. Can you hear those animal noises? There are pumas and jaguars here. Poisonous spiders and snakes and stuff. It's not safe."

"Just two minutes," she says, pleading. "At least let me

know you've thought this through. What makes you think we're in Calakmul in 653?"

"I reckon Montoyo's changed the coordinates," I say. "Only, I don't know how because I thought only a Bakab could activate the Bracelet. . ."

Ixchel interrupts, "How do you know that?"

I hesitate. "Montoyo told me." Then it hits me. "He must have lied. He *did* set the coordinates, probably before I even got to his apartment. Maybe he got one of the other Bakabs to do it for him. . . Everything else, all that pretence of not being able to change the coordinates. . . It was all show."

She lets out an anxious gasp. "What else did he tell you?"

I think hard, remembering the conversation. "Basically – he said his goodbyes. In case he never saw me again." Montoyo's little speech of things that "need to be said" is starting to make an awful kind of sense. "I said I'd look after my mum if anything happened to him," I say bitterly. "Carlos said he'd make me the same promise, 'if the situation were reversed'. Which, I guess, it actually was. Thanks to him."

With an air of resignation, Ixchel says, "He tricked you."

"Good and proper," I agree. "The coordinates were set before I even touched the Bracelet. AD 653 Calakmul. I don't know the exact date, but that's the year."

"The year the Ix Codex was stolen from Ek Naab and taken to Calakmul," she says. "But why?"

Over the next few minutes I explain everything to Ixchel.

At this point, there's no good reason to keep any secrets from her. She's astonished by my claims about Tyler – like everyone else, Ixchel has no memory of him. When I've finished, I notice that my eyes have adjusted to the faint starlight. It washes a ghostly shimmer over the interior of the forest. I can make out Ixchel's silhouette and the tiniest sparkle of her eyes.

"If Montoyo had to ask another Bakab to set the coordinates, why didn't he get someone else to do this mission?"

"Isn't it obvious?" I say bitterly. "Because this is about the Ix Codex. No Bakab but me can touch it and live."

However horrible the job might be . . . it's mine. From the minute my father died.

"Montoyo really thought this one through," I reflect. "Except for you. He didn't bargain on you walking through his door." I pause, then ask, "Why did you?"

She stalls. "What did you expect?"

I say nothing, waiting.

"I knew something was going on," Ixchel admits after a while. "You acted strangely; it's not like you to avoid me."

"I didn't want to avoid you. Montoyo asked me to help him; I just wanted to get it over with."

Ixchel shakes her head slowly. "He sent you into the past with no plan, no idea where to go, nothing to protect yourself . . . not the greatest way to think it through."

"A lot of effort, when he could have just asked me."

"Would you have agreed?"

I give a sardonic laugh. "I'd have told him he's mental."

"I think you'd have done it."

"Well, *you* think I'm crazy-reckless," I remark. "But most times I don't go out to do anything I think is going to be all that dangerous."

"Maybe you aren't very good at assessing risk."

For some reason, Ixchel's comment makes me angry, so much that my cheeks actually burn red for a few seconds. Luckily she can't see me. I can only hope she thinks it's a strong-silent-type response.

"Montoyo went to a lot of effort to make sure he got me here," I say coldly. "But he forgot I could just hit the safety to get back."

A horrible thought occurs to me. What if there's a way to turn off the safety . . . like with a gun? Could Montoyo have done something to the Bracelet so that I wouldn't be able to escape?

Beside me, Ixchel tenses. "Did you hear that? An animal . . . moving . . . in the trees just behind. . ."

Just before she gets silenced, Ixchel manages to cry out. I throw myself forward, grabbing uselessly for her in the dark, landing chin first on the ground. The second I try to budge, I feel the sharp edge of a blade against the back of my neck. A fierce voice hisses at me, spitting the words. It takes me a while to realize that I can just about understand what he's saying. He's speaking Mayan. It sounds a lot like Yucatec, though the accent is strange and so are many of the words. Basically, he's saying, "Lie still or I'll cut you open like a pig."

Someone grabs my arms and twists them behind me. It only takes a few seconds for my attackers to bind my hands so tightly that the twine cuts into my wrists.

In a voice edged with panic, Ixchel calls, "Josh, don't say anything. . ." Then she cries out. I can't see what's happening to her but it sounds like she's being slapped around. I'm too scared to protest, but I can't help wincing from the pain when they drag me to my feet, then knock me down again so that I fall on my knees.

I can hear at least three people – all young men – in the woods with Ixchel and me. Now that they've captured us both, their mood relaxes. When I concentrate, I realize I can understand most of what they're saying.

"Where's Fish Face?" one of them shouts, irritated. "I told him to bring that light, the stupid. . ."

The rest of the sentence, I don't understand, but it must be a rude insult because all three of our captors break out in merry chuckling. Montoyo was right – Classic Maya is quite a bit like Yucatec.

Ixchel is an expert in lots of languages – probably understands every word they're saying. Yet – she's saying absolutely nothing. Probably wise.

"What *were* you kids doing out here?" All three snigger. "Sacrificial runaways, I bet." This time they make thoughtful sounds of agreement. There's a long silence. Then, "Where is *idiot* Fish Face with that light?!"

Our captors sound young, probably not much older than us. I still can't believe how silently they stalked us. I hadn't heard the slightest unusual sound. Behind my back, I move my hands, trying with my right hand to reach the Bracelet on my left forearm. It's useless. Even if I could reach, I wouldn't be able to bring myself to leave without Ixchel. I don't even have to think about that one. If I couldn't leave her in Brazil with those kidnappers, I won't be able to live with abandoning her to these Mayan warriors.

Ixchel, I can hear, is shaking again – I can hear her teeth chattering. The sound of her fear only adds to my own sense of creeping doom. Our captors just ignore us now, talking amongst themselves so rapidly, using so many words I don't know, that it's impossible to follow their conversation.

I take a few deep breaths, force myself to be still and not panic. I try not to let myself think through the terrifying things that might lie ahead, but it's almost impossible. Ending up as a sacrificial victim is my biggest worry. It's conceivable that some pretty nasty things might also happen to us before that.

What a day this has turned out to be – more like a nightmare with every minute.

95

Yet deep down I can't find it in me to be angry with Montoyo. The job of repairing the Ix Codex is mine. There's no point protesting. Anyone else just can't risk getting close to that book – the bio-defence toxin will kill them.

He tricked me into doing my duty. *There are higher duties that bind me*, he said. *Ultimately, I'm a servant of this city and our mission.*

He was talking about *me*. My duty, my mission. Montoyo might have seemed overprotective in the past, preventing me from handing myself over to the kidnappers in Brazil. It wasn't because he cared about me getting hurt.

The darkness seems to close in around us. With a sickening heart I face up to the harsh truth.

Montoyo was saving me for tasks like this.

Through the trees, probably twenty metres away or so, there's a burst of orange light. Dancing behind slender black shadows of countless tree trunks, it approaches. Our captors let out a sarcastic-sounding cheer.

"Here he comes."

"Fish Face!"

"Where've you been? We missed you!"

The flaming torch continues on its path, bobbing through the woods. Eventually Fish Face steps out from the thicket. He's short and walks with an awkward shuffle, looking embarrassed but also annoyed. He holds up the fiery torch, and for the first time, I can see Ixchel and our captors.

They can see us too – and they react with loud exclamations and gasps of disbelief.

I was right – they're aged somewhere between sixteen and eighteen. All look shorter than I am and are dressed in suede loincloths decorated with shells and beads. Their chests, shoulders and faces are marked with black and red body paint: horizontal stripes across the chest and eyes, lips painted black, vertical lines all the way across their foreheads. Their long, straight black hair is pulled into a topknot and then either loose or tied up into a twisted plait. Each warrior, I notice, has an armband made of what looks like the mottled skin of a jaguar. Just above their knees they wear bands encrusted with sharpened beads and shells. All wear leather sandals and have chunky necklaces of seashells.

It seems hard to believe that we could appear frightening to them, given how scary they look with all that war paint and blades made of black volcanic glass in their hands. Yet scared is exactly what they are, at least at first. They stand up slowly, poking our skin and clothes with their knives, then their fingers, muttering in amazement.

The guy nearest to me drops slowly to his haunches and stares at me for what seems like ages. I'm suddenly aware of how strongly he smells, because there's an abrupt change in the wind. He absolutely reeks – they all do. I don't think I've ever been this close to such a strong-smelling human. It's a harsh, almost metallic smell.

He's as fascinated with me as I am with him. He beckons Fish Face closer with the torch. When Fish Face doesn't react, he leaps to his feet yelling and grabs the torch, shoving the shorter warrior so hard that he crashes into a tree.

Then he crouches down again, holding the flame so close to my face that I flinch from the heat.

"Are you blind?"

I stare back at him, shrugging. Involuntarily I glance at Ixchel. The warrior boy touches a finger to my right eye. Awestruck, he asks, "You can see out of this?"

They've never seen blue eyes before.

"Don't answer, Josh," Ixchel warns, speaking English. Another warrior boy pushes a knife against her throat.

"Shut up, beautiful," he says in a playful voice. "We don't take orders from women. Even when they smell as sweet as you."

The third snorts, "What a liar! He does nothing but takes orders from a woman."

"I take orders from a *princess*," replies the guy with a knife on Ixchel. He's annoyed.

"Why don't you want to talk to them?" I say, looking right at Ixchel.

The minute I speak, Warrior Boy Number One shoves me hard. This time I'm ready – he hardly shifts me. I can see the surprise in his eyes, as well as a flash of respect.

"Don't talk to her," he yells at me, in Mayan.

"I don't take orders from you, mate," I reply, in English.

"What's he saying?" he asks. The other three guys make various noises of puzzlement.

"Who are you?" says Warrior Boy Number One. I notice

that he's slowed down his words now, speaking very clearly. "Not from the Snake Kingdom. So, where?"

I couldn't reply even if I wanted to. I can understand fairly well now that he's taking care with his speech, but I can still hardly string together a decent spoken sentence. All the same, I'm amazed at how much of what he's saying I can actually follow.

"I'm Rain Son," he says, pointing at his own chest. Without taking his eyes from mine, he points at the guy who's still holding a knife to Ixchel, although less fiercely now. "He's Mountain Jaguar." With a nod he indicates the third warrior boy. "Tree Frog."

My eyes go to the guy with the torch. "Fish Face," I say slowly, in Yucatec.

All three burst out laughing. Ixchel, I notice, is still frozen, crouched on the ground.

"Fish Face, that's him. And you?" Rain Son jabs his knife against my T-shirt.

"Josh," I say, leaning on the "J" sound.

Rain Son repeats the word slowly a couple of times, nodding.

All four guys are focused on me now. Rain Son is still pointing a knife at me but for the moment he doesn't look too threatening. It's clear that they're taken aback by everything about us. They prod and tug at our clothes and hair; they sniff the air around us. I guess it's the smell of all

100

the various soaps and perfumed products we've used in the last few hours.

"Josh," Rain Son says reasonably, gazing at the multifaceted blade of his knife, "I think you're lying." Slowly, his eyes move to mine. He lifts the blade to a point just under my eye. With great deliberation, he adjusts the angle, then presses it against my skin. The blade hardly touching me, he slices across my face with utmost care. There's almost no pain. A trickle of blood makes its way down my cheek.

"Look at those eyes," Rain Son says with a chilling smile. "They're like something on a demon."

"Get away from him!"

Everyone jumps slightly, startling at the sound of Ixchel's voice. Her voice trembles with fear and rage. We're riveted.

She speaks the same language as them, a kind of Yucatec. With a slightly strange accent and words I don't understand. My best understanding is that she's saying something like, "Yes, he is a demon; he's not from this world, can't you see? He's dragged me straight out of *Xibalba*. You'd better take us both to your lord. Or he'll take you back to *Xibalba* with him!"

At first, they seem completely thrown at hearing Ixchel speak. Only a second or two later, though, they go back to ignoring her. It's though they aren't even sure all those words came out of Ixchel. As though she were some helpless, mute creature that couldn't possibly have spoken.

Rain Son puts his finger to my eye socket and touches the cut he's just made on my face. Then without taking his eyes off mine, he tastes my blood on his finger.

"Hmmm. Looks like blood. Tastes like blood. Strange demon."

"The Hero Twins were in *Xibalba* too," Tree Frog says, frowning. "They were cut into pieces and they *bled*."

"The Hero Twins are just a story," Rain Son says, sounding haughty. "Any child knows that. This 'Josh' is no demon." He sniffs deeply. "Who ever heard of a demon that smelled of firewater and herbs?" His voice drops to a low, icy whisper. "And he understands me. Don't you, 'Josh'?"

Mountain Jaguar seems to have noticed Ixchel again. Hesitantly he stretches out a hand to her hair, touches it gently, then starts to stroke it. I react immediately with a dive in his direction, yelling at him to get away from Ixchel. Rain Son grabs me around the shoulders and wrestles me to the ground. He's incredibly strong. The second he puts the blade to my throat again, I freeze.

In the flickering light of the flames, I see Rain Son's eyes glitter with menace. He barks out orders to Tree Frog and Mountain Jaguar. They drag Ixchel into position behind me and fasten wooden collars around our necks, looping the collars together so that we're linked. We're both forced to our feet.

Mountain Jaguar's eyes are still fixed on to Ixchel. He

walks around her, murmuring with appreciation. Then he approaches me. His mouth falls open as he stands in front of me, gazing intently into my eyes. For a few seconds we stare at each other. I'm determined not to let these guys – or Ixchel – see how terrified I am.

"Touch her and I'll end you," I hiss.

It earns me a punch to the ribs. I double over, badly winded, trying to catch my breath. From behind me I hear Ixchel sighing. "Josh, stop talking. Please."

When I straighten up, Mountain Jaguar notices the Bracelet of Itzamna. He gasps, impressed. He's about to touch it when Rain God's hand snaps out, grabs his wrist and twists it until Mountain Jaguar cries out.

"But look, it's. . ."

Rain Son interrupts, "I know, I've seen it."

"It's. . ." Mountain Jaguar seems desperate to share his revelation. Rain Son, however, is just as sure he won't let his friend do that.

"Quiet! I said, I've seen. I know what we have to do."

The two warriors glance at each other and reluctantly, Mountain Jaguar nods. He takes two steps backwards, once again rests his eyes on Ixchel.

Rain Son checks all the bindings and the collars, and then tightens the cord around my wrists. With a swift kick to my calf, he mutters, "Move. Now."

12

Tied up as we are one in front of the other, both with our hands trussed up behind our backs, it's impossible for Ixchel and me to look at each other or even to touch. I've been running on adrenaline since we arrived in the forest; my head is all over the place.

I have to risk checking on Ixchel. "Are you OK?"

"I'm OK," comes her hissed reply. She doesn't sound OK. She sounds as petrified as I am.

"Enough of your demon talk," Rain Son warns, aiming another kick, this time to my thigh. All his roughing up is really getting on my nerves. At this point I'd love to take a swing at him. The truth is I daren't risk any kind of resistance. Alone, maybe I could bring one of them down with my legs; just maybe I could get hold of a blade, maybe cut myself out. . .

It would still leave me with three guys to beat and Ixchel to rescue. The odds aren't great. But I reckon I do have a

chance . . . if we can just stop moving for a bit. The forced
march through the jungle keeps Ixchel and me busy enough
just staying upright. Every time we slow down, one of us gets
a kick.

Fish Face pipes up, "What are we going to do with
them?" His voice sounds high, as though it's only recently
broken. Rain Son ignores him. Fish Face starts up again,
whining, "Well?"

"Quiet! No more words!"

We all trudge along in silence, apart from the rustle of
low branches and undergrowth as they whip against our
legs. Ixchel and I are wearing jeans at least, and good
trainers. I wouldn't want to be doing this bare-legged like the
Mayans.

My thoughts go to Mountain Jaguar's reaction to seeing
the Bracelet of Itzamna. Rain Son's reaction was even
stranger.

Was it the metal? I know the Mayans of this time don't
use metal for weapons or tools, but I'm pretty sure they have
gold, copper and silver jewellery. The Bracelet is made of
something else – I don't even know what. But it looks slightly
coppery, especially in some lights.

Or perhaps it's something specific about the Bracelet?

We walk for almost an hour. Eventually, the forest gives
way to fields of maize. We march between two fields, green
stalks of leafy maize blocking out the moonlight that's begun

to light up the horizon. Beyond the maize fields are other crops, low-lying vegetables – maybe squash? Even with moonlight, I can't tell for sure.

The land seems highly organized. Not much different to the plantations on the surface of Ek Naab. Nothing, in fact, to suggest that we're walking around in AD 653.

Then the moon appears behind what I'd taken for a hill in the distance, throwing the outline into silvery-white relief. That's when I realize that the "hill" is actually a gigantic, monumental pyramid.

Ixchel spots it too. She stops in her tracks. My collar yanks me backwards as she stalls.

"Holy mother of God," she breathes. "The Snake Kingdom."

Hearing this, Rain Son chuckles. "Even demons like these are impressed by the Snake Kingdom." Then he shoves Ixchel so hard that she crashes into my back. "Come on, demons. Move."

As we get closer, we round a curve that takes us on to a path which leads directly into the plaza in front of the main pyramid. It's just staggeringly massive – the largest pyramid I've ever seen in the Mayan world. The closer we get, the more ominous its presence. An enormous, hulking monument, seemingly as wide as it is tall; a looming shadow that seems to swallow you up as you approach.

The moon has risen clear of all the temples now, shining

106

down in roughly three-quarter glory. There's enough light to see the scattered groups of warriors posted around the main palace structures. Each group of two or three warriors holds at least one fire torch.

In front of the giant pyramid is an open plaza lined with temples, a broad avenue. We're led to a smaller structure that's closest to the main temple. As we approach the three-strong guard at the temple, Mountain Jaguar, Tree Frog and Fish Face begin to get fidgety, chattering in quiet voices. They sound nervous and excited. Rain Son alone stays calm, almost solemn, puffing his chest out as he walks.

In a gruff voice, one of the temple guards shouts, "Rain Son! What have you dragged out of the forest now?"

Rain Son is practically bursting with pride. He struggles to keep his voice even as he replies, "Two strangers. Found them alone, unarmed." Rain Son tugs at the wooden collar around my throat, pulling Ixchel and me towards the temple guards. The rest of our captors hang back.

When I'm face to face with the main temple guard, he lifts a torch and stares at me for ages, grimacing. I want to grimace back but I'm way too scared. Rain Son himself, he's pretty fierce-looking, with his black-and-red face paint. But the temple guard is much older, with stern, grizzled eyes, his cheeks covered in rows of ornamental scars, nose pierced, lip pierced, as well as black paint lining his eyes and lips. Even his jewellery looks fierce – a necklace made of animal teeth, arm bands embellished with vicious-looking thorns. He looks and smells like a hard-as-nails Hell's Angel.

I practically quake under his gaze.

"What's this. . .?"

Rain Son says, "The others think he's a demon, Crunching Jaguar. I think he's just a foreigner. Calls himself 'Josh'."

Crunching Jaguar's eyes flash. He stares at me again, prods my face and eyes with a horny fingernail. "'Josh'," he repeats, rolling the word around a couple of times. "This 'Josh' – is he blind?"

From behind me, Ixchel pipes up again. "He IS a demon, he will bring the curse of Ek Naab upon you all. He brought me here from *Xibalba*! Beware, don't cross him. . ."

Rain Son seems mortified at Ixchel's outburst. He's just starting to tell her to shut up when Crunching Jaguar raises his hand.

"Is this a *girl*?" He looks Ixchel up and down. She's dressed more or less the same as me; jeans, T-shirt and trainers. Our clothes must look pretty weird to the Mayans.

"I'm the demon Josh's servant," Ixchel replies venomously. "He rescued me from the underworld. He can take you back there whenever he pleases."

Her words certainly have an impact. I can't tell if the guards believe her or not, but the fact that she's saying it at all and in such a confident, angry way is forcing them to stop and think.

"Try to persuade them not to split us up," I tell Ixchel in English. "As soon as someone unties my hands I'm gonna grab you and use the Bracelet to get us home."

Rain Son struggles to restrain himself from telling me to shut up, but I can see he's livid. Crunching Jaguar, on the other hand, seems delighted to finally hear my voice. He smiles for the first time, a taut, toothsome grin.

"The demon speaks!"

Ixchel insists, "He asks that you untie him and present him to Lord Yuknoom Ch'een."

Crunching Jaguar's head swivels, fixing a penetrating gaze on Ixchel. "You speak for the demon, do you, little sister?"

"He brought me from *Xibalba*, from the underworld, to speak for him," Ixchel says. I have to hand it to Ixchel, she's a good actress. She manages to sound haughty and angry when I know that she must be as frightened as I am.

Rain Son coughs, bowing his head. I wonder who this Crunching Jaguar is to him. Someone he respects hugely, that's for sure. His father, perhaps?

"Crunching Jaguar, look at his arm."

Crunching Jaguar grabs my left forearm from behind me and pulls it close, examining the Bracelet of Itzamna. I'm twisted around as he looks, so I can't see his expression, but I hear the reaction in his voice. He gives a low whistle, drops my arm. Violently he grabs my chin, forcing me to return his gaze. His grip intensifies; his hand applies crushing pressure to my jaw.

"You're no demon, boy," he whispers in a voice that oozes menace. "You're a foreigner; anyone can see that. But even worse – you're a thief."

When he finally releases me, I notice that one of my back teeth feels loose.

Crunching Jaguar grins, his eyes beady with sadistic anticipation. He's so close that I can smell his rotten-cabbage breath. He turns briefly to Rain Son with a quick nod, takes a step back into the shadows.

Rain Son steps into the torchlight, holds his knife at eye level. Unlike Crunching Jaguar, his expression seems pompous and grave. Trying to show us that there's important work to be done and he's just the serious guy for the job. He lowers the blade until its black, chiselled edge touches the sleeve of my T-shirt. Carefully, he lifts the sleeve, slices upwards, cuts straight through the cotton weave. His eyes bore into mine. He lowers the knife to my skin. A fresh sweat breaks out all over my skin as he slides the blade down to the Bracelet of Itzamna on my forearm.

He's going to try to cut it off. Our only way of escape. . .

Rain Son slides the weapon between the Bracelet and my arm. As he turns it against the metal, the edge bites into my skin. It's like broken glass; it cuts easily into my flesh, releases a thread of blood. Instinctively I twist and slide my arms upwards until his blade slices through the twine around my wrists. We're locked together for a few seconds as Rain Son tries to figure out what's happening, and how his knife hand managed to get all tangled up with my arms.

When I spring free of him my hands are untied. I stagger forward, break the fall with my hands. That's when I notice there's blood streaming from deep scratches in both my arms.

His blade is insanely sharp. I hardly felt a thing.

Rain Son leaps forward with a yell. He lunges at me with his blade, but I sweep a *gancho* kick right into his blows. It's not the most effective execution of the move, because I'm still attached to Ixchel by the collar. Yet Rain Son seems flabbergasted that I'm putting up any kind of resistance. My kick connects with his knife arm, right on the funny bone – a very useful move. In the second during which his arm is paralysed, probably jangling with electrical weirdness, I grab it with my left hand. I slam his blade down on to the cord between our wooden collars. It cuts through; the cord snaps in two.

Ixchel and I spring apart. Euphoria surges through me; I can move freely for the first time since they captured us. I feel ready to bounce off the temple walls.

Rain Son, eyes blazing with fury, leaps at me with his knife held high . . . but I'm already diving under his legs in a defensive roll. When he lands, he has to twist to find me with his eyes; I'm already behind him. I dive, land on my hands, arc my upper body into a *meia lua reversao*: the spinning heel kick. The first kick catches him across the jaw with a satisfying crack. I keep pivoting, follow through with another kick half a second later.

Rain Son doesn't know what's hit him. He slumps to the floor, stunned.

I don't think I've ever struck anyone that hard. Frankly I'm amazed at the power of the kick when it's done for real, not as part of a capoeira play. I bounce lightly, flexing my still-stiff arms, watching Rain Son as he tries to get back up. My chest heaves with the effort of breathing, heart pounding away inside.

For one golden second every one of us simply stares in total disbelief at Rain Son lying crumpled on the floor, almost merging into his own torchlit shadow.

Then Crunching Jaguar comes to his senses. A deep roar erupts from his throat; he throws himself at me. He's fast – but with an acrobatic *mortal de frente*, I flip right across his back. There's an audible gasp from the temple guards. After a tiny hesitation, Mountain Jaguar and Tree Frog attack next, together. I dodge Mountain Jaguar with a handflip, but Tree Frog seems to have realized that I always end up behind my attacker. He's there waiting. Before I can prepare a kick, he slams his body against mine and knocks me to the ground.

I'm still seeing stars when Fish Face appears in the air behind Tree Frog, squealing like a pig. He lands on top of Tree Frog and squashes us both beneath his stocky bulk.

It knocks the wind right out of me. I'm about ready to suffocate when both guys are unceremoniously dragged off me by Crunching Jaguar and his men. I'm next, hauled to my feet by both arms, each in the firm grip of a temple guard. Everyone is rigid, waiting for Crunching Jaguar to react. But he just stands there, hands on his hips, staring at me, impassive.

Without taking his eyes from mine, he approaches slowly and in a quiet voice asks, "What was that?"

Everybody, Ixchel included, waits in silence. I don't know how but I can tell that Crunching Jaguar knows that I understand him. Confused, I glance at Ixchel, but she looks as indecisive as I feel.

"How can you move like that?" he asks. "Tell me or die."

With those simple words, Crunching Jaguar puts his knife to my throat.

I gasp a few times and cough, trying to get enough wind to speak. "A dance that is a fight," I mumble, trying out the words in Yucatec. "From a land far away."

My answer seems to surprise Crunching Jaguar. "A *dance* that is a fight?" He lowers the blade but continues to stare at me expectantly.

I clear my throat. "For play. For fighting also."

Crunching Jaguar's stern features break into a wide smile. "You were *playing* with Rain Son?" In a low voice, he chuckles. The temple warriors holding my arms follow him, beginning to laugh.

I don't know what else to say, so I nod. Crunching Jaguar gestures at the temple guards to let go of my arms. He grabs my left wrist and raises it so that the Bracelet is between us, almost at eye level. Still fixing me with a glare, he says, "You took something that does not belong to you."

"It's mine," I tell him softly.

"This is a holy object," he bellows, "and it belongs to the *Chilam Balam*!" His outburst is so unexpected that I actually jump in alarm. As I'm reacting, he gives my wrist a quick snap. Before I know what's happened I've fallen to my knees in agony. One arm is twisted behind my back in a searing lock. Crunching Jaguar slides the Bracelet down my forearm and over the wrist. When he looks at me again he raises the Bracelet of Itzamna, touches it reverently to his lips. Then he frowns, contorting his scarred, painted face into a grotesque mask. It's almost theatrical – as if he's doing it to impress the other warriors. "The *Chilam Balam* – our Jaguar Priest – will deal with you in the morning."

He backs away then, signalling with his hands to the temple guards.

"Take him inside the palace. Tie him up again – this time

his feet too." Then slowly, Crunching Jaguar turns to Ixchel. He strolls over to her, drawing himself up, pushing out his chest and chin. He circles her, looking her up and down with a critical eye, like a farmer inspecting a horse. The temple guards pull my arms roughly behind me as I helplessly watch Ixchel being weighed up in this creep's mind. I watch in silence; meanwhile they bind my hands again.

Ixchel has the sense not to stare back at Crunching Jaguar. He's got that look about him now, nostrils flared, eyes wild, teeth bared – as though he's won a battle. I notice that he's slipped the Bracelet on to his wrist. He rolls it casually around his arm as he makes up his mind about Ixchel. She keeps her gaze low, somewhere in the middle ground between herself and me.

In empty space, our eyes meet. We gaze at each other then – it only lasts a few seconds, maybe three. But in that one look, I know; I feel it, just as keenly as if she'd said the words, and it's like a miracle, I think, that you can say so much with one look; I didn't know it was possible.

Time is suspended. In that moment, everything we mean to each other becomes crystal clear. Ixchel is terrified of being separated from me.

I can hardly breathe.

Ixchel nods once, and then Crunching Jaguar sticks his face right against hers and yells, "You, foreigner, better say farewell to your 'demon' lord, *girl*. You're a slave here, nothing but a slave!"

Ixchel is shivering, eyes wide with fear. Tree Frog and Mountain Jaguar are practically smacking their lips together as they start to haul Ixchel away, dragging her by the wooden collar. Ixchel breaks into a sob. At the sound of her terror, I can't stop myself – I struggle against the guards, elbowing them both in the side, yelling with frustration. It's no use. The instant I begin to resist they grip mercilessly, dig sharp into my arms. At the scratch of a dagger against the back of my neck, I freeze.

"Don't you dare hurt her!" I blurt in English. Then I rattle off a few choice curse words in English and Spanish too. I'm almost spitting with rage. For a second, I can see they're impressed. Crunching Jaguar turns on his heel, slowly. I can tell that he means to intimidate me. It works. He crosses the circle of glowing orange light that surrounds the one temple guard who hasn't budged since we arrived in the Snake Kingdom. Centimetres away from my face, he stops and puts his head on to one side.

"What is she to you?"

I don't know how to answer him; I don't have the words. "Don't hurt her," I manage to say, pleading with my eyes. Crunching Jaguar nods, not without sympathy, although he doesn't seem to have changed his mind about anything.

"The girl is a slave," he says gravely. "Found in the king's lands – she belongs to Lord Yuknoom. He will decide her fate. These warriors will not harm her. She belongs to their king. Clear-Eyed Demon, do you understand me?"

I nod, trembling. They pull Ixchel away then, less roughly, but pretty insistently. She's still sobbing. In another second she's vanished into the shadows of the pyramid.

Only minutes later, I think back to that moment, and I wish I'd said something, anything. Later, I think of any number of bold and memorable things. Any one of them would have been fine last words for a girl you're crazy about and might never see again. That's when I decide.

I'll see Ixchel again, somehow. I'm going to make that happen; that's promise number one. Number two is this: I don't care where it is or what is going on around us, next time I see Ixchel I'm going to say it.

They haul me inside the stone palace. I don't have the energy to resist. There's a single tunnel inside, leading to rooms lit by torchlight. I can't see inside the doorways we pass; they're blocked by curtains of woven palm fronds. Probably bedrooms, judging by the snores, most likely quarters for the priest class. The temple guards pause in front of one of the doors, then push me to the ground. One guy busies himself with tying up my legs, nice and slow. He hums tunelessly as he works. Then they sit with their backs against the opposite walls. With a single word, one orders me to sleep. They glare at me until I close my eyes and try to relax.

It's hard to imagine how I'll get any sleep, lying on hard stone, hands and knees bound so tightly that it hurts. After a while I notice that I'm still trembling all over. My mind races with images of all the horrific things that might be happening to Ixchel. A slave, in this place, in this time. What could that mean? It keeps hitting me, harder every time, just what a nightmare situation we've been forced into. Hard to believe things could get worse than this – trapped in the Mayan past, prisoners of a violent warrior who probably answers to an even more violent king.

I take a few deep breaths. I wish I could cry, just sob away like a heartbroken little kid. But I can't. My eyes are dry; my chest feels blocked up. Something's shifting inside my brain – something is taking control. I might even believe that I'm numb with fear, if it weren't that there's something I'm even more afraid of than being trapped here, waiting for my fate. Something that, if I let it get hold of me, will finish me for ever.

Fear itself. That's the killer. That idea seems very concrete now. I can sense part of my mind just ready to shut down and give in, to collapse and start blaming people for what's happened, to panic, to surrender.

But I've been here before. The night I was lost in the woods after Camila died was the first time. I thought the fear was going to eat me alive then, until I remembered that in a survival situation you have to stay calm, make a plan.

Sometimes, it takes a miracle or the help of good mates to save you. My mum would say that it's God, but I'm not sure I can agree. There must be plenty of people who prayed to God and still died. Still, I figure a prayer can't hurt me. It might even help focus my mind. So I say a few Hail Marys. I whisper them over and over until I start to sound like my mum and her religious friends saying the rosary. For some reason, that makes me laugh. One of the guards pokes me with his foot. Weirdly, though, I do feel better, calmer.

Use this time. Make a plan.

I try to remember some of the Mayan history I've been studying. Yuknoom Ch'een II was the greatest king of Calakmul, which was known as the Snake Kingdom by the Maya. He ruled for fifty years, led a victory over the other great Mayan kingdom, Tikal. I wonder what kind of person he was. There's almost no Mayan history recorded – only what you find in temple inscriptions. Since the kings order what is inscribed on temples, I guess it might not be completely truthful.

Tomorrow, I'll meet the *Chilam Balam* – the Jaguar Priest. They reckon that I stole my Bracelet of Itzamna off him. Their own Bracelet can only have been brought here by the agent of the Sect of Huracan.

Maybe their agent is *still* here? Even if he isn't, somewhere along the line, that other Bracelet has been taken by the Jaguar Priest. People know about it here; they've seen it. Crunching Jaguar called the Bracelet a "holy relic".

I stretch my legs and try to get comfortable. Now that I've started to think this through, I'm struggling with a tiredness that hits me like a wave.

Two Bracelets? I guess it makes sense that there would be more than one – the Bracelet doesn't seem to be designed for transporting more than one person. Ixchel felt really sick after hitch-hiking along with me, said it was a horrible experience. It felt fine for me, though, as the Bracelet-wearer.

Maybe Itzamna the time traveller made two Bracelets. Or maybe he *found* two? It makes more sense that he found them, when I think about it. Itzamna is from the future – he wrote the four Books of Itzamna, including the Ix Codex, in English, a modern language. The Bracelet seems to be Erinsi technology – just like everything else in Ek Naab. Itzamna didn't create any of that knowledge – he found it on a temple wall near a place called Izapa and copied it down.

So who were the Erinsi? I think through all the facts I know about them. The original time-travelling race, who built the Revival Chambers, who created mysterious technology that will protect the earth from the galactic superwave in 2012.

It dawns on me that I can't be sure if Itzamna is from the future after all. He might know English – but if the Erinsi used time travel then they might know English too. Itzamna could be one of the last surviving Erinsi.

Could Itzamna still be alive, travelling in time? Ever since I found out about Itzamna and Arcadio I've wondered: could they be the same person?

And how does the Sect of Huracan fit in? They want to let the superwave blast the human race into some nightmare apocalypse, so that billions die and the planet can start to recover from whatever having seven billion people living here has done to it.

That doesn't make any sense either. I'm pretty sure Planet Earth can take care of itself. It's been around for way longer than anything that's ever lived here.

Benicio told me once that whatever the Sect's real purpose is, it will be something that makes sense, even to us. It'll be about power, or money; how the Sect will have lots of power and influence once our technology-based civilization collapses.

Whatever it is, the Sect must want it pretty badly, to risk twisting the timeline. Or maybe whoever is in charge is a nut job? I can see how having something like the Bracelet of Itzamna can make you insane. I felt a little crazy when I first thought about using it. All that power to change the destinies of billions of people. I just wanted to change things for me and my family by saving my dad. Ixchel and Tyler were shocked, though, I remember that very clearly. They warned me how dangerous it could be, how it might change other things. At the time, though, I really didn't care.

When it didn't work, my plan to save my father, I kind of got the hint. Some things are just meant to be; what happens, happens.

Which is why this all feels so wrong. Waking up in a world you realize has changed . . . and you're the only one who remembers how things used to be.

It's a kind of madness.

What have the Sect done with the Ix Codex? Is there really a chance that I could stop them, fix things so that everything goes back to how it was?

As sleep descends, I become more and more confused. *Two Bracelets*. The image just won't go away.

Just before I finally can't resist any longer, I remember: I *have* seen two Bracelets. I think back to when I found my dad in the cell under Area 51 – we'd stood face to face looking at each other through the bars, Dad with his Bracelet, me with mine.

Yet it was the *same* Bracelet.

Dad was wearing the broken Bracelet that he'd been given by Blanco Vigores. After months of wondering how my dad ended up on the slopes of Mount Orizaba, I actually watched Dad zap himself out of the Area 51 cell. He must have landed on the icy volcano. Dad lost his memory and stayed on the mountain, confused and terrified, because all he could remember was that someone was after him.

Months later, I showed up on Mount Orizaba, led there by Arcadio's mysterious coded message. Dad died saving my life – and he gave me the broken Bracelet of Itzamna, with its crystal burned out. The Bracelet could transport someone in space but not time. Without the controlling Crystal Key, the Bracelet of Itzamna was nothing more than a teleport device with no control over where you ended up.

Arcadio – whoever he is – led me to Mount Orizaba, to my dad, to the Bracelet, because somehow, it matters. I thought it was just for me, so that I could fix the Bracelet and save my dad.

But what if there was another reason? In his letter to me, Arcadio talked about destiny. He quoted that writer, Borges: *Our destiny is not frightful by being unreal; it is frightful because it is irreversible and iron-clad*.

So maybe this is it. My *iron-clad* destiny is wrapped up with the Bracelet of Itzamna.

Blanco Vigores found the broken, burnt-out Bracelet of Itzamna in the ruins of Izapa. He gave it to my dad. My dad gave it to me. I found the Crystal Key – I fixed the Bracelet. When Dad and I faced each other in Area 51 it was with the *same* Bracelet.

Remember this, I mutter, dimly aware that my breakthrough insight might be lost in the fog of sleep. There can be two Bracelets – but they could be the one and the same. Suddenly it seems incredibly important that I've realized this.

The Sect of Huracan has a Bracelet of Itzamna. But maybe it isn't *another* Bracelet. Maybe it's mine.

One from the future, one from the past.

15

When I wake up in the morning I feel like I've been kicked
around all night long. Every part of my body feels bruised,
every muscle aches. My mouth is completely parched. My
stomach cramps with hunger. I move around a bit, groaning.
Then the two guards wake up.

One of them cuts through the binding around my feet.
The other starts coughing and spits against the wall. I look
on, bemused. There is going to be some grossness in this
place. I'm kind of curious to see what form it takes.

I don't have to wait much longer. The haul me to my feet
and march me out of the sweaty air of the temple into
sunlight so dazzling that for a second, it blinds me. The
guards don't fare much better, I notice. They shield their eyes
and mutter under their breath until our eyes adjust.

Under a white morning sun I get my first proper look at
the city. Unbelievable. It's like being shrunk down and
walking through one of those models they make in

anthropology museums. A stone city cut neatly into the brilliant green jungle of Mexico.

The buildings that dominate the citadel are not grimy limestone, like every ruin I've ever visited. No: this city blazes with colour; temples glisten with deep hues of blood red, blue, ochre, green. They look like giant versions of those museum models, hard lines etched against a clear blue sky.

The ground has been cleared; no grassy banks between temples. No vegetation anywhere inside the citadel. In places the ground is paved; small limestone blocks in a rough mosaic. Elsewhere the soil has been tamped down and swept.

People are everywhere, thousands of them. In front of the giant pyramid, they're assembling a market. Semi-naked workers in loincloths erect stalls of wooden trestle tables and cloth sunshades, whilst richly dressed men and women oversee servants who bring baskets of fruit, caged animals (lizards, monkeys, birds), jewellery, pots. The air carries a powerful mixture of smells: hot chicken fat, beeswax, fresh blood, wood smoke and the acrid smell of quicklime. As we pass near one of the longer temples which flank the main causeway, I notice that part of the surrounding trees have been chopped down. There's an enormous pile of smouldering logs in the middle, glowing red at the centre. A line of weary-looking workers ferry baskets of broken limestone rocks, taking turns to toss them on to the bonfire.

The limestone processing plant – they're turning quarried limestone into powdery quicklime, making the cement and stucco for building and waterproofing the pyramids. The reason why these buildings will last for centuries, and I'm watching it. *Now*.

In spite of all my anxiety, I turn my head as we walk, amazed at the sight. My dad used to tell me about this. Now I'm seeing it for real. Incredible.

If only Dad could have seen this. He should have been the Bakab Ix, the user of the Bracelet of Itzamna. Not me.

For a minute or two I'm just reeling at the spectacle, watching the ancient city breathing, growing, pulsating with life. The guards push and kick me to keep me moving along. As we pass, every single person stops what they're doing. Some simply gape in amazement; others whisper excitedly and point. Dozens of eyes home in on me.

"We should sell his clothes," one guard says. The second guy just grunts. "You want to die?" he says. "Lord Yuknoom might want his clothes too."

We walk past the entire market, making straight for a green thicket behind the main pyramid. Passing by its flank, I notice that on the broad platform of the enormous lowest tier, there's a crowd of people. It sounds like there's some kind of argument going on, or a fight. I can't see what's at the centre of the crowd, but the people are getting pretty agitated.

The temple guards notice me staring up at the gathering. One of them grins nastily.

"Shall we watch?" he suggests to the second guard. They exchange looks of cruel satisfaction, glancing at me, then at the crowd, then at each other. They push me ahead, forcing me to climb the first terrace of the temple. We walk along to where citizens are buzzing around something.

The guards start pulling people out of the crowd so that we can get through. The citizens catch wind of the guards moving through their midst and start to step aside. Again, mouths fall open when they look at me.

Silence sweeps through the crowd like an infection. The final layer of bystanders peels away. We can see clearly to the centre of the crowd: the cause of all the tumult.

In the middle of it all, about three metres away, stands Ixchel. She stares defiantly at the slender Mayan women who come up to her and, with intense curiosity, prod and touch her hair, skin and clothes.

"What's the highest bid?" asks the second guard, laughing.

Next to Ixchel there's a man dressed in a two-piece outfit made of a purple-dyed cloth. He's about thirty years old, with pierced ears, nose and lips. His tense smile stretches across wide angular features without an ounce of spare fat. A taut, muscled arm grabs Ixchel by the wrist.

"No one bids more than Lady Seven Sky," he says, throwing out the words with triumph.

Ixchel and I, we look at each other. I mouth, "Are you OK?" She nods in response, just once.

"You see, Clear-Eyed Demon, no harm will come to your girl." The second guard tugs at my arm, making me sway back and forth like a drunk. "Look at him! He's drunk with love for her!"

The whole crowd erupts with laughter. Now that they can see that Ixchel's outfit of jeans, T-shirt and trainers isn't entirely unique, they seem to have relaxed. But still, I'm sensing an edge of uneasiness. No one will look me in the eye.

"Lady Seven Sky will have to be disappointed today," another voice drawls. The voice sounds like it should belong to a headmistress. She approaches, followed by an entourage of three young serving girls. All four females frown haughtily at the crowd. They all seem fully aware of their impact, which is electric.

"Lady Black Shell," stammers the trader in purple. Whoever Lady Black Shell is, she's wiped the smile right off his face. "It's an honour."

"Name your price," snaps Lady Black Shell, cutting him off. She swivels around and takes me in with a glance. "I'll have this one too." Then she stops, stares deep into my eyes. She takes a step closer. "What have we here?"

The crowd murmurs its appreciation. The second guard speaks up. He seems to enjoy the attention. "We call him the

Clear-Eyed Demon, milady. The girl claims he's a demon straight from the underworld. But he bleeds just like the rest of us."

Lady Black Shell approaches me until she's centimetres away, peering into my eyes with her own: shiny, black and narrow. I'm surprised at how young she looks, but she's probably my mum's age at least. She's wearing a red dress, its edges decorated with embroidery, shells and beads. Around her neck is a rope of gold necklace; her arms are covered in bangles, bracelets and arm bands. Pure gold and silver, encrusted with pieces of jade.

I can't help staring back at her. Is this the queen of the Snake Kingdom? She seems grand enough.

"The king's sister would have these foreigners for our own daughter," she purrs, stroking my cheek with one long-fingered nail. "What strange eyes you have," she adds. The way she stares at me is pretty unnerving. "Strange, yet beautiful. Like water. My daughter will enjoy you."

The second guard coughs self-importantly. "The Clear-Eyed Demon is not for sale, milady. We're taking him to the Jaguar Priest."

Lady Black Shell says nothing. But behind her eyes there's coldness, a vacuum. The first guard's hand tenses on my shoulder. I sense ice at the base of my spine.

This woman is dangerous.

Now she's about to have Ixchel in her grasp.

The two temple guards get behind me and start shoving again, this time pushing back through the crowd around Ixchel. I resist for a second, dig in my heels as I stare at Ixchel, trying to find the words.

"Just let her go, demon," grumbles the first guard.

"Ixchel," I call out. I hesitate. This is nothing like how I imagined I'd be telling her.

But I promised myself.

My cheeks burn red. "I'll be back for you," is all I manage to say.

Amazingly, Ixchel smiles. That smile is the last thing I see as the second guard grabs my head, turns it around and shoves me hard in the middle of my back.

"Stop talking, demon. If we don't get you out of here, Lady Black Shell and the Jaguar Priest will tear you in two and fight over your bones."

After the crowd disperses, the guards scurry down the

pyramid steps and back towards the woods behind the citadel. When we're properly behind the giant pyramid, we veer to the left. Towering behind the trees is another pyramid, one I hadn't noticed before. It's some way back inside the jungle, not part of the main citadel but apart – raised slightly on a hill. A pyramid acropolis decorated with squared-off pillars.

By now the sun is high enough to make the air begin to sizzle. I break into a sweat. The temple guards don't look at me again; they just keep applying the pressure, pushing and shoving me all the way.

I'm finally going to meet this *Chilam Balam* – their Jaguar Priest.

Better hope I'm right and there really are two Bracelets of Itzamna, or I'm in for some serious grief.

We climb the steps to the gleaming white stone of the plaza in front of the pyramid. There seems to be some kind of class in progress. Around twenty boys no older than ten are sitting cross-legged listening to a guy dressed in a blue tunic. On the other side of the plaza, there's a ring of guys around my own age. In the centre of the ring two boys seem to be training to fight with short obsidian knives. The silence descends again as I pass. On one side, solemn-faced little boys with long hair in topknots turn to me; on the other, its sweaty teenagers.

"You should see this boy fight," the first guard calls out to the knife-fighters. "He flies around, like a howler monkey!"

They perk up immediately. A couple of them nod, painted faces breaking into expectant grins.

A capoeira demonstration? You've got to be kidding. Not now.

"First the Jaguar Priest," insists the second guard, grabbing my left arm and pulling me towards the steps of the pyramid. I look back towards the audience of boys, shrugging.

Relief washes over me for a second, only to be replaced by more tension as we begin to climb the steps.

This pyramid has only one flight of stairs; they lead to a thatched-roof structure on the summit. The walls of the pyramid are red and decorated with multicoloured friezes of god-masks and other images I don't recognize. Stone columns – *stelae* – rise from the staircase at various intervals. They're also painted red and covered with carved inscriptions.

We head for the narrow black opening. Inside, flaming torches are placed at intervals. They light up the paint on the walls. We stop in front of a doorway. The second temple guard makes an announcement that I don't catch. A barrier of woven palm fronds is pulled away from the doorway, from the inside.

There's a pause. Then the temple guards shove me, pushing me through the door.

It's a small room and he dominates it, the Jaguar Priest. His back is turned to me when I arrive, covered by a long, deep blue cloak. He's arranging his headdress or something. There's a strong, rusty smell of blood in the room, and smoke from the flaming torch.

The Jaguar Priest turns around. He's tall – taller than any of the Mayans I've seen. It's not just the headdress, although feathers, shells and bones are arranged in a fearsome creation that sits on his grey, smooth hair. He's also older than any of the Mayans I've seen. In his late fifties, at least. Like all the others his face is painted; swirling black lines and red dots. His lower lip is plugged with a tiny, crescent-shaped stone of deep jade. But there's something else that's strange about his face too. Something different.

He doesn't look very Mayan. His eyes, his nose and lips are completely European.

Neither of us speaks for several seconds. The Jaguar Priest eyes me with a strange, sardonic air, looking me over. He breathes loudly through his nose, as if he's trying to inhale me. I don't dare to look him in those black-lined eyes, which look even fiercer than Crunching Jaguar's. I can't avoid looking at his arms, though.

On both his arms, just beneath the elbows, is an identical Bracelet of Itzamna.

He laces his fingers and cracks the knuckles a few times. A slow smile spreads across his face. His teeth gleam white. Not the brown, worn-down stumps I've noticed in the older people here – shiny white teeth.

I look at him; he keeps looking at me. Smiling. He begins to nod. Still not a word has been spoken. The Jaguar Priest speaks first. The moment he opens his mouth, I realize: *I know him.*

"Hello, Josh."

Even though by the time he finally speaks I've already guessed the truth, I still gasp.

"You're . . . you're. . ."

"Marius Martineau? That's right, Josh. We finally meet."

His smile is radiant now. He steps forward and grabs me by the arms.

"My dear boy, you simply cannot begin to imagine what a great, what an extraordinary pleasure this is."

"Huh?"

"After all this time, after everything that's happened. . ." Quite gently, he takes hold of my chin. "May I?" he asks, staring into my eyes. "My goodness, it worked. They're quite, quite blue, aren't they? Melissa's genetic engineering. She really is remarkable, that woman. Did the rest work too?"

I pull away. I don't like having him anywhere near me. "I don't know what you're talking about," I mutter.

He just chuckles. "I rather suspect you do. But no matter; it can wait. Your eyes are blue . . . they suit you, by the way. Which means, almost certainly, that the other genetic changes have also taken place. Thus, you are now endowed with the many gifts of the Bakabs."

136

"How did you get here?" I ask. I want to get off this topic . . . for all I know he's trying to trap me into confirming that their genetic experiment worked. Without testing my blood, they couldn't know for sure.

"You must think me rather foolish," he says with a grin. "I'm afraid I'm not in the business of giving away secrets, any more than you."

"You've got another Bracelet of Itzamna," I say, nodding at the two devices on his arms. "Where did you get it? Did Blanco Vigores give it to you? Is he on your side now?"

Again, he laughs. "Blanco Vigores? How interesting that you should mention him. Why, do you have your suspicions already, dear boy?"

"How's Simon Madison?" I say suddenly, with venom. "Did that cow Ollie dump him yet?"

Martineau's smile vanishes. "Simon and Ollie don't exist; they haven't been born. Stop thinking of time travel like aeroplane travel. Once you leave your own timeline, for all intents and purposes it is gone for ever. Unless you return immediately, there's little guarantee of ever returning to the time, the place, the people you once knew. Simon and Ollie *don't exist*. It's possible that they never will."

I gaze at him in the flickering torchlight. His words have a terrible ring of truth. I feel sick to my stomach at the idea. I don't want to believe him.

"But. . ."

"Every action has its consequences," he snaps. "Every consequence is magnified in subsequent repercussions. Have you never heard of the butterfly effect?"

"Uh . . . it's a film?"

Martineau rolls his eyes. "Dear lord, how can such an ignoramus have got the better of us on so many occasions?" He fixes me with a stern gaze. "Anything that you or I do in the past is likely to change something in the future. The consequences are unpredictable, because they magnify. Time travel, therefore, is extraordinarily dangerous."

"So why are *you* doing it?"

There's sarcasm in his voice now. "Because, dear *innocent* young Josh, has it not yet occurred to you that our entire existence has already been compromised by one foolish time traveller?"

"Who . . . Arcadio?"

Martineau pauses for a minute, as if he's surprised by what I've said. "No . . . not Arcadio. But how interesting that you should suspect . . . Arcadio."

I get the feeling that he meant to finish that sentence with something else.

"Who, then?"

"Itzamna, naturally! The original time traveller. His meddling interfered with the plans of the Erinsi to protect the world from events like the galactic superwave. Where you and I come from, civilization has paid a heavy price for Itzamna's interference."

Now I'm confused. This isn't what I've been told by Montoyo. "Civilization is in danger . . . *because* of Itzamna? But isn't he the one who stored the Erinsi knowledge? Who, like, kept it for the future? Isn't that how come we've got any hope of handling the superwave in 2012?"

"Really, my boy, why do you think Itzamna went to such efforts to copy the Erinsi writings, to create the Books of Itzamna? He's a time traveller. Why get involved?"

He has a point; I've never asked anyone that.

"To save the world?" I suggest.

"Yes, possibly. Generous of him, don't you think? To worry about people thousands of years in the future?"

I think about that for a few seconds. Is it especially generous? If Itzamna was from the future, he might know *absolutely* that if he didn't go back in time and change something, all the people he cared about would be different. Maybe they wouldn't even exist?

Martineau's words break into my thoughts. "Guilt is what motivated Itzamna, I'm almost certain. It's a powerful force, Joshua, guilt. Itzamna – or whatever his real name is – he knew that his meddling had already doomed us. The superwave and other disasters wiped the Erinsi civilization from the globe. But they found a way to preserve their technology, their knowledge. Itzamna, that interfering busybody, found the time-travel bracelet. He meddled. Oh, no doubt he meant well enough. But the result was – the Erinsi plan was disrupted."

"Are you saying that their plan . . ." I begin, incredulous, ". . . was interfered with?"

Martineau sighs. "For all their brilliance, the Erinsi failed to foresee the possibility that time travel could be their undoing."

"Itzamna . . . he tried to fix things . . . by copying their knowledge into the four books?"

"So it would appear."

Now I'm really suspicious. Martineau seems to know so much more about Itzamna than I do. Maybe even more than Montoyo. "How do you know all this?"

He gives me a tired look. "This isn't my first outing with the Bracelet."

Accusingly I say, "Then you're just as bad as Itzamna, aren't you?"

Lightly he replies, "I didn't create the reality in which you and I were born, Joshua. Have you not felt, throughout your life, that things were very wrong on our world?"

I shrug, peering at Martineau. His eyes glint like polished stones in the torchlight. Now that I know who the Jaguar Priest is, the costume seems ridiculous. What is a university professor doing dressed up like this? How has he conned Lord Yuknoom into accepting him?

For the first time, I glimpse the advantage I might have here.

Martineau can't risk that I might talk, tell the Mayans that he's an imposter. Which means he'll have to kill me pretty quickly, before I can talk to anyone else. . . If he does that, how will he explain killing me to the king?

His only other choice is to make me his friend.

The way he sounds, it feels like he's trying to be friendly. But this is a guy who gave orders to have me captured, shot at, tortured and experimented on. His organization threatened to murder my mother and best friends.

Does he think I've forgotten any of that?

Martineau falls silent, watching me form a question. Eventually I say, "So . . . you want to fix what Itzamna did?"

"I doubt that's possible. We don't even know *what* he did. I plan to ensure that the Ix Codex never falls into the hands of your friends in Ek Naab. Of all four books, it's the most dangerous."

An outrageous idea hits me. Is it possible. . .? "Was it you, then . . . did you get Yuknoom Ch'een to bring the Ix Codex out of Ek Naab?"

Martineau's lips stretch very thin. "You give me too much credit. Lord Yuknoom did that all by himself. But for your interference, Josh, it's likely that the Ix Codex would have remained lost for ever. Well," he says, in a voice that's turned suddenly steely, cold, "I'm going to get my hands on that codex. Things will turn out different, you'll see; better. In

2012, the superwave will blast the human population back to a manageable level. Those of us who rebuild society will be able to ensure that our new civilization develops in an orderly, managed way. There'll be no splurging capitalism, no environmental wreckage. The new world order will be at one with the planet."

He's smiling by the end of his speech. There's something wild about that smile, and it's not just because of his alarming face paint. I don't know much about new world orders but I can't see the difference between Martineau and all the other crazies who think they should run the world.

I can only see the similarity. However these things turn out, people like him are only interested in ending up on the winning side, the side which makes the decisions and controls everyone else's lives.

In our twenty-first century, the Sect has their training camps in Switzerland; they're rich from money from Chaldexx, the pharmaceutical company that Melissa DiCanio runs. They have agents all over the world. All the males are Bakabs – descended from the rejected Bakabs of Ek Naab. The Bakabs have genetic abilities that I don't even understand.

New world order? Yeah, right. With the Sect of Huracan at the heart of everything.

Martineau runs his tongue over the top row of his miraculously gleaming teeth. "I'm going to get my hands on that codex, Mr Garcia. And you are going to help me."

Martineau reaches around his waist, under his flowing blue cloak. From a jade-studded leather belt he pulls out a short, squat blade. Like all the others I've seen, it's made from meticulously crafted black volcanic glass. I look from him to the knife, confused.

"Turn around," he orders, mildly. "I'm not going to kill you; why would I waste my time talking if that was my intention? You're far more useful to me alive, as you will see."

With that he cuts through the bindings on my wrists. I turn around and silently rub at the rope burns on my arms.

"I'm going to take you to meet Lord Yuknoom," he says gravely. "Now remember this – the king is a man in his prime. Fifty-three years old, and he's ruled the Kingdom of the Snake Dynasty for almost twenty years. He'll rule for another thirty. A period of prosperity and growth, and one of the most magnificent Mayan cities in all their history. The Mayan world

will not see his like again. He is not a man to be trifled with."
Solemnly, he gazes into my eyes. "Do you understand?"

I nod.

He continues, "You will speak only through me. If the
king believes that you can communicate directly with him,
there will be no reason, no excuse, to always have me
present when you are with him." He pauses again, then adds
quickly, "Before you start wondering if that wouldn't be to
your advantage, understand this: you know nothing of this
world, this time. Whereas I have studied the ancient Maya all
my adult life. That's how I'm able to operate as a Jaguar
Priest. With *everything* that entails."

The way he stresses "everything" gives me a sudden
shiver. I glance up, my question unspoken. He nods slowly,
grinning like a death mask. "Yes, Mr Garcia. I've killed. I've
taken human lives for sacrifice." He lifts his right hand,
holding the knife high. The Bracelet of Itzamna on his wrist is
right in front of my nose. "With this very hand, with this very
knife, I've cut flesh, spilled blood. Men, women. . ." He nods.
"Even children." His voice drops to a whisper. "Most Jaguar
Priests leave bloodletting to the *ah nakom*. But what I
discovered was this – I enjoyed it." His eyes burrow into
mine. I realize I'm holding my breath. "There's an urge to kill
that's tamed in our society. In this world, though, killing can
be seen as a powerful, a positive thing."

Finally I find my voice, hollow with disgust. "The

Mayans . . . they really believe they need to kill people to make it rain, to make food grow. But you. . ."

Martineau smiles. "I know that they don't? With my modern mind, I understand that rain and weather are all part of an uncontrollable miasma of natural forces?"

"Yes," I whisper.

"We kill to eat," he murmurs. "We kill to stay alive. We kill because someone orders us to. You think it's as simple as that? Joshua, it's even simpler: some of us kill because we're born to it. We're better than the rest; their lives are ours for the taking, when the wish takes us."

If he's trying to scare me, it's working. I don't know where to look; I only know I want to avoid those flat, pitiless eyes. Fear rises in me again, like a metal claw closing around my heart and lungs. It's so strong it threatens to blot out everything else.

Martineau grabs my arm and leads me to the doorway. He leans closer until his mouth is right next to my ear. "Follow my lead and we'll have the Ix Codex, and a glorious new future. One wrong move, though, and I'll add you to the list of sacrificial victims for the next sacred festival. I'll cut your heart out myself, Joshua. And I'll enjoy it."

He drags the palm-frond barrier away from the door and pushes me ahead of him into the passageway. The two temple guards are waiting outside, stretched lazily in the sun, on the steps at the summit of the pyramid. When they see my hands untied, they seem surprised.

"The boy is with me," Martineau says. He doesn't even glance at them as we begin the descent.

"Goodbye, Clear-Eyed Demon," sneers the second guard.

"Clear-Eyed Demon," Martineau mutters, in English. "How amusing. Looks as though you've found your Mayan name, Mr Garcia."

A numb feeling settles over me. I almost glide down the steps. Martineau says something to me but I barely hear him. The sun beats down on the city now, on every pristine stone on the temple, every column and frieze, on the hot skin of every man, woman and child. How many hours have I been here? Yet the shock of it is still slapping me in the face.

This is just unreal.

If only it were. Martineau's dagger is all too real in its glinting sharpness. He's obviously persuaded Lord Yuknoom that he has all the mysterious knowledge of a Mayan priest. No wonder, after all his years studying the Mayans: their history, mathematics, religion, language, customs.

In the Mayan Snake Kingdom, Martineau can pass himself off as a prophet, a seer.

I'm completely stupefied as he leads me across the acropolis, through the tree-lined path to the main citadel. We walk along the side of the enormous main pyramid. For a second or two I enjoy the cool of its shadow. We pass the low palace structure where I slept the night before. We cross the crowded plaza, winding our way past a jumble of traders, beggars and peddlers selling animals, dead and alive, caged birds, skinned iguana lizards with their tongues hanging out, stacked banana leaves tied into parcels with dry palms, baskets woven from shiny green palm fronds, fish sliced open, filleted and dried in the sun, clay pots filled with charcoal, gourds of every shape, hollowed and rattling with beans. A plump woman lumbers by weighed down with hundreds of shell and bead necklaces, and tugs at Martineau's cloak. He ignores her completely and pulls me away with greater urgency.

She's the only person who doesn't get out of our way, who doesn't stare. Everyone else stops what they're doing. Martineau and I carve a line of stunned silence into the crowd.

A young child speaks clearly into that silence. "Look! The Jaguar Priest has a son!"

The kid's mum tells him to shut up and the silence becomes a flurry of whispers. I glance at Martineau to see his reaction. His lips are pressed together, hard. He returns my glance and says, "It's your complexion. I was the whitest person they'd ever seen until you. At least my eyes are brown. The king will believe that we aren't related. However. . ." He pauses. "It may be a useful rumour to spread. I intend to keep you close, Mr Garcia. When we return to the twenty-first century, we will return together."

18

The temples are arranged on opposite sides of a wide causeway. At one end of the giant avenue is the main pyramid, which overshadows the citadel like a mountain. It's a complex series of tiers, platforms, columns on the lower tiers, niches at every level. As with every pyramid, on the summit there's a thatched-roofed stone building with arched doorways. At the other end of the avenue is the second-highest pyramid, with one long flight of steps up the front of its three tiers.

We head for a lower, broad temple structure at the opposite side of the causeway. Its wide staircase is almost as broad as that of the giant pyramid, but there's only one flight. Martineau leads me up the staircase to the building on top, which is watched by ten guards who stand out because of their red garments. They don't shift from their positions as we walk past, but I sense them bristle, fingers reaching for the handles of their daggers.

Martineau stops, addressing the guard at the door.

"I bring the foreign prisoner to our lord. Guard him while I speak alone with Lord Yuknoom."

Then he disappears inside the temple. I wait for a few minutes, squirming under the harsh gaze of the king's guards. Then he's back, standing in the doorway.

"Mr Garcia," Martineau says to me, speaking loudly, almost self-consciously. "Lord Yuknoom will see you now."

Inside, torches light up walls painted brightly in yellow and red. Reclining on a bed of dark cushions and woven blankets is a man dressed simply in a red tunic, drawn in by a belt. He's wearing a collar necklace with a big jade stone at its centre. There's black make-up on his face, but only around the eyes. His cheeks are lined with meticulously arranged swirling lines that are scarred into the flesh. From pierced ears dangle large golden earrings. His mouth is wide: full lips, a jaw that juts out slightly. Behind closed lips he grinds his teeth. Incense burns in a clay brazier decorated with the mask of a Mayan deity. It fills the room with a heady aroma of earth and spices.

Lord Yuknoom gazes at me impassively for so long that I grow even more nervous. He picks up a banana leaf next to him that's laden with ground maize, roasted and swollen, cooked with oily meat. The king picks at his food with two fingers and a thumb, drops small portions into his mouth and slowly chews.

While I watch, while I wait.

I'm starving, starving. Haven't eaten since last night. It's been a massively demanding sixteen hours. I want to gaze longingly at his food but I daren't.

Finally he gestures at me to sit. There's no seat or anything so I sit on the ground, cross-legged. He motions me closer. Martineau remains standing, less than a metre away. Even I can tell that he's nervous.

Lord Yuknoom clears his throat. When he speaks his voice is high, crackly. Like a man much older than his fifty-odd years.

"Where are you from?" he asks, speaking Mayan.

I glance at him, then at Martineau. Martineau nods once, then repeats the question, in English.

"What should I say?" I ask Martineau. He seems irritated by the question.

"Address the king, not me. Tell him you're from a far-off land called Oxford. Why not, that's foreign enough. . ."

"Are you instructing the boy?" Yuknoom asks Martineau, sliding his gaze over to him. "We shall hear his answers. Not yours."

"Apologies, my lord. The boy did not understand your question. He does not speak our language. I was translating."

Yuknoom says nothing but gives Martineau another hard look.

"I'm from Oxford, sir," I reply. "It's far away from here."

The king speaks, Martineau translates. "How did you come to the Kingdom of the Snake Dynasty?"

"I was transported here," I say.

There's a pause. Then Martineau says, "The boy claims that a demon transported him."

The king's eyes flash with anger. But he doesn't move.

"Why were you wearing that bracelet?"

"It transported me," I say slowly. Martineau tells the king, "The demon placed it upon his arm."

Yuknoom looks up at Martineau. "So you were right about that bracelet. It is from the underworld."

Martineau bows his head. "I suspected as much, my lord. The place where I found it was inhabited by many demons."

"You found yours in a city to the west," Yuknoom tells Martineau, thoughtfully. Seems to me he speaks with more than a hint of suspicion.

Martineau nods, his eyes closed. "Yes, my lord."

Once again, Yuknoom faces me. "My temple guards tell me that you have some magical way of fighting. You fought three of them."

"It's not magic," I mumble. "And the temple guards beat me. It's just movement. Not meant for fighting with weapons."

As Martineau translates, the king looks thoughtful. He peers closely at me for several seconds. I try to relax, to face him properly without too much show of fear.

"You will show us this magical fight," he says after a moment, "this movement. We will decide whether it is useful for fighting with weapons or not."

Drily Martineau says, "It appears we'll be having a demonstration of your pathetic Brazilian martial art."

Pathetic, hey? It was good enough to beat Martineau's son Simon last year by the river in Oxford. The memory of that perfect *mariposa* move almost makes me smile. But instead I nod, lower my eyes. "Professor Martineau . . . can you please ask him if I can have something to eat first?"

Martineau chuckles. "Well, it would be a shame if you passed out with hunger before I've got you working for me. I'll ask His Majesty." Archly he adds, "Is there anything else?"

I hesitate. But I might not have another chance. "Could I see Ixchel? I think she was bought by Lady Black Shell."

Martineau practically spits with disdain. "Forget about the girl. Lady Black Shell is a harsh mistress. It's unlikely that you'll ever see her again."

As I take time to absorb that, Martineau translates everything I've said. The king starts eating again, not looking at me. "Take him to eat with the temple guards. Have him escorted to the Temple of the Jaguar, and prepared for battle. I want him ready to fight. With a knife."

Lord Yuknoom gazes at me, expressionless. "For what use is a warrior if he is afraid to spill blood?"

The temple guards and the king's personal guards are fed in a thatched-roofed hut some way inside the woods, behind the royal temple. When he takes me there, I don't wait for Martineau to start eating, just wolf down the hot, tasty food. He's leisurely, watching me throughout.

When my stomach finally stops complaining, I stop eating. The old woman gives me a knowing look and passes me a bowl of water that she scoops from another pot, this one set in the recesses of the hut. Only when I'm finally satisfied do I let my thoughts turn to the next problem.

Capoeira with a knife? That's asking for big trouble. Use the knife right and you'd kill someone with one move. Capoeira isn't a fighting technique that works for any kind of long, drawn-out fighting, either. It's way too exhausting.

I don't want to kill anyone. But then again I don't want to die. That would leave Ixchel totally stranded. She's here because of me. It's up to me to get her back.

Again. No wonder Ixchel doesn't want us to be together – I really am a bad-luck charm.

The only thing to do is to aim for a quick knockout. Like I did with Rain Son last night. I don't need the knife for that – I can hold it in one hand while I go for a massive kicking strike.

I take a few deep breaths to calm my racing heart. Martineau leads me back through the trees to the city. The whole way, I can feel his eyes on me. But I don't return the glances.

"You're brave, boy – I'll give you that. You're the subject of many conversations, I wonder if you realize."

Because I keep scuppering their plans?

"It's rather galling to think that a young man of such apparently limited resources can be the source of such inconvenience," he drawls, almost talking to himself. "You really would be a valuable asset."

I don't reply. Martineau must be insane if he thinks I'd switch sides and start working for the Sect. It's bizarre enough to be eating and talking with him.

Once we leave the cover of the trees, the sun's rays start to pelt down in earnest. I notice a mosquito feasting on my arm and slap it. I don't even bother to wipe away the trail of blood.

There's going to be a lot more blood soon. Unless I hit someone very fast, very hard.

By the time we reach the temple my face is dripping with

sweat. It must be almost forty degrees centigrade. Looking around me, though, I see that no one else seems that bothered. No one but me is slick with sweat, fighting off the mozzies.

There's a crowd of around fifty people assembled to watch. Most are temple guards, or the same trainee warriors and young boys I saw earlier today. Then a call goes out; the crowd parts. The red-caped royal guards lead Lord Yuknoom to the front.

This time he's wearing the kingly regalia, including a large headdress made of green feathers and a gruesome red mask over his forehead, which I'm guessing is a serpent's mouth, complete with wild eyes, forked tongue and fangs.

Lord Yuknoom stares at me, eyes round, excited. He takes a blade from his belt and hands it to me, making a big deal of the gift.

"Use it well, Clear-Eyed Demon. Defeat one of my warriors with your fighting magic and I will reward you."

How, I wonder? An image flashes into my mind – me defeating the warrior and asking for Ixchel's freedom.

Martineau translates the king's words, keeping his head bowed throughout.

"Don't make eye contact with the king," he warns. "Take my advice – kill the warrior if you can. Forget your twenty-first century morals."

I weigh the knife in my hands. Black obsidian, knapped

edges as sharp as cut glass, with a handle of polished bone. It's warm, solid. A warrior not much older than me advances, his own blade glinting in the sun.

When I step forward, it's like an out of body vision, just for a second.

This cannot be happening.

But the salty taste of sweat on my lips, the slick damp of my hand trying to grip the knife, the squint of my eyes in the sunlight; they tell me something different. The stink that's pouring off the Mayan warrior boy who's been set loose on me – this is *aggression*.

Aggression has an actual smell. Before today, I didn't know that.

I feel my own blood rising. This guy wants to cut me, wants to see me bleed. Well, can't have that.

I go straight into *ginga*, moving my arms across my face as I bounce from side to side, waiting for him to lunge. The split second he moves his arm I'm already diving over it, on to on my hands and into a *meia lua de compass*. I land two hard kicks, one to his head, one to his shoulder. Covering my face, I launch into a three-hundred-and-sixty-degree *martelo* – a high snap kick with a full spin adding an extra strike.

My trainer connects hard with the side of his head. The guy totters for a few seconds, eyes closed. The dagger falls from his fingers. He crashes on to the floor, knees first.

Three kicks to the head. I'm not surprised he's feeling dodgy.

Adrenaline is pouring through me now. The crowd of spectators react only by gasping. When I look, the king is watching me. His brow is furrowed; he looks angry. He holds my gaze for a long moment, then stares into the crowd. After hunting another guy out, he nods. The second warrior is older, bigger. As tall as I am and much, much harder.

Lord Yuknoom frowns at me. "Use your knife!" he shouts.

The second warrior doesn't wait for a cue. He leaps forward with a snarl, dagger held high in his right hand. At the last minute he leaps, pouncing at me. A low dodge roll gets me out of his way – just.

This one is bigger, but slower. I calculate that I could dodge him for a while, let him tire. Then when he's flagging, give him a few hard whacks to the head and chest. We carry on for about two minutes. He doesn't manage to land a finger on me; I'm over him, under him, behind him before he knows what's happened.

But diving around so much, I'm the one who tires.

My first warning sign is when his dagger nicks my arm. It's a small cut, but the shock of blood streaking down my arm is enough to wake me up.

This guy may be slow but he's fit. A hundred times fitter than I am. I pull back to get a proper look at him. He's pretty ugly. His face is all cut up – not decoratively, either. He looks like he's had some nasty injuries.

He's survived injuries. This guy is a veteran of some brutal fights.

As if a switch had been flipped inside my head, I feel myself move on to a whole new level of alertness.

I'm going to kill this guy.

The thought is in my head before I even realize it's there. I push it away, focus instead on listening to a *berimbau* playing in my head. A warrior rhythm, but also a playful one.

I really don't *want* to kill. Especially not to entertain some psychotic old men.

He lunges at me again. The blade shreds a sleeve as I float past and into a cartwheel. Landing, I launch a series of high kicks, *armados*, right into his knife hand. The first time, the blade slices into my jeans and bites into my calf muscle. The follow-up knocks the dagger out of his arm. A red wave descends. Fury.

He's cut me twice now. I want him to feel this pain too.

Joelhada – the knee blow. Then a move that I've never tried before – *suicido* – a high double kick. I catch him just under the chin with both toes. A blow to the windpipe. It can be lethal. He gasps, clutching his neck for a second. Then he crumples.

Silence. Nobody moves. I'm catching my breath when finally, the king utters these words: "Cut his throat."

158

I'm hunched over, clutching the dagger between my fingers. My head is pouring with sweat, dripping from locks of hair. Breathing hard, I glare at Martineau.

"Tell him I won't."

"They're dead anyway," Martineau replies, irritated. "They lost a battle – they'll become sacrificial victims. You can cut their throats, or I'll cut out their hearts."

Terrific. Does that go for me too? In which case either I kill or I'm killed.

In the crowd, there is a low murmur. Fifty pairs of eyes are trained on me, standing underneath the acropolis temple in black jeans, white T-shirt and trainers. Blood seeps from my arm, shoulder and a deep cut in my calf.

Resignation clouds my thoughts.

I can't cut someone's throat, another boy. I just can't do that.

A blank expression falls across the king's face. He starts looking into the crowd again. Most of them go quiet immediately, practically quaking under his gaze.

Then there's a voice I recognize. "I'll fight him, my lord."

The king nods. A whisper of appreciation from the crowd. I can't see who's spoken until he makes his way through the crowd of warriors.

Rain Son.

Looks like he's recovered totally from the knockout blow last night. In his eyes there's hunger for revenge. I made him look stupid last night. It's payback time.

"Rain Son," I mutter. Martineau is close enough to hear. He seems to stiffen at my words.

"You know him?"

"He captured me."

Martineau hesitates, winces. Then he steps closer, right behind me, in fact. I feel a jab, a sharp bite as something sharp plunges into the base of my neck. Instinctively I turn around, clutching my neck. I'm staring at Martineau, stunned.

What has he just done to me?

There's not another second to wonder. Rain Son dives at me, blade twisting, swivelling in his hand. I drop back on to my hands, a *queda de quarto*, and trip him over my outstretched legs. Rain Son goes down, but not too heavily. I'm about to choose my next move when, as clear as if he'd showed me a picture, an image of Rain Son punching me with one fist and swiping his blade across my throat comes into my mind.

Automatically, my own knife arm shoots out, ready to block the punch. The blade catches his fist and cuts deep into the soft tissue of his palm. Rain Son can hardly stop himself letting out one anguished cry. It only lasts a second. His eyes flash with rage. My knife is smeared with his blood.

Then there's another image expanding in my mind. Me with my throat cut, a long red wound. My torso opened up from the base of my throat to my stomach. The shock of it stops me in my tracks. I'm paralysed. With what seems to me like lightning speed, Rain Son grabs my knife arm, twists it until I drop the weapon. Then he knees me twice in the guts. As I fall forward, he catches me by the hair, lifts my face and then kicks me hard, under the chin. I fly backwards, head ringing with pain, tasting blood in my mouth as my teeth bite into my own cheek. He kicks me a few more times, lands heavy blows to my ribs. I can't move, just lie there groaning, begging him to stop. A few kicks later, Rain Son stops and jumps over me, straddling my body with both legs.

He lowers himself until he's sitting on my chest. Staring deep into my eyes, he slowly lifts his blade to where I can see it. Terrified, I glance at it, then at him.

He opens his mouth. "Time you returned to *Xibalba*, Clear-Eyed Demon."

Martineau shouts at me, "Tell him to drop his knife. Speak clearly. Look into his eyes."

Confused, my eyes go to Martineau. He's got to be kidding.

"Do it!" he urges. "Now!"

Rain Son brings the dagger closer. He positions it against my throat. The tip of his blade jabs into me. My heart is almost bursting out of my chest. It can't end like this. Not here, not now.

In Yucatec I tell Rain Son, "Drop the knife."

Rain Son's eyes widen in disbelief. He stares at his own

fingers as incredibly, they unfold around the handle of his blade. With his dagger lying harmlessly on my chest, Rain Son continues to stare at his fingers, as though they are completely foreign to him. My arms are trapped at my sides, pinned in place by Rain Son's thighs. I can't get to the knife, can't shift him off my body.

"Get off me," I hiss, glaring.

He meets my glare with a sneer. Yet within a fraction of a second, something changes. His confidence seems to slide away. With a slight shiver, Rain Son stands up, slowly, reluctantly. He steps aside. The Mayans are open-mouthed with amazement, gasping, urging Rain Son to attack me. Rain Son himself looks as baffled as anyone else. When he faces me, I can see it in his eyes.

He's afraid.

I've made his own body betray him. Rain Son has no idea how I did it. Neither do I.

Things happen pretty fast now. The audience of warriors and students scatters in the time it takes me to check my ribs, arms and legs for cuts and bruises. I don't even get off the ground, just lie there with silent tears of pain streaming from my eyes. My torso aches badly, which makes me wonder if Rain Son cracked a rib.

I've never been beaten up this badly in my life. Rain Son was ready to cut my throat. One swipe from his blade and I'd have bled to death in minutes. You'd think I'd be relieved to still be alive. Truth is, I'm distracted by the throbbing ache of bruises, the rawness of sliced skin. I let out a couple of gasps as I turn over to find a less painful position. Really need to get my mind off the pain.

What did Martineau do to me? He injected me with something, but what?

Words start to come back to me; things Ollie said, and others in the Sect. *Your Bakab ability is just the tip of the iceberg* – didn't Ollie say something like that? Martineau too – he implied that there was more to the genetic changes they made to me; way more than being able to resist the four different poisons that protect each of the Books of Itzamna.

Rain Son did *exactly what I said*. I spoke, he obeyed. As if he was under hypnosis.

I don't know how it happened, but it's connected to those genetic experiments. Martineau knew what to expect. He planned it.

He saved my life because he needs me to get the codex for him. But why? If he's Madison's father then he has the Ix gene too – he can touch the codex and not die. I can't figure it out. Whatever the reason, it's why I'm still alive. Martineau is going to use me to get the codex. He'll do whatever damage he plans to inflict on the book. Then he'll transport us both back to the twenty-first century. A parallel timeline in which there's no way to stop the 2012 superwave.

Leaving Ixchel completely marooned in the Mayan past.

I shift again, moaning softly. Martineau and the king are watching me out of the corners of their eyes. They're having some sort of quiet discussion, just the two of them. Martineau is scheming, no doubt.

Thinking about Ixchel actually helps me to handle the pain. I take my mind back to one of my favourite memories: me and Ixchel on the bus together, riding to Tlacotalpan. The nostalgia of it actually brings tears to my eyes. Hard to take in just how much has happened since then – it's like thinking back to a simpler time. There was her and there was me and we were riding into the night together. The warmth of her skin as she leaned against me. Perfect. What I'd do for a chance like that again. I wouldn't waste a second.

I make a decision. All this fighting is exhausting me. I can't keep it up; there's no energy left. I can't make a complicated plan, can't concentrate on two things. Between saving Ixchel and ruining Martineau's plan, I choose Ixchel.

The king and Martineau finish their discussion. Yuknoom blots out the sun for a moment as he takes another long look at me. "Find out the truth, *Chilam*," he instructs Martineau.

Martineau is still bowing long after the king's footsteps fade away.

We're alone when he finally reaches out a hand to help me up. I feel totally humiliated. Beaten up in front of a crowd and left to bleed on to the stones, without a single friend to help.

Martineau hauls me to my feet. I'm unsteady. He makes these irritated noises, like I'm some annoying, uncooperative child. After a minute or two he supports me with his arm. I almost burst into a sob right there, accepting help from him, from Martineau, after what he and his son and his stupid organization have done to me.

But I keep going, for Ixchel. I have to find a way to get to her.

Instead of heading towards the main citadel, we turn down a path into the woods. We walk for about five minutes, me stumbling most of the way. Then we reach what looks like a small village. The trees are thinned out here – just the occasional few for shade.

The suburbs of the Snake Kingdom?

There's a big wooden trough in the centre, filled with water. It reminds me of the wooden troughs I saw in Switzerland, for watering cattle. Martineau takes me up to it, grabs a dry gourd that's hanging from a post and dips it in the water.

He passes it to me. "Drink, use it to rinse your hands. Then clean your wounds."

I do my best. I have to take my T-shirt off to get to all the cuts and bruises on my chest. That's when I notice villagers are stopping in their tracks, looking at me. Martineau notices too. He glares at them and they keep away, but still steal little peeks at me when they think he's not looking.

"Your skin is so pale, they can't take their eyes off you. Makes me wonder if your mysterious Ek Naab isn't hidden underground somewhere," he remarks. Our eyes lock for a second. I hold my face muscles rigid, determined not to give anything away. Then to my amazement, he bursts out laughing.

"Foolish child. Of course I already know that Ek Naab is

underground. Your poker face, though! Most impressive. Yes – I'll remember that."

Just how many Sect spies are there in Ek Naab?

When I've cleaned all the blood away, I look at my T-shirt. It's soaked with sweat, stained with blood and dust. I don't much want to put it back on. I check the cut on my calf muscle. It's still bleeding a fair bit. I rip the sleeve off my T-shirt, douse it in water and rinse out the dust. Then I tie it over the cut.

Martineau inspects the damage. There are the knife cuts from the fights last night, all over my forearms. Rain Son's carefully carved scratch on my cheekbone. Fresh cuts from today, which are deeper, on my arms and leg. Bruises all over my ribs from Rain Son's kicks. It even hurts to breathe.

After a while he looks up. "I have medicines that I brought from the twenty-first century. But you don't need them. This can be treated easily with what the Mayans have." He smiles very slightly, a cold, empty smile. "You might enjoy being taken care of in the medicine hut. They'll make a fuss of you, I'm sure of it."

Martineau brought medicines.

"You injected me with something," I say slowly, accusingly. "Something that made me do something to Rain Son. Didn't you?"

Martineau purses his lips, gives a secretive look. "Yes, of

course. Did you enjoy it? A little something that Melissa's lab developed. We call it 'hypnoticin'."

"Melissa DiCanio – the boss of Chaldexx Biopharmaceuticals? They've found a way to hypnotize people?"

"I've already told you," Martineau replies, "you'd be an asset to the Sect. We can get things out of you that no one else can."

He won't say any more, just leads me by the elbow towards a wide hut. There's a strange smell coming from inside – a mixture of smoke and incense, herbs and spices. An old woman emerges from the hut, wearing an embroidered poncho. Her mouth is a curved line in her face; her expression doesn't change one bit as she gazes at me. She holds a pot between both hands. For a second she reminds me of the images I've seen of the Mayan goddess Ixchel. The Healer – of course.

In complete silence, the old woman spreads the sticky grease from her pot on to all of my cuts and bruises. It smells faintly of pine.

"Tea tree oil mixed with white willow bark and arnica," Martineau comments. "Antiseptic with pain relief. Now go inside and lie down. You'll feel better soon."

Then he leaves, taking both Bracelets of Itzamna and my only chance of getting out of here. Resigned, I follow the old woman inside the dark of the empty hut and lie down on a narrow cot bed made of palm leaves. I breathe out slowly. Pain begins to ebb away from my wounds. The sensation of it leaving me is almost ecstatic. Small noises from the village filter through the woven palm walls. Quiet conversations, children laughing, crying, playing. Footsteps, wood being chopped. The sounds are soothing. Close my eyes and I could be in Ek Naab. I concentrate on an image of Ixchel and me lying on a beach somewhere, a perfect beach where there are no hotels and no tourists. Nothing and no one to disturb us, nothing to distract me from what I want to say.

The medicine seeps into my blood. I feel as if I'm floating away.

It's dark when I wake up, alone. I notice the dancing flames of a fire through chinks in the walls of the hut. The smell of roasting pig fat is everywhere. It makes my mouth water. In the shadows of the hut, I hear something stir. Before I can sit up properly, there's a sudden sound from behind me. Two arms wrap around my neck and chest from behind. A hand clamps over my opened mouth before I can make a noise. Against my ear I hear a curt whisper.

"Quiet. It's Marius."

He moves around so that he's facing me. I can hardly make out his face in the dark.

"They think you're out cold. The king has been asking questions. The whole city is talking."

Astonished, I whisper, "About what I did to Rain Son?"

Martineau nods. When he speaks again, I can hear the strain in his voice. "You have them worried. You appear from nowhere wearing strange clothes; you fight with an acrobatic

170

technique that they've never seen before. Then you command a warrior. Why capoeira?" He seems exasperated. "It doesn't even seem particularly effective. So much flying around – rather wasteful, I'd have thought. Very attention-grabbing." He pauses, staring, his eyes black hollows in the darkness. "The king is beginning to believe you may indeed be a demon from the underworld."

"And that's bad?"

"It could be extremely bad for you. Right now they're wary, cautious. The king wants to see how much support you have amongst the gods. There's going to be a special religious ceremony in an hour or so, at dawn. They will make a sacrifice. Every class of society will provide a victim."

I stand up. "What *did* I do to Rain Son?"

"What?" he hisses. "Forget that. Listen to what I'm telling you! When the sun rises, the sacrifices begin. The king expects an answer to his question: are you a demon to be appeased, or destroyed?"

"Who's he going to ask, you?"

"He asks the gods." There's a smile. "Naturally, we priests speak on the gods' behalf."

Seconds tick by while I think through what he's said.

"You're running out of time," he says quietly.

"Give me a Bracelet," I beg. "Take me to where Ixchel is. Just let us have a chance to escape. Please. You can do what you want with the codex. I don't care any more."

I hear the smile, the nasty smile in his voice as he replies, "What an innocent! Mr Garcia, even if I wanted to help you I couldn't. You see, I suspect there was a reason for Ixchel's rather hasty purchase by Lady Black Shell. Her family is long overdue to surrender a household member as a sacrifice."

"Not Ixchel. . ."

"I'm afraid she's the most likely candidate. Far better to lose a new, untrained servant like Ixchel than one of Lady Black Shell's own trusted household staff."

My tongue almost sticks to the roof of my mouth. "You're saying that . . . Ixchel is going to be sacrificed?"

Martineau shrugs. "Probably. There's nothing you can do."

I hardly dare to ask. "How . . . will it happen?"

"She'll be covered in jewels and purified in a steam house, with the other sacrifices. As the sun rises, they will all be hurled into the *cenote*. The death that drowns." He pauses, seeming to relish the silence in me as I flinch at his words. After a few seconds he continues, "Obviously, Lady Black Shell's household will be on high alert. It's not unusual for sacrificial victims to run away before their time comes."

"Please. You've got to let me go to her."

"Indeed I will not. As I've already explained, without you I can't get the Ix Codex."

"Why not? You've got the Bakab Ix gene too. You must have – Simon has it. You're his dad."

172

There's a long intake of breath. "Ah, well, it's more a matter of where the codex is, to be perfectly frank."

"Where?"

Deliberately, he says, "In a hidden tomb underneath the royal palace. One of the K'aan, the Snake Dynasty's ancestors. Only someone of royal blood can enter the royal palace at night."

"So that's me out."

Through tight lips he murmurs, "Leave the guard to me."

"Huh. . .? But if the guard's no trouble, why use me?"

"It's the second layer of protection that defies me, sad to say."

"Which is?" My mind is beginning to drift away from Martineau's plan and back to the idea of rescuing Ixchel. But how? Right now I can't think of a single thing I can do. Not without the Bracelet.

"Snakes!" he pronounces, almost triumphant.

That gets my attention.

"The most valued treasures of the Snake Kingdom are protected by deadly poisonous snakes. Rather apt, wouldn't you say?"

I swallow. "You're afraid of snakes?"

"Most certainly. Particularly the deadly variety."

"I'm not going into a thing with poisonous snakes. . ."

"You don't have a great deal of choice. The bites will hurt, definitely. But you'll get out in time. I'm full of confidence in your determination. When you reach me, I'll provide the antidote."

I hesitate. "What kind of poison?"

"The wound becomes excruciatingly painful, swells and begins to rot. The only remedy known in this time is to amputate the limb."

We're both silent for what seems like ages.

"You're kidding," I say eventually.

Only he isn't. I know, with a deep sickness in my guts and a chill of blood in my veins, he is totally serious.

When Martineau says nothing, I whisper, "What if I won't?"

"There's no other way out of this for you, boy. The king stands ready to order your capture. If the priests advise him that you're a demon to be destroyed, you'll be sacrificed. Marched up to the summit of the great pyramid and your chest cut open, your heart ripped out, still beating."

My heart's beating twice as fast already, just hearing his threat. My eyes go to Martineau's arms, searching in the shadows for the telltale bump of the Bracelet of Itzamna on his wrist. As if he's read my mind Martineau says, "I'm not wearing it. Naturally I realize what a threat to you I've become. I'm sure you'd stop at nothing now, to get your Bracelet. But you'll return to the twenty-first century with me – only with me."

Gulping, I murmur, "You can't send me into a pit of deadly snakes. I might never get out alive."

"I'd ask the same of my own son."

I believe him. He's thought nothing of using Simon Madison as an agent of the Sect – his own son, putting him in danger, ordering him to steal and lie and kill.

"What's a few snake bites amongst friends?" Martineau says with a low chuckle. "Don't you trust me to provide the antidote?"

I become conscious of the sound of my own breathing, rapid and anxious. I don't reply to his question and instead turn away, rubbing my eyes with both hands. If I want the Ix Codex, this is the only way I'm going to get it. If I don't take this chance, it's all been for nothing.

Get bitten, get the codex, find a way to defeat Martineau. That's my only way out of this.

In that moment, I feel powerless, numb with fear. Martineau has forced me into this. I hate him for it.

"I'm going to take you to the palace now," he continues in a level voice. "Royal guards will be arriving here any minute. We need to leave before they get here."

The cuts on my arms and leg still feel raw. There's a dull ache in my ribs. Nothing like as bad I felt earlier but also, not the ideal physical state for breaking into a secret chamber guarded by snakes.

Snakes. Jeez. I'm not scared of them, not specially. But poisonous ones? I've had a snake bite before, the first time I was lost in the jungle of Campeche. It's like being stuck with a hot poker.

We sneak out of the hut through a gap in the wall near the back. Martineau pushes me towards the trees, away from the centre of the village where they're enjoying the hog roast. I wish I hadn't smelled that meat cooking. Hunger is the last thing I need to worry about right now.

Once we're in the cover of the trees, we speed up, moving steadily alongside the path that winds between the village and the citadel. Martineau grips my arm the whole time, hard enough to leave a bruise. It crosses my mind to try to escape, but where would I go? They'd catch me within an hour. Anyway, Martineau is my only link to the Bracelet of Itzamna. Without that, Ixchel and I really are doomed.

When huge dark shadows rise against a paling grey sky, I realize we've arrived at the citadel. I don't think I'll ever get used to seeing those massive stone structures at night. The way they seem to rise out of the ground, loom over you, blotting out starlight; monstrous, inescapable shadows.

The edge of the sky is turning pink. Soon the sun will rise. The sacrifices will begin.

I'm struggling to take in the enormousness of what's going to happen, but Martineau doesn't let up. His head is down as he leads me behind the royal palace. There's a narrow, low opening in the second tier. Martineau pushes down on my shoulders until my knees buckle.

"Get down, we're going inside."

"Wait . . . the antidote? I want to see it."

Martineau chuckles. "Ah yes. I almost forgot." He kneels down and fumbles inside a leather pouch that hangs from his belt. Out come a tiny torch, no longer than a thumb, and two syringes. He switches on the light, shining it into the tunnel. My eyes, though, go straight to the two syringes. One is tiny, with a needle no longer than the end of a pen. The other is much bigger with a long, wide needle. Martineau pops the cover off the needle of the tiny syringe and taps it smartly into the back of his neck.

He's dosing up on that hypnosis drug. This must be his plan to get past the guard.

Martineau holds the second syringe in the palm of his hands. "Here, see? Antivenom. I'll inject you afterwards.

"We'll be back in the twenty-first century by then, Josh. You and I."

"And Ixchel," I say firmly.

"What? Don't be foolish; if she's on the list of sacrifices she's already lost."

"You can talk to the king. Save her."

Martineau looks massively exasperated. "Oh, all right. I'll do what I can. But first, the codex."

I nod. "Fine. Good."

"I suppose she'll be of some comfort to you in the twenty-first century. Where we're going, she may not even exist."

My jaw drops. "What. . .?"

In the dispersed light from his torch, I can see that Martineau is smirking. "It'll be a brave new world, young Garcia. I told you; this isn't my first outing with the Bracelet. It's evident that what I attempted last time didn't change the future enough. This time, I'm removing the codex from history. Taking it from the seventh century direct to the twenty-first. The Ix Codex won't exist for your grandfather to find. Your grandfather might not even meet your grandmother." He smiles slowly. "*You* might not be born. Won't that be interesting for you, Mr Garcia? To arrive in a parallel reality in which you don't exist, where you have no family."

I stare at him, speechless.

"Now, pay attention. The duct leads to a small chamber that is guarded. In the centre of the chamber is an ornamental clay brazier. Move it carefully. Underneath you'll find the opening. The drop shouldn't be more than a couple of metres. Take the guard's fire torch – it might keep the snakes at bay. "

"Where's the codex?"

"I've never been inside the tomb," he says. He's struggling to sound patient. "I'll deal with the guard, then wait for you in the jungle."

I push my back against the pyramid. "No. You have to stay and help me get out of the tomb. What if it's too high for me to climb out?"

"If I actually go into the chamber with you, the guard will see me," he says sardonically. "I'll have to kill him and blame it on you. Are you happy with that?"

The guard doesn't deserve to die. If anyone does, it's *Martineau*, for what he's making me do.

"You've got to help me out of there," I insist. "Or I'll get bitten to death and the codex stays with me."

We stare at each other, breathing hard.

"All right," he concedes. "I have some sedative. I can inject the guard, knock him out."

"Why didn't you say so?"

He sighs, leans back and gives me a long, appraising look. "Don't get clever, Mr Garcia. I'll still blame the incident on you. More evidence of your demonic alliance."

I turn away. Every word he says makes me feel sick with guilt and rage. I wish I dared stand up to Martineau. But I won't risk being stuck here. Without Ixchel, I wouldn't survive, I know it. My thoughts go back to what he said about Ixchel being sacrificed. I can barely stand to think about it.

I can't let it happen. I have to get the Bracelet back. Before sunrise, I have to find Ixchel.

The duct is narrow – just wide enough for one person, not tall enough to stand in. We both have to bend our knees and dip our heads. Ahead there's the glow of firelight. It's coming from a doorway.

We don't reach the doorway before the tomb guard emerges, his knife drawn. When he sees me, he charges, weapon high in his left hand, the torch in his right.

"STOP!" calls out Martineau, in Mayan. It's just as well because in my panic, I was still trying to remember the word for "halt" or "stop".

The guard stops immediately. He's young, stockier than most of the Mayans I've seen. Flabby, even; slow-moving, looks out of condition. His eyes narrow, creases that are almost lost in his chubby, paint-lined cheeks. He peers past me, trying to get a look at Martineau. The guard doesn't lower his weapon or the torch, just stands in the passageway, blocking our path. He looks puzzled yet still pretty fierce.

"Give the torch to the boy," intones Martineau, still behind me. The guard frowns, even more confused. He can't take his eyes off his own arm, stretching out, offering me the torch.

"Drop the dagger," orders Martineau, soft as a whisper. The guard stares at his left hand as it opens and the dagger falls to the ground.

"Don't move," he says, finally, this time almost casually. He pushes me in the small of my back. "Go ahead, boy. Your chance to prove yourself."

I walk up to the guard and try to pass him. He won't budge. I give him a little shove, try to shift him to one side. He growls at me, but still won't move an inch. This hypnoticin stuff is incredible. A few words from Martineau, that's all it took. My head reels with the possibilities of mind-controlling drugs. If the Sect has developed a something that lets them hypnotize people, who can stop them?

Martineau speaks again, very slow and clear. "Turn around." The guard obeys. Martineau pushes me aside, takes the torch out of my hand and swings it violently against the guard's shoulders. The guard cries out in surprise as much as anything and staggers. Martineau whacks him again, on the head. The poor bloke crumples.

It doesn't seem fair. I daren't say anything. The hypnotic drug doesn't seem to have any effect on me but . . . I can't be sure. The last thing I want is some kind of suicide instruction from Martineau.

Martineau does this stupid little bow. "After you."

I stare from Martineau to the Mayan guard on the ground.

"Did you have to whack him? What about the sedative?"

Martineau scowls. "Waste not, want not."

The way is clear for me to get to the tomb. Inside the chamber it's just as Martineau said: the small room; the brazier, glowing hot with burning charcoal and incense. I push it aside, watched by Martineau. There's a woven mat of coarse sisal fibres. I toss that aside. Then I'm gazing into an opening a little wider than me, a dark hole.

"Drop the torch," orders Martineau.

I do it. Immediately there's a reaction from the hole. A collective slither and hiss. Where the torch falls, the ground clears. I can just make out the snakes at the edges of the clearing. In the shadows I can see a roiling mass of serpentine bodies. A shiver goes through me; my skin seems to crawl with a million ants. I position myself over the hole. Then I jump.

The instant I drop, the snakes hiss louder. I guess they've caught the scent of an intruder. I reach for the torch. The sudden movement provokes a dull ache in my calf muscle, where Rain Son wounded me. In the corner of my eye there's a sudden movement. I swing the torch, hit the attacking snake and a few others. Another chorus of hisses. They sound furious. But the fire keeps them at bay. I wave the torch low, sweeping in an arc in front of me. They move away, seething the whole time. I take a step. Then another. And another.

At one end of the pit I can see a dais, on which there's the unmistakable shadow of a dead body. It lies on a mat that is laid across five ceramic vessels. The body seems to be coated with a red pigment. I take a few steps closer, waving the snakes away. A real Mayan tomb – with an actual body. I can hear my own heart thumping. When I get closer I can see that there's a mosaic jade mask over the leathery skin of the face. Three pairs of jade earplugs, a jade ring, jade beads, three jade plaques, thousands of shell beads and a stingray spine. And lying on the chest, the boxy shape of the Ix Codex.

Incredible.

I've stopped moving for a second. The snakes begin to close in again. I jab at them, stabbing the torch right into the heart of the writhing mass. They slither away, almost moving as one. The tension in the room rises. Even I can feel it; they're angry.

I take more steps, batting the snakes away until I reach the body. The skull is covered with wisps of rotten hair. I catch a whiff of the putrescence. Faint as it is, the stench worms its way into my brain. My stomach heaves; I retch. The snakes react, hissing. They sound bitter. I spin around, brandishing the torch.

"Shut up, you FREAKS!" I yell.

A hundred eyes glitter at me, tiny glints of reflected flame. Some of the snakes back up, raising themselves a metre off the ground.

"Back off!" I yell, louder this time, angry.

When I turn towards the body, I can sense them behind me, staring at my back. I reach out, grab the codex and spin around. One touch is enough to activate the toxic gas in the codex's deadly cover . . . but I'm immune.

The snakes have drawn closer. They're almost touching me. Yet none of them strikes out. Carrying the codex makes it harder to dodge or to attack them with the torch. For almost a minute I'm like a statue. Waiting, watching the snakes. They hardly move.

I watch their heads twitching. They smell something. They're interested. I'm rigid with terror, waiting for the attack.

Then something weird happens.

The closest ones are the first to go. They start to writhe frantically, striking out at their neighbours, biting and hissing. Within a second there is utter mayhem. The snakes turn on each other. They've gone completely wild, totally insane.

The blood starts to circulate in my veins again. I toss the torch along the ground, watching the long slithering bodies wriggle out of the way. I leap into that cleared path, landing under the opening in the ceiling.

Martineau was right – it is low enough for me to jump out, but only if I use both hands. Freeing my hands would mean I'd have to throw the codex up to him.

Yeah, right. And watch him leave me with the crazy snakes?

"Give me your hand," I yell. "Come on, help me up! The snakes have gone mad! They're killing each other!"

"It's the toxin," says Martineau's disembodied voice. "It does something strange to their physiology."

There's a jolt to the back of my leg. I almost jump out of my skin. "Just get me out of here!" I scream. Two snakes are flung against my jeans, their mouths closing over each other's bodies.

After the initial shock, I realize I'm OK. I haven't been bitten. But any second now, I will be. They're everywhere now, sinking their crazed fangs into one another. It's only a matter of time before I'm caught in the crossfire.

"Get me out!" I scream, panicked.

Martineau's legs come into view; then an arm pops through the hole. I grab hold and pull myself up until I can put both arms on the top of the hole.

I'm out. In the crypt below, the snakes look as though they're being boiled alive. Martineau is inscrutable behind the bright light of his torch. He reaches out for the codex. I back away. There's a startled gasp, then a chuckle.

"You surely don't think you can keep me from the codex now, Mr Garcia?"

"We had a deal," I tell him, breathing hard.

"Yes – I helped you out of the crypt. I'll inject you with antidote."

I shake my head, backing further down the narrow tunnel. "No. I'm not bitten. You're not coming near me with another needle."

His silky, persuasive voice. "You really should trust me."

I'm backing away again, the codex held firmly behind my back. I'm almost outside the pyramid now. "Give me the Bracelet. Help me find Ixchel."

He laughs again. "Ridiculous!" He follows me out of the tunnel, his torch beaming directly into my eyes.

Then we're standing on the ledge of the royal palace, against the ominous gloom of the jungle. In the grey light of dawn, I can see his face, half-shadowed.

"Be reasonable," he says. "You've nowhere to go. Once you're caught in the jungle with the codex, you'll be finished."

"I won't get caught," I breathe.

His voice drops. "Give it to me, boy. You're becoming annoying."

There's movement in the shadows underneath the base of the royal palace. Flame torches appear; dancing lights approach from the front. Voices call out the second they notice Martineau and me a couple of metres above them on the ledge. There's confusion, then a terrified cry.

"He has the cursed book!"

Instantly, the guards scatter, some into the jungle, some back towards the front of the palace. Within a minute their leader manages to bring them back into some sort of order, at a safe distance. They aren't happy, though, not a bit. I can hear the whispers.

I move away from Martineau. He's hesitating, won't come any closer. I'm ready to attack him. In my mind I'm already running through all the capoeira moves that I could do on the small space of the ledge. I'd get some good kicks in, maybe enough to knock him off the ledge. Martineau's in his fifties at least – a two-metre fall could break a bone. He's in no shape to tackle me up here. From his wary stance, I can tell that he knows it.

In fact, the moment he sees the guards, he stops moving towards me. As if he's also afraid of the toxin. But he's immune . . . what's going on?

The leader is getting vexed. "The boy! He's holding it – the cursed book!" I recognize the voice – it's Crunching Jaguar.

"Yes," Martineau booms. "The demon – he has it."

He smiles as he betrays me, hands me over to them as a demon.

There's another voice then, the high, reedy tones of the king. I spot his elaborate headdress bobbing amongst the crowd of guards. The king works his way to the front of the crowd, but no further.

They've dealt with this poisonous gas before. I remember Blanco Vigores once told me the story of when the Ix Codex came to Calakmul – the Snake Kingdom. Dozens of warriors died, screaming, their insides turning to bloody liquid when the toxic gas hit them.

"If the boy can defy the book's curse then he is no demon but a messenger of the gods."

Stunned silence.

"Are you, boy?" the king continues. "Do you bring a message from the gods?"

I glance at Martineau. He's rigid, looking from me to the shadowy huddle of guards.

"He commanded me with a god's voice," calls someone else. It's Rain Son. "I could do nothing but obey."

"You dare speak in the presence of Lord Yuknoom!" shouts Crunching Jaguar. There's a scuffle in the crowd, the sound of a fist hitting flesh, then a groan as Rain Son goes down.

Martineau yells, "Detain the demon!"

There's silence, again. But nobody moves. Furiously, Martineau repeats the order. Still no movement.

For a second, I'm as confused as they look. Why isn't the hypnosis drug working for Martineau?

Concentrating, I struggle to string words together. "I bring a message," I begin. The crowd gasps, almost with one voice. It's the first time they've heard me talk in Mayan. "A message," I repeat, louder. "From the gods!"

"We will hear your message, boy," calls the king. "Speak!"

"The book is cursed," I shout, echoing their own words. "The Bracelets – they are cursed! The Jaguar Priest is. . ." I hesitate, no idea how to say "an imposter". "The Jaguar Priest is not your friend. I must take the Bracelets, the book and the Jaguar Priest. They are cursed!"

The guards look up at us, then glance expectantly at the king.

"The Jaguar Priest is wise beyond any other priest," Lord Yuknoom admits. "And yet it is true . . . there is something strange about him." The king raises his eyes to Martineau, a long, thoughtful look. "A Jaguar Priest who dares to command his king. We have never seen such a man."

"He is . . . not of . . . the Snake Kingdom," I say, stumbling over the Mayan words.

"The *demon* clouds your thoughts," Martineau urges, almost hysterical. "Seize him! Now!"

They want to obey him, I sense it. The whole crowd
moves closer. I bring the codex round to my chest, clutch it in
front of me to ward them off. They stop moving. Some of
them make a noise like a child crying with frustration. They're
fidgeting, rocking back and forth, confused. They want to
surge forward. But they can't take their eyes off me with the
codex.

*The hypnosis drug . . . it can't make them do something
they think will kill them.*

Martineau freezes. He dips his head towards me. He
chuckles, then smiles. He reaches inside his garments, to a
red pouch hanging from his belt. From it he pulls a Bracelet.
In front of everyone he pushes it on to his wrist. I watch,
mesmerized. Words catch in my throat.

His hand remains hovering at the Bracelet. All he has to
do is push the Crystal Key and he'll vanish. Along with any
hope I have of escaping, of rescuing Ixchel.

Finally, he speaks. "The codex . . . for your Bracelet, Josh.
The best deal you'll ever get from me."

Martineau reaches out with his right hand. He takes two
steps forward.

"Wait."

He halts; his nostrils flare in disbelief.

"This purification ritual for the human sacrifice," I say.
"Where do they do it?"

Martineau begins to laugh. "You surely don't think. . ."

"Tell me where she is. . ." I interrupt. "Or no deal."

"Your better nature will be the death of you, Mr Garcia. Mark my words." He gives a dramatic sigh. "The steam house is part of the new building, at the summit of the great pyramid. That's where they'll have taken the sacrificial victims."

That's it, then. Game over for the codex – he's beaten me hands down. I step forward, reach out with my left hand open, palm facing up. "Give me the Bracelet."

Martineau reaches into a second pouch, on the other side of his belt buckle. His fingers pull out another Bracelet. "You mean this?" he says, nonchalant. "Put the codex down. And I'll drop the Bracelet. We pick up on three."

I do as he says, not taking my eyes off his hands. Beneath the pyramid the king watches with his guards. I can sense their tension. They're holding their breath.

We start the count. On three I lunge forward and grab the Bracelet. Martineau gives a cry of delight as he holds the codex. Before I can react, his left hand slams on to the Bracelet on his wrist. His eyes glint with satisfaction as he watches the Bracelet activate the countdown.

"Farewell, young Garcia. I doubt we'll meet again."

There is a faint sound, like a crackle of electricity. For a fraction of a second his whole body is engulfed with white light. It wraps him up, eats him out of the air.

There's a tiny moment of stilled shock. Below, the Mayans

gasp. Then the guards drop to their knees, moaning and wailing in panic. I've never seen people fall apart like this. Only the king doesn't react. He gazes right into my eyes as I fasten the Bracelet of Itzamna on my left wrist. There's no fear in his eyes, only menace. I start to back away. Then I turn and run.

I reach the end of the pyramid in just over a second, leap high and land on grass-cleared ground. Somewhere behind me I can hear the king urging his guards to get up. I don't stop to listen to what he's saying, just get my head down and run – as fast and as far away from the guards as I can, and towards the central plaza.

All the guards must be on the other side of the royal palace with the king, because the plaza is empty. I sprint across the main causeway, heading straight for the great pyramid. My trainers fly across the hard, dry ground. My heart pounds, once, twice. From behind me, I hear the charge.

The guards. They're coming.

I reach the main pyramid in another second. Its many staircases stretch across the end of the plaza. One wide staircase all the way across the base of the pyramid, to the first tier, where they auctioned off Ixchel yesterday. Then one main staircase in the centre, flanked by two narrower staircases, crossing as many as five more tiers. I swerve around the stone columns at the base, bound on to the lowest staircase, land four steps up. I start climbing, two steps at a time.

The first guards are less than fifteen metres behind. They've found their voices now, and courage too – they hurl abuse at me. I keep climbing, diagonally, heading for the main staircase that runs up the centre of the pyramid. The guards reach the base of the pyramid. They swarm up the steps. Out of the corner of my eye I notice one guard breaking away. He's approaching me fast. He scrambles across the first-tier staircase, leaps on to the lowest platform and bounds across to the main staircase.

No more than ten stairs behind me.

I don't look back. I push on, panting with the effort of climbing the steep, narrow steps. It's shattering, this staircase. Endless. With each step the pounding pain in my wounded calf muscle just gets stronger. Somehow, I have to ignore it. I climb one, two, three more tiers of the pyramid. The summit still towers overhead. Above, there are voices. I glance up – at the end of the staircase there are two guards, waiting. My spirits plummet. I'm done for. Behind me, there's a terse yell. "Hold him. He's mine."

That voice. I know it – Rain Son. Again! Won't the guy ever give up?

I cut across the central staircase, heading for the next tier. It's one layer below the platform at the top of the staircase, where two guards are waiting. When they see me changing

193

course, one of them crosses to the edge of their platform. It's a long drop to the level below. Even so, he jumps.

But I'm already there, waiting. I don't give him time to get up. He gets two punches across the jaw and then a sharp kick to the front of his chest. The second guard loiters on the platform above, still getting the nerve to drop down.

I think I've put him off.

I cross the platform, moving to the right of the multilayered pyramid. There's a series of connected platforms here – no stairs, but the tiers are close together. None are too high to climb. I clamber across the layers, approaching the top.

Now I can see it – right on the summit there's a whole extra temple. It's a smaller pyramid, set far enough back that I hadn't seen it from the front. It's this extra bit that makes the giant pyramid really tower over every other building in the city. It's new, too. There are baskets of fine, powdery white lime everywhere, waiting to be applied as stucco to the outside of the temple. Powdered lime – worse than sand in the eyes, much worse. I grab one of those baskets and step carefully, avoiding small heaps of mixed cement that have been abandoned by the builders. The air is strong with the clean, acidic smell of freshly mixed stucco.

There's another smell too, floating down from somewhere above. Perfume. For a second I stop moving, breathing it in. Steam, scented with fragrant oils.

The ritual steam bath. It's in the summit temple.

I glance down – to see Rain Son one level below. He yells up, "Believe me, demon, you will die."

I'm so high up now that I can see across the whole of the citadel, all the way across to the sun rising near the horizon. The red, yellow and green painted friezes of the pyramids begin to glow at the edges, touched by the pink light of dawn.

The second guard at the top of the temple finds the nerve to jump on to the lower platform. Now he's only a couple of steps behind Rain Son.

I race across to the base of the summit temple, where the stairs begin. There are about twenty-five steps up to another platform. I can see an opening in the structure above. Rain Son is crossing the final platform now. When he hits my staircase I'm only seven steps ahead. He's close enough for me to hear his lungs wheezing.

I reach the summit. No more guards here, but dozens on their way, swarming all over the platforms below. I calculate that I have about three seconds to get out of here. I turn to face Rain Son as he reaches the top of the stairs. He runs his tongue over his lips as he draws a knife.

This guy is really getting on my nerves. He's going to get everything I've got. Everything that's owed to him and more.

I swing the basket around my head and chuck lime powder into his face. His eyes go wide with fright; too late he sees what I'm doing. When the powder hits, he screams, falls to his knees, hands to his eyes. I follow up with a couple of *chapa baixa* kicks, rapid strikes across his head and shoulders.

Rain Son goes down face first, moaning in agony. His chin hangs over the edge of the top step. His knife clatters to the ground. I reach forward and grab it. Two other guards have just started up the final flight of stairs.

Then I'm round the side of the summit temple. The doorway is open. Steam pours out. I step inside. There's a narrow corridor. All around me, the sweet smell of exotic flowers and pungent pine resin. A few steps down the narrow corridor, I pass through another doorway. This one is blocked. A heavy wooden panel lies across the opening. I get a shoulder to it and heave. The panel totters; I step aside as it falls across the corridor. Now I'm blocked in too. The steam room is ahead. I take one more step.

I'm inside a room no more than two metres square. There's a thin stream of light from a narrow slit in the ceiling. Clustered together on the floor are five bodies. Young women, children too. At first glance the women look the same. They're wearing white linen shifts that cling to their skin. Their hands are bound together. They almost look like they're praying. Nothing on their feet, nothing on their heads. But on their arms, their wrists – the unmistakable yellow of gold. I move between the bodies of the young women. Looking for Ixchel. They're all unconscious, their skin flushed and glistening from the steam. I lift one girl's chin carefully. It isn't Ixchel. There are two little boys, no older than seven. I can feel my heart breaking with a slow, painful crack.

I can't save them all. They're practically on the verge of death right now. I wonder if they'll even notice it when they're thrown into the chilly waters of the *cenote*.

I check a girl in the corner. Her hair is tied up, Mayan-style. When I touch her cheek, I know it's Ixchel. I speak her name. She doesn't respond. I turn her head. It's her. I put an arm around her waist and shoulders, pull her against me. She droops, no resistance. Not a single response. I stare down at her closed eyes. I wonder at how someone can look so peaceful when they must have been so scared. I lift one of her hands. That's when I notice the bloodstains on her knuckles. The skin broken and bruised.

Ixchel tried to break the door down. It should have moved easily. Someone must have held that panel against the doorway until she stopped thumping, stopped screaming, crying, begging. Until there was no sound from inside. Until the heat overwhelmed them.

The steam house fills with the sound of guards. They're all around the summit, outside. I hear them approach the temple's entrance. I hear the wooden panel being moved, the corridor outside unblocked. I see a guard at the opening of the cramped, steamy room, his blade in one hand. My finger is on the Bracelet of Itzamna, on the crystal. He looks at the

197

bodies, then at me, at Ixchel in my arms. My finger presses hard on the crystal. The royal guard stares at me. He's paralysed. All the ancient horror of the unknown is reflected in his eyes, aghast at what they're being forced to witness. I see him disappear, torn from my sight like a page ripped out of a book. I see the sun explode into view, blazing overhead. I see the sky turn blue. I see grass expand under my feet. I'm standing there, all dirty jeans and bloodstained top, holding a girl in my arms, a half-dead girl, and it's like the most everyday thing. I see sweet turquoise water stretch endlessly in front of me. It laps against a lakeside dotted with lily pads. I see the girl I'm holding open her mouth, just a little. She screws her eyes tightly, reacting to the sun. I see houses around the lake, hardwood trees, fiery orange tree blossoms, coconut palms, the water's surface dotted with rowing boats, tall reeds swaying with the breeze. In the distance there's a restaurant with a thatched roof and a mariachi band playing on the waterfront.

I see the future materialize before my eyes; the most dazzling thing I've ever seen.

I fall to my knees and gently lower Ixchel to the ground. Her eyes flutter open. I watch her, conscious of my heart beating so hard that it hurts, of the pulse in my ears, of every single beat. I could die from this feeling, I think, but I never want it to go away.

Ixchel's skin feels hot and clammy, like she's running a high
fever. She's awake but hardly able to move or speak. I empty a
couple of hundred-peso notes and my Ek Naab mobile phone
from my jeans pocket, kick off my trainers and then pick up
Ixchel and carry her to the water's edge. I jump in, still holding
on to her. The water is warm but still a little cooler than her
skin. In the water, Ixchel flops. I have to support her completely.
After a few minutes she starts to relax and begins to float.
With one hand still under her back, I dip under the water and
rub at my head and neck. I swallow a few gulps of the lake
water. It's amazingly refreshing. I keep wading, chest deep in
water, until we're beyond the reeds and lily pads. The water is
so clear I can see all the way to the soft, sandy bed of the lake.

After a few minutes in silence, Ixchel wriggles free. She
drops her legs and stands in the water with her arms spread
out, looking at me. I look back at her, not knowing what to
say.

"You're still dressed," she begins.

"My clothes got pretty rank," I say, blushing. "They could do with a rinse. Anyway. There wasn't time. You were overheating."

Ixchel doesn't answer except with a resigned nod. I realize then that she's close to tears. I want to reach out and hug her but she won't look at me, just stares out into the middle of the lake with an expression of anguish on her face. It's also obvious that she doesn't want to cry, or that she's trying to stop herself.

More than ever before, I want to kiss her. The urge is so strong that it's almost overwhelming. But she won't look at me; there's obviously something wrong. I start talking fast to take my mind off the idea of just grabbing Ixchel.

"This is Lake Bacalar," I begin. "At least I think it is. Freshwater lake, all turquoisey blue. Do you think it is? Yeah. It looks like the place I dreamt about, when I dreamt about Camila showing me the Sect's lake house in Bacalar. See? My dream vision was right – again! Too bad Benicio isn't here, right. . .?"

Ixchel doesn't answer.

"So if we're at Bacalar . . . and the Sect had a place in Bacalar . . . then we must have Martineau's Bracelet. They must have got mixed up in the confusion! He must have left from the Sect's place. That's why we've returned. But Martineau, he's got my Bracelet. So he's gone back to Ek

Naab – to Montoyo's apartment, where we set out from, but ten minutes earlier. That's gonna be kind of a shock for Carlos. . ."

Finally, Ixchel manages to speak. "What do you mean . . . ten minutes earlier. . .?"

For a second I want to squeeze her, I'm so happy that she's starting to come round.

But I just give an enthusiastic nod. "That's how the safety on the Bracelet of Itzamna works. You go back in time to ten minutes before it was last used. Same place, ten minutes earlier."

Ixchel thinks this through for a minute. "Omigosh . . . you're right!"

"So Martineau has gone back to Ek Naab – with my Bracelet. And we've come to the Sect's place in Bacalar."

"If we're at the Sect's place – where is the actual house?"

I concentrate on the scene before us. The lake, clear and blue, the opposite bank empty of all buildings: a wildlife reserve. The developed side, with the occasional villa, condo and cultivated garden. The restaurant in the distance, where the mariachi band play.

"Maybe Martineau used the Bracelet from a different part of the lake."

She looks at me. "I'm hungry. Are you? Thirsty too."

"I've got a couple of hundred pesos maybe. We'll find a shop, as soon as I've had a chance to call Ek Naab."

"I can't go to the shops like this, Josh. This dress is soaked through." She lowers her eyes, embarrassed. "It's going to be practically transparent."

Now it's my turn to be embarrassed. "Right! Good point. And you know what, there's another thing." I point at her arms. "All those gold bracelets. They'll attract attention. We'd better hide them."

Ixchel looks down at her arms, as if it's the first time she's noticed that they're draped in at least fourteen bands of ornate gold, some studded with jade, others with silver. Her mouth falls open. "Wow! Amazing."

"Yep. It would have been a bumper harvest for the Mayan gods. . ."

Ixchel's eyes flash with anger. "Don't make jokes. I was with those people when they were getting ready to be sacrificed. They probably still are. Little children. . . You can't imagine it, Josh."

"I know," I say quickly, as solemnly as I can. "I don't think it's funny. It's just . . . I didn't know what to say."

"Look at you," she says. "You're a mess. Your clothes are ripped. You're all cut up. Your arms, your face even."

"Just scratches," I reply, blushing. But the knife wound in my calf is a bit more than a scratch. It's turned into a steady, pulsating pain.

Ixchel dips her head backwards into the water and smooths back her hair. I watch, mesmerized, while I swallow another mouthful of the lake water. "I can't believe that you came back for me," she says, when she straightens up. She looks right at me. "You could have just used the Bracelet to get yourself out. Instead of climbing all the way up that pyramid."

"I said I'd be back for you," I tell her. Feeling like a coward. Why can't I tell Ixchel how I feel? This is a perfect opportunity. I give her a look that's half miserable, half hopeful. "Leave no one behind – that's me."

"You're a good friend, Josh," she says after a few seconds. She lowers her eyes.

It's like being stabbed in the heart. For a couple of seconds I can't speak. I'm a *friend*. That's all I'll ever be to Ixchel.

Slowly, we wade back to the edge of the lake and climb out. I peel off my soaking jeans and socks. One sock has turned rust red at the top, where it soaked up most of the blood from my leg wound. I untie the bandage I made for the cut, rinse it out in the lake water and then take a look at the wound. It's about four centimetres long, but it doesn't look too deep. On the other hand, it won't close. Ixchel watches in silence. She looks a bit worried. I tie the ripped piece of T-shirt back around my leg, then wring out and stretch the jeans and socks to dry in the sun. Then I open the Ek Naab phone. It lights up, yet the signal-finding icon just keeps rolling over and over. I hold the phone up high, but it makes no difference. Every movement I make is slow and laboured. It's as though hearing those words – *You're a good friend, Josh* – has sucked away all my energy.

Eventually, Ixchel looks up. "No signal?"

"Nope."

"That's very strange," Ixchel says, frowning. "We have total coverage in Yucatan. You shouldn't have problems this close to the city."

She looks anxious, as if she's just remembered a bit of bad news.

"You think it has something to do with Martineau using the Bracelet?" I ask.

"I don't know, I don't know," she mumbles. "I need to eat first. I'm not sure that I'm thinking straight."

"OK," I say, standing up. I put on my trainers and pick up the two hundred-peso notes, leftover from the last time I was in the outside world. It's a disappointingly small sum of money – not even ten quid.

I probably look pretty ridiculous in boxer shorts and a bloodstained wet T-shirt with one sleeve ripped off. But I can't see any sign of a shop and the nearest road sounds like it's at least two hundred metres away. By the time I reach a neighbourhood shop, I'll probably be dry. "Will you be OK if I go and find us some food?"

"There's no one around," she replies, lying down. "I'll get some rest and dry off. If I get too thirsty I'll drink from the lake. But I'd prefer a soda if you can get me one. And some potato chips."

"I'll do my best."

"And a Gansito," she adds.

"Gansito," I say, managing a grin. "Gotcha." Any excuse to get away quickly. Before I start to act like I'm angry, which I am, a little.

Forty minutes later I'm on my way back to Ixchel, thinking about what a weird time I had in the shop. The crisps and drinks had old-style brands. No canned drinks, only glass bottles. They had no fridge for the drinks, only an old-fashioned drinks cooler that used a huge block of ice. There were a couple of teenagers in the shop drinking *guarana*, a fizzy drink I've only ever seen in Brazil. When I went to pay the hundred and forty pesos she charged me (which seemed like an insane amount to pay; normally it would be around fifty pesos for some drinks, crisps and Gansitos), the shop lady almost wouldn't accept my money.

She didn't recognize the peso notes. I managed to blag her, saying I'd just come from Mexico City and they were the first of a new design. She gave me sixty pesos change, rolling her eyes and muttering, "Looks pretty weird to me, but . . . OK. Seeing as God spared Mexico. . ." She was all "whatever" but I could tell she was pretty suspicious.

For a minute in the shop, I even wondered if we'd somehow missed the right date and gone back into the past, the 1980s or something. So I checked a copy of *Time* magazine they were selling.

It was from the right year. We're not in the past. So what's the explanation? Because something is very wrong with this timeline.

I speed up, feeling myself break out into a sweat.

My phone to Ek Naab didn't work.

What if it isn't just the outside world that's different? What if there's something wrong with Ek Naab too?

Ixchel is lying down under a tree. She hears me strolling through the long grass and sits up. As I get closer, she even smiles. I try to smile back. Kneeling next to Ixchel, I pass her one of the bottles without saying a word. After the first refreshing slug, I point to the brand label.

"Antarctica guarana."

Ixchel smiles, puzzled.

"Have you ever seen that in Mexico?"

"I don't know. I guess not?"

"Also, there were no canned drinks," I say. "Only glass bottles. The money is different too. The drinks were kept in an old-style cooler. No 7-Up, no Sprite or Fresca or diet drinks."

Ixchel looks even more confused. "So . . . what are you trying to say?"

"Right here is where my sister, Camila, showed the Sect around a lake house. If they ended up renting it, they were never more than two hours from the gateway to Ek Naab. Camila saw Simon Madison and Melissa DiCanio ages before we'd heard about them. The Sect," I repeat, "was *here*."

I can tell from Ixchel's expression that she's cottoned on to what I'm saying.

"But not now?"

"Not in this . . . reality? Timeline? Parallel world?" I hesitate, nervously. "Maybe there's a reason why I can't phone Ek Naab."

Ixchel drinks from her bottle in silence, thinking. I tear open the cellophane wrapper on the Gansitos and give one to her. "Eat it. I think we're going to need the sugar."

Ixchel nibbles on the chocolate. I take a bite from my own.

"Tastes different," she says.

She's right. All the elements of the traditional Gansito are there: yellow sponge, white vanilla cream, sticky red jam and a plain chocolate coating. But somehow It's different. Like the ingredients aren't in balance.

"Maybe we're in the past?"

"I saw the latest copy of *Time* magazine – we're not."

Ixchel looks thoughtful. "You're sure that this is where the house was?"

"As much as I can be. There aren't many landmarks. Why would it be anywhere else? What business would Martineau have being anywhere else in Bacalar? You think maybe he was in the middle of a hiking trip and suddenly decided to zap himself to the Mayan past?"

Ixchel looks upset. "What's wrong with you, Josh? You don't have to be mean."

I look out towards the lake. "Martineau left from that house, I'm sure of it. I reckon he got himself up as a jaguar priest and then zapped himself into seventh-century Calakmul."

"Wait a minute. Martineau left from here in Bacalar . . . so *his* Bracelet brought us back to the same place, but ten minutes before he left?"

"Yeah. Meanwhile he's gone back to Ek Naab."

I watch Ixchel trying to get her head round this. She's still confused. No wonder – there's a lot I still haven't told her about how the safety device works. If I do, I'll have to come clean about meeting my dad in Area 51.

"Look," I begin, "Martineau's Bracelet – the one we've just used – I think it's mine. I don't know how he got it. But somewhere in the future of this Bracelet, Martineau finds it, starts using it."

Ixchel scrunches up her nose in disbelief. "You're serious? How do you know?"

"I don't know, not for sure. Maybe there are two Bracelets. Maybe Itzamna made two. I don't know, though . . . that doesn't feel right."

"Why not?"

"It's more of a hunch, really. Something tells me that if there were two or even maybe more Bracelets floating around in time and space . . . there wouldn't be so much grief about finding one of them. D'ya get what I'm saying? It could be my imagination, but from the first minute I put the Bracelet of Itzamna on my wrist, I've felt this, like, electric charge. As if the Bracelet *itself* recognized me. As if the Bracelet is one of a kind.

"The thing is, Ixchel, I've seen two Bracelets of Itzamna together once before. That time, it was the same Bracelet. One from the past and one from the future."

"What. . .?" She's almost speechless. "You never told me. When?"

My shoulders droop. It's all going to come out now. "The last time I used my Bracelet. That second Bracelet – it was on my dad's arm. But it was the *same* one. It was the Bracelet that my dad gave me later, the broken one that took him to Mount Orizaba."

26

I rip open the big bag of crisps, offer the bag to Ixchel, then begin, slowly, to explain. There's no point holding back information now – this is too hard for me to figure out by myself. It might even be too hard for both of us to think through together.

I tell Ixchel what really happened in Switzerland. How I used the Bracelet and went back to where it was last used – the deep underground military base in Area 51 where my father was held in secret. He'd been chased and captured by the National Reconnaissance Office. They faked his death so that no one would come looking for him. Then kept him prisoner, in secret. Until one day he used the Bracelet. It transported him to the slopes of Mount Orizaba. But the Bracelet wasn't working properly – the Crystal Key had been burnt out long ago. Without that, the time travelling part of the Bracelet couldn't work. So he didn't move in time, only in space.

He was lucky not to die – Blanco Vigores warned me of the dangers of using the Bracelet without the Crystal Key. Without that crystal, the control circuit doesn't work – there's no way to know where you'll end up. You could end up being teleported into outer space, or into the middle of a rock. Luckily for Dad, he suffered only one side effect of the Bracelet – he lost his memory.

That burnt-out Bracelet without the crystal was the one Dad gave to me, just before he fell to his death in the ice chasm.

"Amnesia is a big problem with this kind of transportation. I dunno why. That's why my dad begged me not to start using the Bracelet. Just to use it once, to get out of the Area 51 base. Then never again. Amnesia is why Arcadio wrote himself all those notes in an old book, and tattooed himself with the reference to the book. Messages from himself to himself, in a book that had been around for almost 200 years. That was his protection – his only protection against the nightmare scenario."

"The nightmare scenario?" Ixchel takes another handful of crisps and crunches them slowly, one by one.

"Yeah – when the crystal burns out and you get hit by the amnesia. That's the worst – if that happens then you're trapped in time. Marooned. You can't fix the Bracelet, you don't know how. You don't even know who you are. Like I say – a nightmare. That's why Arcadio had the tattoo; that's why he left all the notes. If he ever lost his memory and the crystal burned out, he could make the Crystal Key."

"You seem to know a lot about this," she observes.

"I've had months to think it over. About what Vigores told me. About what my dad told me."

"Why didn't you tell me this right away?" Ixchel watches me keenly.

I turn red. "I'm sorry," I say in a low voice. "I just. . ."

"Is there anything else you haven't told me?"

"I keep certain things from you . . . for your own protection."

"You don't trust me."

"No . . . no! Of course I do. It's. . ." I stop talking and breathe heavily, blowing a stream of air through my lips. "Wow . . . this is hard to say."

She looks at me expectantly. Neither of us speaks for a moment.

"It's this Arcadio thing. You think I'm him. And. . ." I stare at my knees and swallow. "And you think that I'm, like . . . going to abandon you. Start travelling in time and forget all about you. It's what you said the other day." For a second I glance up, accusingly. "That's why you prefer Benicio to me." I close my eyes, feeling ridiculous. Ixchel touches my arm. When I open my eyes she's gazing at me with a soft expression.

She says, "I'm sorry."

I can only nod. Ixchel speaks carefully. "Josh . . . do you think that you're Arcadio?"

"I just . . . don't know! I don't know anything about my future. Montoyo once met Arcadio, but he couldn't tell me if I'm him. My dad, he'd met Arcadio too, years and years ago. I think that my dad was afraid I'll become Arcadio. But did he know for sure?" I shrug. "Who knows? The worst thing, though . . . is having everyone make these assumptions about who I am and what I'll do. Cos none of that has anything to do with me, does it? I'm just me, just living my life day by day. I don't even get to make plans. Not my own plans, anyway. It's like I'm living out some kind of plan, but no one ever really asked me."

"It's like that for all of us in Ek Naab," Ixchel agrees. "So I know what you mean about living to someone else's idea of your life. That's why I left."

"But you went back to Ek Naab," I say. "Why? Was it cos of Benicio?"

Now Ixchel is the one lowering her eyes and blushing. "It's complicated. But maybe now you understand why I felt trapped."

"Yeah, yeah." I lean against the tree trunk, stretch out my legs. "I get why you left. I want to know why you came back."

Might as well hear it now. Did she come back for Benicio? Is that how much he means to her?

Very softly she says, "I came back for you."

We stare at each other. She keeps talking, very quietly now, glancing down every few seconds. "The way your dad died. You seemed so heartbroken. The way . . . things were between us . . . on that trip." She gazes at me intently. "You didn't feel something?"

I nod, just once.

"I couldn't leave Ek Naab again. I knew you'd try to fix the Bracelet. Yes, I wondered whether one day you'd become Arcadio, forget about me and leave. It got worse the more I thought about it. Then you and Benicio came back to live in Ek Naab. He came looking for me right away, you know, Josh."

I say sullenly, "I bet he did."

"He told me he'd been waiting for ages to ask me to be his girlfriend. That he had given me a chance to see if I liked you – he didn't want to spoil the arranged marriage plans, after all. But since I didn't like you. . ."

"You said that?"

She looks flustered. "No. But I kept thinking about Susannah St John and Arcadio, how crazy she was about him when they were younger. I thought about how difficult it would be to be. . ." She swallows. "To be . . . the girlfriend of a time traveller. It's just not normal! I really didn't think I could handle something so strange. And there was Benicio. I'd always liked him."

Inside me a mixture of emotions are bubbling away. A minute ago I felt ready to make some grand declaration to Ixchel, to go all out and get properly soppy. Now she's talking about Benicio again. I really can't stand to hear another word.

"I've never met Arcadio and already I can't stand him. He's ruining my life!" I get to my feet. "You can't judge me by what Arcadio does. He's not me, even if he *is* me. You know what I mean. He forgets about you and goes off with someone else and that is something I would *never* do."

I'm seething with rage, wondering what to do with it. Obviously I can't storm off. Ixchel stares up at me as if she's never seen me before.

"But there's another possibility."

Distracted, I say, "What?"

"You said that we might have crossed into another timeline. A parallel reality, where things in Mexico are a little different."

"So?"

Ixchel stands up, facing me. She grabs my hands. "Maybe you don't exist in this reality."

"Oh, great."

"No . . . but think about it! If it's possible for someone using the Bracelet to end up in a parallel reality . . . then maybe Arcadio is a future version of you . . . but from another parallel."

I take a few seconds to process that. A parallel world where I don't exist – Martineau talked about that. Ixchel's right, though – if using the Bracelet can take you to different realities, then who can say where Arcadio came from? He might share my last name, might know all that stuff about me, might have my genetically altered blue eyes.

But that doesn't actually *make him me*.

With that one comment, Ixchel manages to brush away a fear that had clawed its way into my heart. Only now do I realize how crushing the worry had become, the idea that my life was already mapped out and I had no say. I can hardly believe how relieved I feel.

Arcadio does not have to be my future.

From the position of the sun in the sky and the stifling heat, I estimate that it's early afternoon. Once we've eaten all the food, our conversation slows down. I've lost all sense of urgency to be open about my feelings with Ixchel. In fact, I can't work out where I stand with her right now. OK, so we've sorted out part of the Arcadio issue. But there's still the Benicio thing. Plus the fact that I'm running out of ideas.

I mean, what the heck do I have to do to get her to fall for me? You'd think that saving her life over and over would be enough. But no. It's not as if I'm asking for much. Right now I'd settle for way less. Like for her to shut up about Benicio for at least a day.

The question of what to do next is unavoidable. We've got almost no money – sixty pesos in a place where a few snacks sets you back by one hundred and forty. The phone to Ek Naab doesn't work, at least not here. Ixchel doesn't even have shoes.

Then there's the small matter that we may well have zapped into a parallel reality in which things are different. Maybe we don't exist here. Maybe no one we know does.

How different could things be?

The last "different" timeline I remember was Ek Naab when I left it. It was almost identical to the world I grew up in. But in that reality Tyler hardly knew me – we had never become good friends.

This time, Mexico itself is actually different. I don't want to think through everything that could mean, definitely don't want to talk to Ixchel about it. Talking about it makes it seem more real.

We need food, a safe place to rest. We can't call Ek Naab; we need another way to get there. These are the kind of problems I can handle.

All of these things require money, which we don't have. But Ixchel's arms are covered in gold bangles. Rare Mayan jewellery that was being offered up along with her, to the Mayan gods of ancient Calakmul – the Snake Kingdom. That's got to be worth something in modern Mexico. The only issue is – how do we find a buyer?

"We could start at the museum in Chetumal," Ixchel says when I mention the jewellery. "It's a big Mayan archaeology museum, right on the main street." She starts to remove the bracelets, very carefully. We've nowhere to put them so she sits down and tears a strip of fabric from the hem of her white linen tunic, wraps the bracelets within the fabric. She keeps one on each wrist. "To show the museum," she says. Then she hands me the linen pouch full of Mayan jewellery. I pull on my jeans and socks, which are almost dry. I fasten Ixchel's makeshift bag to a belt loop. The Bracelet of Itzamna sits hidden in my front jeans pocket, never more than a few centimetres from my hand.

Chetumal is around twenty minutes' drive from Bacalar. We talk about how to get there. I could walk but Ixchel can't, not without shoes. The bus might just be affordable. Safer than hitch-hiking, too. But then we've blown all our cash. I fill the two empty guarana bottles with lake water. It tastes a bit reedy. Like cold, weak tea.

Without another word we both start walking towards the lakeside road. From there it'll be another few minutes to the main coastal highway.

We reach the highway in twenty minutes. The heat and humidity stifle any idea of conversation. Walking alongside Ixchel I get to thinking about all the time we've spent walking next to each other. About how we've talked over what we're doing and what problem we're trying to solve. Hardly ever about anything fun or light-hearted. Never mind one of those deep meaningful conversations that girls seem to want to have right before they let you touch them. I haven't quite got the hang of that kind of talk.

So after about ten minutes I'm pretty surprised to feel

Ixchel reaching for my hand. We don't say anything; we don't even look at each other. But for the rest of the way we walk with our hands firmly clasped, fingers interlocked. After a minute or two it feels completely natural.

The weather is a killer. Ixchel doesn't complain but it can't be easy walking barefoot on this hot tarmac. Neither of us mentions it but the highway looks different too. It's not the dual-carriageway, fancy new road that I remember riding along with my sister, Camila. Just a single carriageway road, like most of the highway up to the big tourist city of Cancun. We find a bus shelter and wait. After a few minutes we're joined by a couple of petite young women carrying bulging, colourful straw laundry bags. Ixchel asks them what the fare to Chetumal is. "Fifty pesos," says one, staring at Ixchel curiously. Ixchel turns to me with a look of desperation. I can see at a glance that she needs to get off the road. I return her gaze.

"You get the bus. Go to the museum and wait for me. Then your feet won't hurt."

The two young women step back and look into the highway. The bus rolls along. I give Ixchel the sixty pesos and reluctantly let go of her hand. She leans forward and plants a kiss on my cheek, right next to the corner of my mouth. She steps on to the bus, I move back, grin and give her a little wave, thinking that we might look like a couple who've been going out for ages.

The walk to Chetumal is pretty brutal. There's no shelter from the sun, almost all the way. I think about hitch-hiking at least fifty times, when cars stream lazily past. Only the thought of some mishap puts me off. I keep thinking about Ixchel. How she's here because of me and that stupid relic, the Bracelet of Itzamna, which has brought me nothing but hassle and grief.

What did I do to get in this situation? This time, I really think it's all Montoyo's fault. There was no way I was going to start messing around with the timeline, not after what happened when I tried to save my father. I couldn't save him; I may even have been the reason why he ended up on Mount Orizaba with amnesia.

Meddling with time is unpredictable. I knew that.

I thought Montoyo was crazy all along, even wanting to risk it. It never, never occurred to me that he would trick me. Weirdly, though, I can't find it in my heart to blame him. For Montoyo, anything is fair in the battle against the Sect of Huracan. I'm his soldier, his pawn.

He may have a thing for my mother but he is never going to replace my father. My dad would have risked anything to save me. With Montoyo, *nothing* is personal. It's all about 2012.

I check my Ek Naab phone every ten or fifteen minutes. Nothing, not the tiniest whisper of a signal. I cling to the hope that the Ek Naab of this timeline must have developed a different kind of phone technology, and mine won't work.

It's too awful to think that the problem is anything more serious than that. Is the lack of signal from Ek Naab connected to Marius Martineau's arrival there? I try to think through the scenarios that could have followed Martineau turning up in Ek Naab. In my imagination, none of them turn out well.

After four hours I've drained both the bottles that I filled with lake water. My clothes are soaked with sweat. I'm hungry, thirsty, tired and hurting from the stab wound.

A motorbike speeds past and I stare at the rider longingly. No helmet, shoulder-length hair straggling in the breeze, a green Mexico national football team jersey flapping around his chest. What I wouldn't do to be that guy right now.

I pass a road marker that says its five more kilometres to Chetumal. The sun is rapidly dropping in the sky; the heat is fading too. Two more hours of walking? It seems unbelievable. I knew that heat and humidity slowed you down but this is pathetic. I'll be wrecked by the time I walk into town. Probably too late to join Ixchel at the museum.

I get to wondering how much money we could get for all the Mayan bracelets. A thousand pounds? That should be enough to get us to Ek Naab, one way or another.

I don't let myself think about what we'll do if we can't get back to Ek Naab. Some ideas are just too horrible. Instead I think about the hotel room, the cool evening swim and the amazing meal we'll buy when we get some money. I cook up this little fantasy that I'm on my way to meet Ixchel for our first proper date; that we're going to get a really fancy dinner with candles and tablecloths and stuff, steak and chips, cheesecake with ice cream, strawberries and chocolate sauce. Then we'll walk to the seafront and stroll along holding hands. We'll stop under a tree and one of us will start the kissing. The technicalities of how this is going to happen are a bit annoying to think about after a bit, so I stop worrying about it and just skip ahead in my mind to the bit where we're actually kissing. An hour passes by very nicely, thinking these thoughts. I don't even feel too tired and my feet and the various cuts and bruises hardly bother me.

What's Ixchel been thinking about while we've been apart? I bet she's been worrying about the bad stuff. If only I could persuade myself that she's been dreaming about me.

28

It's dark when I arrive in Chetumal and street lamps light up the buildings with a sour white glow. The town looks different, that's for sure. The same mixture of shabby modern low-rise, painted concrete block and glass-fronted buildings with the occasional slightly more glitzy small hotel or monument. Even I can tell that they aren't in the exact same places. Heading into town from the coastal road, I get a strange feeling of disorientation. Nothing is quite where I remembered it being. Until I reach the hospital and then the church – buildings that I do recognize.

First a bed, some food, some rest.

The big Mayan museum is more or less where I remembered – opposite where the Dolphin Hotel was, in my Mexico. I glance across the road glumly, hoping against hope that the hotel is still there. But instead there's an ice-cream parlour. No Hotel Delfin. Anxiety gnaws away at me. It's a sense of disconnection so deep that I really can't bear to face it.

What if I don't exist here? No me, no Mum or Dad, ever. How could something like that have happened? What else would it mean?

I don't recognize Ixchel when I first see her. I only notice that a cute girl in a yellow and white sleeveless dress with long, loose hair is waving at me. There's a chunky pale green, lime ice lolly in her hand. The minute we make eye contact she grins. A huge grin, delighted. She stands up and rushes to me.

"You might want to stand well back," I say about half a second before she tries to hug me.

"Wow. You need a shower!" She's full of smiles; her hair smells of green apples. With a hand over her mouth to mask a laugh, she hands me the ice lolly. I grab it and bite off so much that within two seconds I've got a lime-flavoured blast of ice-cream headache.

"Ow."

She laughs even harder. "Poor Josh! I'm so, so sorry. Kind of a long walk, huh?"

I mock-smile. "Oh yeah, it's a cakewalk. Whatever that is."

"Is it like that other thing you sometimes say . . . a 'walk in the park'?"

"Yeah, that's it. It's a picnic." I mime looking at a watch. "A mere six, seven hours. It's boiling hot, too, did you notice?"

Ixchel laughs. "At least you're in a good mood."

With breathtaking ease I say, "It's because I'm so glad to see you."

There. I didn't even have to force that out. Ixchel seems to notice. She does this quiet, rapid intake of breath. "I'm glad to see you too."

To distract my eyes, I look down at her feet. Two crisp white canvas tennis shoes with little red flashes and short white socks. "You got some shoes!"

"Oh yes I did." She grins widely. "I got some stuff for you too, at the covered market. I figured you'd be too tired to go shopping."

"Aw, honey, you bought me clothes? Baby, you are so sweet."

I'm on fire. Being drop-dead exhausted has turned me into a flirting *machine*.

Suddenly Ixchel's hands are on my waist. There's a teasing smile on her lips. "That's right, 'honey', I bought you clothes. Now, it might not be exactly what your mama buys, but. . ."

"Hey!" I say, pretending to frown. "My mum *so* doesn't buy my clothes. . ."

The mention of my mother threatens to bring a serious edge to our conversation. I like Ixchel this way, teasing and flirting with me. I don't want that to stop. So I change the subject. "You sold those two golden bracelets?"

Ixchel tugs at my damp T-shirt. "I sold them for a *lot*. Josh, you have no idea how valuable they are." Her hand goes to the linen pouch. "We can sell the rest of them too. This jewellery, Josh – it could change our lives."

She leads me down the street to a hotel owned by Sanborns. It's a really famous restaurant and department store chain, but I don't remember them having hotels. I'm also fairly certain that there was no Sanborns Hotel in the Chetumal I knew.

Inside, behind the reception desk, there's the familiar Sanborns logo, the outline of three owls on a perch with a new moon dangling in the background. The three receptionists wear the usual old-fashioned uniform with colourful, hoop-patterned long skirts and brightly coloured matching collars.

"Did Sanborns own hotels?" I whisper to Ixchel as we breeze through the lobby, trying to act as if we own the place.

She doesn't look at me but shakes her head. "Our room is on the first floor, overlooking the pool," she says.

"Where's the Internet café?"

"I was going to tell you about that. There's no Internet."

"Wi-Fi in the rooms, then? Maybe we can borrow a laptop."

Ixchel turns to me. "No, Josh, *there's no Internet*. In this version of history, there is no network of computers called 'the Internet'. Or anything like it. I asked as soon as I got to town. People looked at me like I was crazy! No mobile phones either."

I stop walking. "No Internet? No mobile phones?!"

"I don't even know if they have computer networks here. None of the hotels I saw were using computers for the checking in and bills."

I'm silent for several seconds. "You're joking."

Ixchel shakes her head. "I'm not. And there's something else. I called Yucatan University, trying to get hold of Carlos Montoyo."

"And. . .?"

"They never heard of him."

There's really nothing I can say. It's almost too staggering to take it, yet I have to. This is the reality of time travel, I guess.

Go with the flow.

Inside the room the twin beds are spread with pink-, orange- and white-striped woven blankets stretched over white cotton sheets and pillows. There's a chest of drawers, two matching chairs and bedside tables, all made of cherry wood. No TV, which surprises me. A bunch of plastic flowers in a blue glass decorates the chest of drawers and on the whitewashed walls hang two watercolour paintings of old Mexican colonial-style churches. Above Ixchel's bedside table there's a small piece of framed embroidery.

On the bed nearest to the balcony window Ixchel has laid

out two pairs of knee-length shorts, one khaki and one bright purple, and a packet of boxer shorts, still in the wrapper. There are two flowery Hawaiian shirts and one traditional white guayabera shirt. Under the bed on the brown marble floor is a pair of leather sandals.

I empty my pockets, pulling out the Bracelet of Itzamna and my Ek Naab phone. Ixchel picks up the Bracelet and the linen parcel of Mayan jewellery and locks them into the room's safe with a stout key. I take one of the Hawaiian shirts and stare at Ixchel. "Orange? Tell me you're kidding."

She giggles. "What?! I like it."

"When have you ever seen me wear anything like this?"

"I haven't and it's about time you tried. I'm bored of grey, green and black." Ixchel steps forward and gives me a little shove in the chest. "The shower. Then we can swim."

As casually as I can, I head for the shower. "Then we can *eat*," I say. But I don't rush the shower. It feels way too good to have the day's dirt and all the dried blood sluiced off by powerful jets of hot water. Under the bright bathroom light I take another look at the wound on my leg, the deepest one. It's looking much better now, almost completely closed up. Whatever that Mayan medicine woman smeared over my wounds, it did the trick.

With a towel wrapped around my waist, I step back into the bedroom. Ixchel is sitting on her bed reading a paperback – *Murder in Mesopotamia* by Agatha Christie. She looks up and hands me a box of stick-on plasters. "For your cuts."

I feel like hugging her. "Thanks," I mumble, staring at the box. The plasters are all one shape and size, but they look nice and sturdy. I stick two over my leg wound.

"You can get dressed in front of me," she tells me. "I'll avert my eyes behind this book."

I grin, trying not to look nervous. It crosses my mind to say something seriously flirty like, "You can watch, I don't mind," the kind of dodgy thing Tyler would have said. But my limit falls somewhere short of that. So I dress as swiftly as possible in the khaki shorts and the orange Hawaiian shirt and sandals.

In my whole life I've never worn anything so ridiculous-looking. But Ixchel seems to love it. She drops the magazine and looks me over, giving an appreciative whistle.

"Look at you, handsome."

I smirk to cover up the blush. "Glad you're happy. Now can we get out of here? I'm starving to death."

We head for the hotel restaurant, which is in the central courtyard, a two-storey quadrangle bordered by traditional colonnades and pot plants. The crickets are singing so loudly that you can hear them even over the hum of restaurant chatter. We sit at a table next to a potted kumquat tree and order cheeseburgers with fries and Coca-Cola over lots of ice. While we're waiting for the burgers, Ixchel tells me how she spent the afternoon.

She'd arrived in good time to find the museum director still at her desk. She'd persisted and managed to get to see her: not easy, apparently. When Dr Monica Velasco, the museum director, had seen the booty, she was hooked. It seems that the bracelets have a jewel emblem that is known to represent the Snake Kingdom. Artefacts from Calakmul – the Snake Kingdom – are almost unheard of in this Mexico, because most of them were taken to Spain after the Spanish explorers discovered the Mayan ruins of Palenque.

"In *this* history," Ixchel tells me with shining eyes, "the kingdom of Palenque overran Calakmul! They invaded, not long after we were there, in the seventh century. Yuknoom the Great and the Snake Dynasty, they were finished. Relics from that era, from the Snake Kingdom, are unbelievably rare. The director gave me one hundred thousand pesos for the two bracelets I had! She admitted that it's less than they're worth, much less. But that's as much as she could give me without approval from her board of directors. And, well, we needed the money."

Ixchel took the money and immediately got a hotel room, then stashed most of the money in the room safe. One hundred thousand pesos seems to be worth about two thousand five hundred British pounds, guessing from what we spent at the little shop in Bacalar. Ixchel isn't too sure about the exact conversion rate. "I asked her how much in US dollars and she just kinda laughed. Like I'd said something sad but also funny. She offered me a rate in Brazilian *cruzeiros*."

"*Cruzeiros*?" I say, interrupting. "Didn't we use something called *reais* in Brazil?"

Ixchel shrugs. "In this history it's *cruzeiros*. Something else that's different."

"Brazilian money, though. . ." I muse. "Why would she mention that?"

"I didn't ask. I was too busy getting the money and finding us a place to stay."

After the hotel room and meals, we have money for a couple of weeks here, plus bus money to Becan, where hopefully we'll find the pyramid entrance to Ek Naab. When we've finished the burgers we order slices of frozen lime mousse pie and chocolate milkshakes. It's not exactly the menu I had in mind but it's every bit as satisfying, especially sharing the meal with Ixchel. She's in the best mood I remember seeing her in, like, for ever.

"Why are you so happy?" I eventually ask, sucking up the last drops of my milkshake through a straw. "I mean, it's like . . . you don't mind that things are so different here. Aren't you even a bit worried?"

Ixchel pauses, looking suddenly serious. "Of course." She casts her eyes downwards. "I'm worried. But I'm also kind of happy. We survived Calakmul! I mean, I always believed that you'd come for me, really. But at the end, right at the end, when I was locked in that steam house with those women and the little children. Then, I. . ." She falters, close to tears.

"Don't think about it," I say quickly. "No point. It's over now."

Ixchel bites her lip and goes quiet for a few seconds. Then she continues, slowly, deliberately. "Then there's this whole thing – a world without computer networks."

Suddenly I see what she's getting at. An incredible idea hits me.

"No computer networks . . . means no worries from the superwave in 2012!"

"It does mean that, doesn't it? I mean – if the whole world isn't dependent on a global network of computers to control money and food and medical supplies. . ."

". . .oil and petrol, all kinds of energy, really. Aeroplanes and trains and hospital machines and just, wow . . . all that stuff . . . then when the superwave comes it's only going to wipe out a few central computers . . . and they can replace them pretty easily. All they need is some decent backups." I nod slowly, amazed at the conclusion we're drawing. "This reality – it's 2012-proof!"

Ixchel smiles. "I think it might be! Just think – no one has to know about this Mayan jewellery, Josh. We didn't steal it – it's ours. We can get a lot of money for them. Enough money that maybe we wouldn't even have to live in Ek Naab."

I stare at her in silence for a moment. "You hate Ek Naab that much?"

"Don't you? Montoyo tricked you, sent you back into the past, to a *really* dangerous time. You could have died. Without you, I would have died." She places a hand on mine, staring into my eyes. "No one cares about us there. We're just chess pieces to them."

A soldier, a pawn. She's right – the same thought has already occurred to me.

I turn my hand over and hold hers in my palm. I ask, "Yeah, but . . . what about Benicio?"

Softly she replies, "What about him?"

My skin bursts with a pulse of energy that shoots all the way through me. Every one of my wounds throbs as blood rushes inside my veins. I watch her fingers tighten around mine; I swallow in a throat that's suddenly dry.

Ixchel is serious about changing our destiny. The question is: am I?

After the waiter collects his money, Ixchel leans forward and lowers her voice. "Dr Velasco is going to call back tomorrow. She's phoning some of the major dealers of antiquities. She's certain that we'll be able to find a buyer."

"This Dr Velasco is being pretty helpful," I say. "Can we trust her?"

"We should put the jewellery in a bank safe-deposit box tomorrow. She was actually pretty open with me. She said to me, 'Because you're young and you can't tell me where you got this, I'm going to take advantage of you. Fourteen bracelets like the one you showed me could fetch twenty, thirty million pesos, for the right buyer. But how is a kid like you going to find such a person? So I'll be straight with you: I'm going to get you a good honest buyer who won't steal from you or try to kill you. But she'll pay you much less than they're worth. Then I'm going to take another twenty-five per cent.'"

I sit up angrily. "What kind of a deal have you got us? Sounds to me like we're getting ripped off!"

Ixchel just laughs. "I knew you'd react like this. That's why I went ahead and agreed to the deal. Can you imagine how dangerous it is for us to have something so valuable? We need to sell fast. Even if we only get a few million pesos."

I say nothing. She might be right, I don't know. But I don't like to think we're getting taken for a ride. On the way back to the hotel room, Ixchel falls silent. She says nothing as we climb the stairs. I risk a quick glance at her – she won't even look at me. There's a tension inside my chest that is almost paralysing. My heart sinks as I even try to imagine sliding my arms around her. I won't be able to make the first move, I'm absolutely certain of that now. And unless Ixchel magically transforms on the other side of a locked door, neither will she.

Well, anyhow. In a way, I suppose I should be relieved. I'm dog tired; in no state to impress a girl with my "moves", not that I know any.

Where's Tyler when I need a bit of man-to-man advice?

Inside the room I can see immediately that I guessed right. While I'm adjusting the air conditioning, Ixchel goes straight to the bathroom, where I hear her brushing her teeth. She emerges dressed in a baggy green T-shirt which almost reaches her knees. Picking up the Agatha Christie book, she leans over to where I'm sitting on the bed, taking off my shoes. "Night, Josh," she says with a yawn. "You really need to get some sleep."

What did I do?

To hide my disappointment I get under the covers and roll away. That's when I notice that she's helpfully placed a slim paperback on my own bedside table – *Death on the Nile*, also by Agatha Christie. I start reading, conscious of the quiet rustle of Ixchel's book. But after a couple of pages I can't concentrate.

What's going on in this reality? Things certainly seem to have turned out differently for ancient Calakmul. Martineau kept going on about what a great leader Yuknoom the Great was, how he reigned for fifty years. Well, not now! It has to be connected with Martineau taking the Ix Codex away. Maybe in our reality the Snake Kingdom had some strange power because of the book. Maybe other Mayan tribes had heard stories about the curse of the codex and stayed away from the Snake Kingdom, out of fear?

Yet modern-day Chetumal doesn't seem drastically different, just as though certain buildings went up in different places and with slightly different designs. It's not much richer or poorer than what I remember. There's still such things as Coca-Cola, Sanborns, Agatha Christie, *Time* magazine. Brazil seems to be an important trading partner with Mexico. But maybe it was before; I wouldn't know. Cars seem kind of old-fashioned, and from what I can tell, either Mexican-built VW Beetles or Japanese. Hardly any American cars, now I think about it; I haven't seen a single one of those SUVs.

Still not a peep from Ek Naab. I gaze at my phone on the bedside table, willing it to ring. That's when I realize that I'm not so sure about going along with Ixchel's escape plan. We have to try to get back to Ek Naab. Even if it's just to avoid the Sect of Huracan. You'd think, after she was kidnapped in Brazil by the Sect, that Ixchel would understand. Anyway, what kind of escape plan does she have in mind? In the restaurant she was all lovey-dovey, holding hands with me and talking about forgetting Benicio. Now she's gone all cool and sisterly when she knows perfectly well that I want to be her boyfriend. Is this what she has in mind, her and me running off together to live like brother and sister? If that's it then she can forget it. I'd rather be in Ek Naab.

Ixchel holds a page thoughtfully between her fingers. I listen intently to her flick it back and forth. Then she closes the book and switches off her night light. "Sleep well, Josh," she murmurs. I mutter something in reply and turn off my own light, listening to her turn over in bed.

I can't take much more of this.

After what seems like ages, I finally relax. My eyes close, relieved by a wave of sleep that obliterates me. Just before I fall asleep an image flashes before my eyes: the embroidered writing that hangs over Ixchel's bedside table. It spells out, "God Spared Mexico". I can't remember where, but I've heard that phrase before. Recently, too.

In the morning I wake to find Ixchel already dressed. She gives me a little grin from where she's sitting on her bed applying make-up.

"Hi, Josh. You slept in your clothes!"

I stretch both arms behind my neck and yawn. "Yeah. So what?" Ixchel looks bemused as she applies some face cream. I can't help feeling that it's a shame I didn't wake up ten minutes earlier.

"There's a message from Dr Velasco. She's going to meet us here at five in the afternoon tomorrow, and take us to meet a buyer for the rest of the golden bracelets. That leaves us free for today and most of tomorrow." She stands up. "I've got another surprise for you, one more thing I bought."

"No more flowery shirts, I hope."

She smirks. "Ha, ha, no. You'll like this."

Ixchel leads me outside and round to a small back-yard parking lot for the hotel. She stops in front of a silver-coloured, slightly battered-looking 125cc Honda motorbike. A helmet hangs from each arm of the bike. I stare at her, then back at the bike.

"It's not a Harley, of course," she says. "I just saw it in the street with a 'For Sale' sticker." Our eyes meet. "I thought you might like it."

She hands me a set of keys. I kneel down, looking the machine over. "Ixchel," I say wonderingly, "I bloody *love* it!"

"You can ride it?"

"Are you kidding?"

"Do you think you could ride it to Cancun?"

I shrug with total nonchalance. "Piece of cake."

"I think it takes something like five or six hours," Ixchel says, quite nervously. "If you're OK to ride there, I thought we could go today. You and me. We could go and spend the night in one of those really fancy hotels. Go shopping. Enjoy some luxury, while we can. See what the Cancun of this history is like."

"I thought you hated fancy hotels and places like that? Cancun and the Riviera Maya. Thought you said it was too touristy."

Ixchel blushes, lowers her eyes. "But you like those places, don't you?"

"Well, yeah, I do. When I get the chance to stay in them, which isn't often."

"Then let's go. Think of it as my way of saying thank you. For saving my life." She gives a nervous chuckle. "Again."

I stare at Ixchel in disbelief. This is definitely the nicest thing any girl has ever done for me, by a long way. "Wow." I laugh. "This is amazing."

She looks shy and for a minute, I remember the first time we met, Ixchel in her jeans and Pumas soccer shirt. "So you like it?"

I can hardly contain the urge to grab Ixchel and spin her around by the waist. "Yeah. Are you kidding? *Yeah!*"

She nods, then smiles. "Good. Great! Let's go to breakfast, then to the bank to leave the bracelets somewhere safe. Then we'll go . . . to Cancun!"

I kneel down, giving the bike a quick check. The tyres look to be in good condition, plenty of tread. There's hardly any rust, just a few dents on the mudguards, a couple of scratches on the side of the fuel tank, a bit of wear on the leather seat. "We should probably stop by a petrol station too . . ."

The next hour passes quickly. We gobble down waffles with whipped butter, maple syrup and glasses of seven-fruits juice from Sanborns. Then we're out at the banks, where morning queues have already formed. There don't seem to be any bank machines anywhere close, I notice.

"No computer networks, therefore no bank machines," Ixchel observes. "Another thing that won't go wrong when the superwave hits." She's right. This reality is looking better and better.

When it's our turn we're given the key to a deposit box in exchange for ten thousand pesos. We pick a small one and discreetly place the Mayan gold bracelets and most of our cash in the locker.

"You should leave the Bracelet of Itzamna too," Ixchel says. "We just can't risk that someone might rob us on the way to Cancun, or even here in Chetumal."

I take off the Bracelet and add it to the pile in the box. Just at this moment I can't imagine why I'd want to use the Bracelet of Itzamna ever again. But you never know.

We divide the rest of the money – about the equivalent of five hundred pounds – between us. It's easily enough cash for a night in Cancun's swankiest hotel. I spread the notes between the pockets in my khaki shorts; Ixchel places hers inside a small canvas backpack that she wears over a denim skirt and a white top. We're so eager to get going to Cancun that we don't even bother to buy food or water for the trip, agreeing instead to stop for drinks and snacks at petrol stations on the way. We fill up at the Pemex petrol station on the exit road from Chetumal and then hit the main motorway, 307. I'm a bit surprised that the road signs aren't already signing for Cancun, but I know that the town Felipe Carillo Puerto is about a third of the way, so I head for that.

The motorway cuts endlessly through the tropical rainforest, past the dazzling blue length of Lake Bacalar, past the mangrove swamps of the Sian Ka'an bio-reserve, past coconut and banana plantations. A haze hovers over the road, silvery shimmering heat mirages on every long stretch. Every ten minutes or so, we zip past a small cloud of yellow butterflies bobbing around at the edge of the road.

Ixchel's arms are constantly around my waist. After half an hour she snuggles closer and leans against my back. There's no tension between us, nothing but a melting feeling of togetherness. With my focus on the motorbike, my world shrinks until there's only the machine beneath me, the balance of its wheels, vibrations from the road, the warmth of Ixchel behind me.

It's like being drugged with happiness.

Ixchel could have suggested that we go to Becan, to get into Ek Naab that way. If she were really keen on Benicio, I'm pretty sure that she'd be desperate to find our way there. Yet she'd rather be with me, riding up the Caribbean coast for a getaway break in five-star luxury.

Behind my visor, I grin to myself.

We stop a couple of times at tiny little petrol stations in the sparse villages we pass and buy crisps and cold drinks. The breeze keeps us from sweating too much but underneath the helmets our hair quickly gets damp. We keep waiting for the road to turn into the major dual carriageway that links Playa del Carmen, Tulum and Cancun. But already six hours have passed and we're still on the same little road, which actually stops being much more than a dirt track every so often and slows down with road bumps as it passes through every tiny hamlet.

When we see a scruffy little hand-painted sign pointing to the cliff-top Mayan ruins of Tulum, I come off the road, take my helmet off and turn to Ixchel.

"What the heck is going on? Where's the fast road? Where are all the big Tulum hotels?"

Ixchel looks uneasy. "Maybe they haven't been built yet. It's only been in the last ten years that Tulum has really developed as a resort."

"Why wouldn't it be built yet?"

She shrugs, but I can tell from her eyes that Ixchel is pretty anxious. "No clue. Maybe the economy?"

I'm tired enough to think about stopping now. We're going to keep going all the way to Cancun, I decide. Then stop and rest properly on a lounger beside a pristine blue infinity pool, being served piña coladas and club sandwiches dripping with mayonnaise.

Another hour passes. The road doesn't get any better, but it does take us almost alongside the coast with a stunning view of the turquoise blue Caribbean Sea and a long line of frothy white surf.

Finally there's a sign for Cancun.

The motorway appears, glistening black, fresh tarmac. We pass a long line of slow-moving trucks carrying tons of building materials – sacks of concrete and sand, breeze

245

blocks, rolled steel joists. Eventually, rolling over the bridge across one of the inlets to the wide, green Nichupte Lagoon, we get our first view of Cancun.

Gigantic cranes scar a cloudless blue skyline, hoisting six or seven huge white buildings. The trucks roll over the bridge. Not a single building seems to be finished. The sea shimmers like a jewel in sunlight, kilometres of empty beaches bordering the concrete pits and construction projects.

Cancun – the gigantic, the premier tourist resort of Mexico – is still nothing more than a building site.

Beside the shiny new road, workers with brushes on ladders paste a gigantic banner on to a blank display. Red and green words against a white background – the colours of the Mexican flag. How many of these signs must I have ignored on our way across the state? This time I can hardly drag my eyes from the words splashed across that roadside poster.

GOD SPARED MEXICO.

The words hit me with a stark ferocity. Words that trip off people's tongues. Words that are everywhere, so much that people have grown blind to their presence. Even me – I've heard and seen those words, dismissed them as a bit of folk wisdom.

In the world I knew, people didn't say "God spared Mexico". If anything, they said the opposite. The worse things got in the country, the more they rolled their eyes and said things like "God's forgotten Mexico".

God spared Mexico . . . *from what*? Ixchel's hands clutch me tightly, sensing my tension. Something bad happened in this timeline. Something *really* bad.

31

In that moment I'm aware of how drained I am by the ride. My wrists and arms ache from the long enforced position on the handlebars. Looking over at the gigantic construction site of Cancun, we watch concrete hotels and shopping malls being put up in a cloud of murky dust, between the brilliant green of the Yucatan countryside and the turquoise sea.

I don't want to be here, don't want to get my head around what this all means; I don't want to know what God spared Mexico from or why. I just want to lie down on a beach with a sandwich and a drink.

Without a word, I slow the motorbike down and do a U-turn beside the long line of trucks. Then we're heading in the opposite direction, travelling south along the coastal road. Ixchel immediately works out what we're doing. I guess she agrees because she seems pretty relaxed behind me. I can still feel the heat of her skin through the thin cotton of my Hawaiian shirt.

At the first sign of a village and a path to the beach, we stop. There's a big hand-painted sign at the edge of the road – **Las Olas – A Surfer's Paradise** – with a picture of a hammock and a bottle. It may not be the Hilton, but at this point, I don't care.

The lodgings are right on the beach. A smell of barbecued fish reaches us immediately. My stomach responds with a hungry rumble. There are nine or ten straw-roofed cabanas, each with a hammock outside, all facing the beach. There's another thatched roof, this time covering a wooden bar where a bunch of people are gathered, drinking beer in bottles. Most of them look like college students, or around that age. There are six guys and two girls, all in wacky beachwear. From a glance I'd guess they're all Mexican, and from the silhouettes of some surfboards racked up beside the closest cabana, I'd guess they're surfers.

One of the guys is steadily strumming a guitar and singing along in a husky voice.

Is you is or is you ain't my baby?
Maybe baby's found somebody new.

Both girls in the surfer group are watching him with a kind of fascination that makes me a bit jealous. He's pretty good.

Strolling up to the bar, I notice that on the beach side there's a big grill on top of glowing wood and coals. The delicious barbecue smell comes from a heap of blackened fish and seafood: red snapper, crab and shrimp. Beside it a tall, portly guy with a moustache and thick, hairy arms, wearing a baseball cap and a white cotton apron, is serving up portions of the cooked fish on to plates of rice and tortillas.

As I stand watching the food, I slowly become aware that the eyes of the bar crowd are on the two of us. When Ixchel's arm snakes around my waist, I realize that they're looking at her. Not in a nasty way, but all smiley and flirty.

Which is quite bad enough, if you ask me.

I lay an arm across Ixchel's shoulders and we face them together, returning their grins.

The guitarist finishes his song. "What's happening, kids?" he asks, speaking Spanish with a strong Mexico City accent. He's fair-skinned and with dyed blond hair. "Shouldn't you two be in school?"

I don't answer. Ixchel ignores him and asks the cook, "Where can we book in?"

The cook grins, not taking his eyes off the food. "Right here, missy." His voice is deep and gravelly. For a brief instant he reminds me of Carlos Montoyo. "Two thousand pesos for the cabana per night," he says. "Four thousand all-inclusive; that's food, drinks, towels." He waves a hand, indicating somewhere along the beach. "You can have either of those two." He glances at me, his eyes quick, dark. "Better get your age right on the registration form or I won't be able to serve you a beer." When Ixchel and I both nod in agreement, he looks over at the bartender. "Hey, Paquito, lazybones, get these two lovebirds set up in number three. Towels, forms, etc." Then for a second his face gets a fierce look. "You can have a beer or two, I don't mind that. But if I catch you smoking weed or anything worse, I'm gonna kick you out and I mean kick! We're a hundred per cent drug-free here, is that clear?"

"Sure, chief," Ixchel tells him breezily. "You don't have to worry about us, we're good kids."

He laughs and looks at his blackened fish. "All the way out here on your own with a boyfriend on a motorbike during school. . . Miss, I doubt very much that you're 'good kids'."

I'm silent, but walking to cabana number three I think about how relaxed Ixchel seems to be with the whole biker-boyfriend, rebel-girl-away-from-home scene.

Is the motorbike her way of making me more like Benicio? What's all this "boyfriend" stuff anyway? In the mood I'm in right now, I decide that I'm not going to put up with another bout of *is you is or is you ain't my baby.* Even as we're strolling along the sand to the cabana, Ixchel is removing her arm from around my waist. Was it just an act? I can't tell any longer. So the minute we're inside the room and the bartender has gone I drop my arm from her shoulders, toss my helmet on the floor and glare at her.

"What's going on?"

Ixchel seems genuinely surprised by my tone. "With Cancun. . .?"

"With us," I say sharply, folding my arms. "With you and me. The motorbike, the shirts. Are you trying to turn me into a substitute for Benicio? The whole girlfriend-boyfriend act just now. Who's that for – for me? For them?"

Ixchel stares at me for a few seconds, breathing in. Her eyes widen but apart from that I can't read her reaction at all. There's no bed inside the cabana, no chairs either, only two hammocks strung between two hooks at either end of the room. She leans briefly on one end of the hammock, then very calmly removes her backpack and puts it on the floor. She looks at me then, carefully. Her hands go to her head; her fingers trail in her hair. Very deeply, she sighs. She seems genuinely at a loss for words.

I shift my stance a little, unsure what to do or say next. I don't know what I expected. Tears? Anger? Instead, though, I seem to have plunged Ixchel deep into thought.

Finally, she speaks. "I'm not the only one with the problem."

My arms drop to my sides. "Huh?"

"You don't exactly behave like you should either. Yes, I can see you're angry about Benicio. Every time you see me with him you sulk."

"I do not!"

"Yes!" she interrupts. "You get that sad, hurt face. And I catch you looking at me sometimes. Staring. When you think I'm not looking."

I feel a little sick. She's right. I have felt a bit like a stalker. But I couldn't help it.

Ixchel keeps looking at me. "What's wrong, Josh, nothing to say?"

I lower my voice. "I don't want to fight with you."

"What *do* you want?" She steps closer. "Why don't you ever say anything to me?" She's staring into my eyes now. "You never *ask* me for anything. You never tell me anything nice. Don't you know how you're supposed to be with a girl that you like?"

Now she's confusing me. "You're supposed to say nice things," she continues. "To chase. You're supposed to write poems and make gifts and . . . all of that."

"But *all of that* is so . . . corny," I say, bewildered. "So *fake*. Guys like Tyler do that. Guys like Benicio. They can get any girl that way. I could do it too, I suppose. But you're not just any girl, you're. . ." I stop then, swallowing as the words run out.

When I glance into her eyes what I see is a look of frank anticipation. Slowly, I exhale.

She steps even closer. Her fingers go to my arms, barely touching my skin. "What . . . am I?"

"You're my destiny," I whisper. "My future. We're meant

for each other. From the day we were born, from the minute we met."

Ixchel laughs. Her hands slide around my neck; I can feel her fingers in my hair. She starts to say, "So you *can* be romantic. . ." but I don't let her finish the sentence. Instead, I lunge forward to kiss her, and she kisses me back. We're both unsteady on our feet and stagger backwards until Ixchel's leaning against the cabana door with me pressed against her. It gives way suddenly, bursts open. We fall through, trip over and collapse on to the sand. There's chortling from the bar, the singer stops singing; there are cheers and then a smattering of applause.

"Kids, cool it!" the chef yells with a good-natured laugh. "Get over here and grab some lunch. You shouldn't fool around on an empty stomach!"

The guys from the bar leap off their stools and chase us both into the sea, roaring with laughter, yelling, "Get them into the water . . . they need a cold shower!" Once we're finally in the surf, being pounded by the waves, they leave us alone.

After a few minutes of holding on to each other in the sea (whilst the bar crowd boos), Ixchel and I drag ourselves out of there and join the surfers at the bar. The bartender passes us a couple of towels. We dry our heads and hands. Still in soaking-wet clothes, we eat grilled red snapper with tomato salsa and tortillas. Afterwards we change into beach stuff, rinse our clothes in the cold-water showers outside the cabana and hang them to dry outside.

For the rest of the day I only live in the moment. Pure existence. Nowhere and no moment in the history of the universe has ever struck me as so beautiful, so perfect. The sun begins to set behind the palm trees that line the shore; the sky turns various shades of peach.

I approach the surfer with the guitar, persuade him to lend me the instrument. I unhook one of our hammocks and carry it about a hundred metres down the coast until we can't hear the catcalls of the surfer crowd. We stretch the hammock over smooth sand.

Ixchel asks me what the guitar is for.

"You wanted poetry," I reply enigmatically, then start to play an Arctic Monkeys song – "The Only Ones Who Know".

In a foreign place, the saving grace was the feeling,
That it was a heart that he was stealing

Ixchel listens intently. But I can't look at her while I'm singing. It's hard enough to remember the lyrics without my lips going numb too.

When I put the guitar down, Ixchel says nothing, just stares at me.

"Well. . .?"

"You're full of surprises, Josh Garcia."

Which calls for a clever comeback, but right now I can't think of one.

We lie on our backs watching the roof of the sky turn a deeper shade of blue. We watch the stars begin to appear, then the moon.

I tell Ixchel that I love her then. I say it once, then over and over again, kissing her lips each time. After the third or fourth time she gives me a shove and sits up. "OK, OK," she says with a chuckle. "Now you are just saying it."

"No way," I insist, grinning. "You wanted poems and romanticness and stuff, remember?"

The rhythmic roll of the waves becomes hypnotic. We stare up at wisps of clouds that drift in front of the moon. When we concentrate on the moon it feels as though we're moving at the speed of the clouds. It's like feeling the Earth turn beneath us.

The problem with falling asleep on the beach is that you're woken by the first light of dawn. I sit up blinking, one side of my face powdery with sand. The sound of the sea seems different; clear and sharp. Ixchel has gone from my side but I can see her standing close to the water, watching two grey herons diving for fish. The sun is rising over the horizon, bleeding pink and purple into the grey sky. I stand up and walk over to Ixchel. Without saying anything, I put my arms around her waist from behind.

"We can't stay," she murmurs.

"Yeaahhh. I know."

"'God spared Mexico'."

Wordlessly, I nod. Ixchel turns around in my arms and says, "We have to return to Ek Naab."

She's right, but I wish we could have forgotten about all that for a few more days. Since we arrived on this beach I haven't wanted to leave. It's as if there's some kind of glue making me stick to it. Something tells me that if I don't leave pretty quickly, I never will.

We leave after breakfast – pancakes cooked on a hot plate by the sea. I barely manage three, that's how sick I feel about leaving. The air cools sharply as we start our journey back along the coast. We don't stop for petrol until two hours later. Then the summer rain starts: a skin-drenching torrent that makes the ride back north even more miserable. A cloud of rain-splash and steam rises into the air. Our beach seems very far behind. Soon, I know, it will feel like another life.

Even though it makes us both heartsick to admit it, we agree that Ek Naab has to be our first stop. So when hours later we finally reach the turning to Chetumal, instead we turn up Highway 186, towards Becan. For the second time in my life, I find myself riding along that arrow-straight road. This time I'm trying not to think about the last time I was here, with my sister Camila. Trying not to look at all the treacle-black swamps that have formed in the ditches beside the road. One of those swamps swallowed my sister, drowned her. It was a shock to my system that made every bad thing that had happened to me before seem mundane.

Yet it turned out to set the whole tone of my life since then.

I grip the handlebars a little tighter, grimacing as rain trickles down my face. In half an hour we'll be in Becan. Then

Ek Naab and . . . goodbye to all this freedom. What will Ixchel do about Benicio? She'd better dump him. This time, I'll insist on it.

Drenched to the bone, we arrive in Becan to find the site deserted; not surprising in such relentless rain. The car park is empty. There's no neat little straw-roofed welcome hut run by INAH – who run all Mexico's archaeological sites. No little maps and Mayan souvenirs. There's only a large canvas tent, the kind I recognize from my dad's excavation trips. We peek inside, first calling out "Hola!" I spot walkie-talkies and a radio, plus some scruffy-looking camping gear. But there's no one there.

We head down the path towards the plaza that contains Structure IX. The heat is unbearable by now, easily 45 degrees and totally sweltering. The mosquito situation is as bad as I've known it. Our clothes are quickly soaked with sweat as we push past the creeping vines and undergrowth that lines the narrow path. It's immediately obvious that the site of Becan in this reality isn't as well-cleared or maintained as what we're used to. In fact, when we reach our destination, we're both shocked to see small trees growing out of the side of the pyramid. Only the main staircase has been cleared. To our right, Structure VIII is excavated only on the front.

The secret entrance to Becan is on the west flank of that giant pyramid – Structure IX. It leads to a secret elevator inside, which takes you down to the Depths, and then the underground tunnel-lift to Becan. This gateway from Becan was built almost a hundred years ago, according to what I've studied about the history of Ek Naab.

So when we find nothing but immovable stone on the side of Structure IX, we're pretty perplexed. After another half hour I start to worry that we'll melt away under the incessant rain. We go from anxious to scared, from scared to panicked, from panicked to despondent.

I lean back against the crumbling stone. I gaze out over the trees, listen to howler monkeys yawping in the distance. "There's no entrance here."

Ixchel looks perplexed. "There has to be."

"No." Exhausted, soaked to the skin and more resigned by the minute, I shake my head. "*God spared Mexico*, remember? Something is very different here. Let's face it, if there's no Internet and all, there might be a pretty serious reason for it." With the back of one hand, I wipe away the rain water that's rolling into my eyes. "No signal on the Ek Naab phone, even here. No Carlos Montoyo at Yucatan University. And no gateway from Becan." I swallow, scarcely able to believe what I'm about to say. "Maybe there's no Ek Naab in this reality."

Ixchel doesn't even raise her voice to argue. She's too drenched, fed up and tired.

Around three hours later we're back in the Sanborns hotel

of Chetumal, showered, finally back in dry clothes and ready to meet Dr Velasco. She arrives in a car that looks old but carefully maintained. Or maybe it isn't old? Generally, I've noticed how different motor vehicle design is in this reality. All pretty boxy. Velasco herself is as tidy as her car: about forty years old, dark brown hair in a sleek, bobbed haircut, neat and elegant in a navy blue linen trouser suit.

We're almost too worn out to stand up. Dr Velasco notices. As we sit in the back of her mercifully air-conditioned Nissan, she asks us what's wrong. Have we changed our minds about selling the golden bracelets?

Naturally, we haven't. Neither of us has the heart to ask our questions, though. Where do we start? *What happened to this world? Why does everyone say "God spared Mexico"?*

Not exactly questions that will help us to keep a low profile.

If there's no Ek Naab, then we are really and truly, terrifyingly, on our own. It doesn't really matter how nice and cosy the Mexico of this reality might be – we'll still need money. As kids with no relatives, no friends, no home and no jobs, we need as much money as we can get.

Right now, those golden bracelets are the key to everything.

As she drives, Dr Velasco talks. "The woman we're going to see is an American; she moved here after the war, married into the Vargas family. They own a big medical supplies company. Her husband is dead now, but they started collecting antiquities many years ago. Not everyone in the antiquities business is entirely honest, to tell the truth. The Vargas family has always dealt straight with me. Mrs Vargas won't be keeping your Mayan gold for herself. She will sell it on. Do you understand what that means?" In the car's mirror, her eyes find mine. I nod, wrapping my fingers around Ixchel's. "She's going to sell for much more than she pays."

I say, "How much do you think we'll get?"

"Leave that to me. I'm taking twenty-five per cent, remember? So I'll do my best to get a good price."

The Vargas house is a lavish mansion. We reach it after a thirty-minute drive, leaving the narrow road and driving along a dirt track, surrounded by wild scrubland. Then from nowhere a marble gate appears, then a straight, palm-lined avenue set in a manicured green lawn. The car passes through a fine mist of spray as the grass is watered. The driveway leads to a red-roofed, Spanish style hacienda covered with dark pink bougainvillea and a tall jacaranda tree in front. Dr Velasco leads us to a caramel-tinted pine door, ornately carved. A minute later the door opens.

I stagger for a second, transfixed at the sight of the woman who opens the door. Instinctively I glance at Ixchel. But she barely reacts, just gazes directly ahead.

Susannah St John.

33

Susannah is more glamorous-looking than I remember; her hair is thicker, she's better-dressed, looks younger too. Before, I'd have guessed her age at sixty-five but now she looks around ten years younger than that. There's no possible doubt – it's her.

And Susannah doesn't recognize us at all.

We watch the two distinguished-looking women greet each other and Dr Velasco introduces us. As we enter the house I'm still buzzing from the shock of seeing Susannah. I hold Ixchel back slightly as the two women stroll casually through a tiled vestibule that's leafy green with hanging plants. "It's Susannah!" I whisper, my eyes wide.

Ixchel nods slightly. "I know! But in this reality, she's married to Vargas."

"And she's lived in Mexico since she was a child!"

Ixchel wrinkles her nose and whispers back, "When did Velasco tell us that?"

"Remember? She said Susannah moved here after the war."

"Right! Then I guess she never met Arcadio."

"Maybe he doesn't exist."

Breathless, I follow Ixchel into a large study. Immediately we're struck dumb by a huge display on two walls. Glass cases protect a giant collage of newspaper cuttings. Photos, headlines in English and Spanish. Ixchel and I can't tear our eyes from those images and words, even with the two women staring at us, amazed at our reaction.

Gigantic mushroom clouds. The Eiffel Tower – a melted, twisted wreck. London in ruins. New York with the Twin Towers, and every other skyscraper in the vicinity, reduced to rubble. Headlines that scream their horrific news.

US IMPOSES BLOCKADE ON CUBA ON FINDING OFFENSIVE-MISSILE SITES

USSR THREATENS TO LAUNCH CUBAN MISSILES

IT'S HAPPENED – NUCLEAR WAR

NATO ALLIES BOMBED BY USSR

MILLIONS DEAD IN FIRST STRIKE ON USA

MOSCOW PAYS THE PRICE

BRITAIN IN RUINS

NEW YORK CITY DESTROYED

EUROPE A RADIOACTIVE WASTELAND

MILLIONS FLEE RADIATION

MEXICO, BRAZIL, JAPAN, AUSTRALIA WELCOME REFUGEES

The images and words are utterly mesmerizing. I'm still struggling to absorb what I'm seeing when Susannah's voice breaks through to me.

"My dear, are you quite all right?"

I face Susannah suddenly, totally unable to speak. Her eyes trail over to the walls; her voice becomes low, her tone reflective. "Quite a shock to see it all in one place, I imagine. I guess your school history lessons are somewhat less intense?"

Now it's Susannah who draws my gaze. That face, that voice. The same woman who looked at me so tenderly last December. The same keen intelligent eyes within a soft pink complexion and fair hair. All that familiarity is absent. Instead there's a cool, businesslike formality. Until she sees how Ixchel and I are affected by the newspaper displays. For a second I glimpse a hint of the same concern we saw before. An old friend looking out for two kids in trouble.

Ixchel is riveted by the display cases. "God spared Mexico," she murmurs.

"You moved to Mexico . . . after the war," I say, suddenly understanding. *But not as a child.* Dr Velasco wasn't talking about World War Two. This world had another war, a nuclear holocaust.

"Indeed," remarks Susannah drily. "Rather fortunate for me that I happened to be visiting this country when the bombs started to fall on the United States. Nineteen sixty-two. . ."

265

It's crushingly obvious now why there's no Internet or mobile phones, why the cars seem so old-fashioned, why there are no American cars and so many Japanese ones, why Cancun is only just being built decades later than in the world we remember. All the other weird little differences too.

This world has been reeling from a global nuclear war. Around fifty years ago, from what Susannah is saying. One headline in particular grabs me, twists my guts into anxious knots.

EUROPE A RADIOACTIVE WASTELAND

"What happened to everyone back home?" I ask.

Susannah seems a little reluctant to answer. "They died, dear, most of them. My people were from Virginia, you see. Near Washington, DC. It used to be the capital of the United States."

"Used to be. . ." I echo in a hollow voice.

"Before Seattle," she says.

Hesitantly, I nod. "Seattle is the new capital of the USA. Right."

"You have a British accent," Susannah observes curiously. "How unusual." She sighs, a sound of deep regret. "I went to England once, before the war. It was quite, quite lovely. Sandstone cottages, emerald-green fields, the rivers, the gorgeous little village pubs. Just dreadful to think that it'll be poisonous for another fifty years."

Tears come to my eyes when she mentions England, the

deep ache of homesickness combined with a sheer disbelief at what she's saying. Susannah doesn't seem at all surprised, just pats my arm comfortingly and says, "It's too bad, I know."

She turns to Ixchel. "How about you? You don't say a great deal, my dear, do you?"

"I'm Mayan," Ixchel says blandly. "And we're not here to make friends. We're here to sell the bracelets."

There's a brittle silence. Susannah gives us both a steady look, then places both hands flat on a huge mahogany desk. For the first time I notice the collection of Mayan stone carvings and paintings. Part of the desk is covered in glass, under which I spot pages of a Mayan codex. I'm immediately distracted.

Could this be part of the Ix Codex?

Susannah's already anticipated a question. "It's from the Madrid Codex. The real thing. A friend of mine went into the ruins of the museum and brought it out. Damaged, of course. He rescued only a few pages; that's one." She runs one hand along the desk past statues, an obsidian knife, a carved-stone incense burner. "I don't collect jewellery as a rule. But I know people who do. Your pieces are quite extraordinary – Monica showed me yesterday." Her voice goes flat. "So tell me, where did you get them?"

Ixchel puts her head on one side. "I already told Dr Velasco: we can't say."

"I'm not interested in buying stolen goods."

"We *could* tell you," I interrupt, "but you wouldn't believe us."

Susannah shrugs. "So tell me. What do you have to lose?"

Ixchel smirks. "The sale."

"The sale, you may already have lost."

I blink twice, incredulous. But Susannah means it, I know.

"A couple of teenagers alone out here? A British boy with a Mayan girl? I thought maybe you were cashing in your family jewels. But your people don't have any money. All the rich Brits went to Australia and Argentina." Slowly she nods. "There's something rather peculiar about the two of you. So, unless you persuade me right away that some gangster isn't going to come after me for buying his treasures, there's no sale."

Ixchel and I share a glance. Then I open my mouth. "Before you married Mr Vargas, your name was Susannah St John," I begin. "You were a nurse. You came to Mexico for a nursing conference . . . in Veracruz." I stop, aware of Susannah's narrowed eyes and Dr Velasco staring at me, open-mouthed. "You visited a little town called Tlacotalpan. With a friend, I think. Another nurse."

"And then the bombs fell. . ." murmurs Susannah, incredulous.

"We've met before," I tell her. "You, me, Ixchel. In another reality. We've travelled in time. With a sort of . . .

device. Sometimes what you do when you travel in time, it changes things. Creates a parallel reality."

I'm panting slightly, hardly believing what I'm saying. The air is crackling with anticipation. Even Ixchel looks stunned.

Dr Velasco erupts with a scornful laugh. "What utter nonsense!" I can see she's furious. "Susannah, I'm sorry. Come on, children, let's go. You've had your fun."

But Susannah doesn't flinch. "No. Stay." She faces me. "You're saying that . . . you changed something?"

My eyes flick from Susannah to Dr Velasco, who looks horrified and embarrassed all in one.

"Not us. We're not the only ones travelling. The time-travel device has had other owners throughout history."

"A parallel world. . ." she murmurs to herself, wistfully.

Dr Velasco grabs Ixchel by the bicep. "I'm sorry, Susannah, but I'm taking these silly children off your hands. Please accept my apologies. I really have no idea how they got that information about you. I swear to you, I don't have such things written down. I had no idea they planned such a ridiculous scene."

"Indeed you will not, Monica." Susannah fixes Dr Velasco with a beady glare.

"But Susannah, time travel? A parallel world?"

"It's an entertaining story. Indulge me."

Dr Velasco looks exasperated. "I'm not staying here to be made a fool of."

"That's all right, my dear," Susannah says gently. "Why don't you go see if Carmita can fix us a snack."

I've never seen an adult woman look as offended as Dr Velasco does then. Susannah must be a very important customer, though. Dr Velasco straightens a lapel on her navy blue jacket and leaves the room, stiff with dignity.

"Tell me about your parallel world," Susannah says smoothly. "Tell me about time travel."

I continue, "Where we're from, this didn't happen, your nuclear war. I was born in Oxford, in England. Almost fifteen years ago."

"England is uninhabitable," Susannah says flatly.

"Not where I come from. In our world, you and me," I tell her, "we're friends."

Susannah lapses into another tense silence. She sounds amazed. "And . . . that's how you know all those things about me?"

"Yeah. You told me the first time I met you. The other-you, I mean. We're trapped here now, in this reality. Alone."

"We brought the golden bracelets from another reality," Ixchel says. "They aren't stolen."

"They're our only way to make money."

"If this is true, then you're risking a great deal," Susannah remarks. "Telling me that you are alone here. Alone, and with a valuable treasure."

I gaze at her steadily. "Like I said, I know you."

Susannah purses her lips. "Do you indeed, young man? *Time forks perpetually towards innumerable futures. In one of them I am your enemy.*" For a second or two I hold my breath, waiting. Then a twinkle appears in her eye and for an instant I catch a sense of that same warmth, the way Susannah acted towards me the morning that we climbed Mount Orizaba.

Hesitantly I mumble, "You're not my enemy."

"I am not. Yet you couldn't know that."

"Unless he's telling the truth," Ixchel adds.

Susannah speaks thoughtfully, almost to herself. "So, you didn't steal these bracelets from your family."

"What . . . how could I?"

"It happens. European refugees with a stash of family jewels, ancient treasures looted from museums before they fled the radiation. Is that what's going on here?"

Bowing my head, I murmur, "You don't believe us."

Susannah stares at me with a knowing look which fills me with dread. In a tiny voice she says, "Oh yes. I do."

I whisper. "How? Why?"

Please don't mention Arcadio.

"I have my reasons." She clears her throat. "I'll give you ten million pesos for all fourteen bracelets."

"How much is that?" Ixchel asks. "Can we live on it?"

"Here in Quintana Roo that money will buy a nice little house, some land for farming and a small business, maybe a shop or a restaurant," Susannah tells us in a mild voice. "I'll talk to Monica. We can all go together to the bank tomorrow. I'll expect the authentication certificates for each item."

"Ten million," I repeat, trying to hold a firm gaze.

"A comfortable life, most certainly. You won't be rich, sure, but you'll have everything you need. If you want to be rich, well, there I can advise you. There's land in this state that is going to become extremely valuable once this new Cancun resort takes off. If you buy the right pieces I really think you could make millions by the time you turn twenty."

Ixchel and I stare at each other, hearts in our mouths. I know what she's imagining – the same as me. The two of us living the rest of our lives by the Caribbean Sea, our own place, some banana and coconut trees, maybe one of those trees with red flowers. Our own surfers' paradise, cabanas on white sands. Barbecued fresh-caught fish, every day. Playing guitar on the beach. And in a few years when Cancun hits the big time, maybe our own really cool, luxury beach house, the kind of dream place you make on *The Sims*. Every night could be like last night, the two of us lying on a soft warm beach, watching the stars appear over the sea.

No ancient destiny. No worries about 2012. Just Ixchel and me, together for ever and finally free.

Susannah leads us out to her back garden, where there's a pool so smooth that the water looks completely untouched. While she and Dr Velasco iron out the details of the deal, Ixchel and I are silent, our fingers touching under the table.

Susannah's history room has hit me very, very hard. I'm finding it tough to adjust to the news that while life in Mexico seems relatively undisturbed, everyone I knew *does not exist*.

My mother was probably never born. Tyler almost certainly never born. Even my dad and everyone in Ek Naab – if Ek Naab doesn't exist then they don't either, the lot of them. *Never born.*

England is in ruins. All those other places too. I feel bad for them of course, but England! Oxford deserted, radioactive, overgrown just like ancient Becan or Calakmul.

The day I returned the Ix Codex to the "invisible city", Blanco Vigores warned me: *Don't imagine that one day people won't stroll through the remains of Manhattan, of Trafalgar Square*. The thought that I could actually do that now makes me queasy. As he also said: *We all exist in the shadow of tomorrow.*

The day before yesterday I was in Calakmul. Not the crumbling ruins in a sweltering forest but the living, breathing capital of the Snake Kingdom, teeming with life. Now, everyone and everything in Calakmul has crumbled away. The same goes for Oxford.

Death, decay and ruin – it's waiting for every one of us. It makes you wonder – what is the point of life?

Yet glancing at Ixchel, I realize that I already know the answer to that. Right now, she's all I care about. Those things that Susannah promised us we could have with her money . . . without Ixchel, they're meaningless.

"I'm flying my jet to Mexico City tonight," Susannah announces.

I nod. "You fly a jet; that's cool."

"Pilot lessons proved more enjoyable than the alternative," she says modestly. "With all the businesses to check on I'm in the air twice a week, at least. Tonight, Josh, Ixchel, I'd like you to join me."

"To Mexico City?" Ixchel says.

I add, "Why?"

"Because there's something I want to show you there tomorrow morning."

"What?" Dr Velasco seems taken aback and even a little put out by Susannah's suggestion.

A mysterious gleam returns to Susannah's eye. "I'd prefer to keep it a surprise. Would you let me? It's something kind of special. We'll stay in my Mexico City apartment – it's a wonderful place, you'll enjoy it."

"So long as you and I can conclude the deal," Dr Velasco says. "Then I guess there's no problem."

I'm pretty keen to see Mexico City in this world. Susannah seems so happy when we agree. I keep catching myself looking at her closely, checking for any possible sign that deep down, she knows me. Do I remind her of Arcadio? Did she meet Arcadio? Is that why she believes our story about time travel?

She believed it very quickly. I definitely get the feeling there's something she's not telling us, too.

We say goodbye to Dr Velasco outside Susannah's house. Until this moment she's seemed entirely confident and comfortable, but underneath her friendly goodbye with Susannah I wonder if there isn't a bit of tension. As though Dr Velasco resented us going over to Susannah.

We shake her hand while she eyes us with polite distaste.

"Be careful," Dr Velasco warns in a strange voice. "See that you don't get blown off course. This is hurricane country."

As she leaves, Ixchel whispers, "What did she mean?"

"I dunno," I reply. But her words give me an uneasy feeling. They remind me of something Blanco Vigores once said to me. He warned me against storms too. But somehow I don't think he was talking about the weather.

Susannah drives us to Chetumal as the sun is setting. We swing by the hotel and the bank to pick up our clothes and the Mayan jewellery. While we're in the hotel Susannah goes to the museum, where Velasco has promised to sign a bunch of authentication certificates for the bracelets. I take the opportunity to grab the Bracelet of Itzamna and stuff it into my pocket. There's no way I'm leaving it here if we're flying all the way to Mexico City. . . From there we drive to a small airport. We park almost in front of her company's white four-seater jet. It's not much bigger than a Muwan. Then I remind myself that there probably aren't any Muwans in this reality.

No Ek Naab, no Muwans, no Benicio.

In the plane, Susannah takes to the cockpit. As we drive on to the runway it's already dark. Looking at Susannah, I have to admit that she's less and less like the other-Susannah we met in Tlacotalpan. There, she seemed lost, unanchored. She'd spent most of her life waiting for news of the bloke she loved. Whereas in this reality, she's a canny businesswoman, collector of rare antiquities, and a pilot too.

We arrive in Mexico City at around 9.30 p.m. As we fly in, the twinkling orange lights of the city extend almost as far as the eye can see. After we've landed, we find a car from Susannah's company waiting on the tarmac.

Ixchel's eyes are wide at the whole experience. "Her own

plane, her own driver . . . she's pretty rich, Josh!" she whispers to me. "History might have killed Susannah's entire family in this world, but she sure did manage to do well."

"God spared Mexico," I whisper back. "No wonder everyone here is so grateful. Their neighbouring country gets blown to bits . . . but Mexico's left untouched."

We drive along raised highways adorned with swirling, flashing lights advertising Coca-Cola, Antarctica, Varig Airlines and mainly Japanese companies like Sony, Nikon, Honda. Apart from Coca-Cola, there are no American brands. The car takes us to an old colonial neighbourhood near the centre of the city. Her apartment is the penthouse of an old palatial building. She leads us out on to a balcony with iron railings and at least thirty pot plants. We watch as she unrolls a hosepipe that's attached to an outdoor water tap and sprays water all over the plants.

"Look at my poor plants," she murmurs fondly. The spicy aroma of geraniums fills the air. "They miss me so." Casually she adds, "I've asked the maid to make up two bedrooms for you. Now, how about some pie and a nice cup of chamomile tea?"

We eat blueberry cheesecake at the kitchen table next to furniture that's oddly strange in design. Powder blue seems to be the "in" colour for fridges here.

"I'd like to talk about this time travelling," Susannah announces.

Ixchel and I exchange wary glances. "Why?"

"Because, my dears, don't you think it's fascinating? I mean, you say that there was no nuclear war in your reality." Delicately, Susannah puts down her fork. "Surely you can see why that idea would haunt somebody like me?"

"*What if. . .*" says Ixchel, almost to herself.

"Exactly," says Susannah. "The big 'what if'. Not a person alive who hasn't asked herself that. What if the nuclear war could have been avoided? In your world, so you say, it was. I'd love to know how."

"Me too," I say, then fall silent.

"Please, dear," Susannah says, with a hint of insistence.

"It's not just us," I say eventually. "There's someone else travelling in time." I watch her reaction. If I mentioned Arcadio now, how would she respond?

"Someone else, you say?"

"I tried to tell you earlier."

But Susannah seems genuinely baffled. "Maybe so, my dear. I'm finding it hard enough to accept that you two young people have travellled in time." With great care, she sets down her tea cup. "So, who is this other journeyman?"

"Marius Martineau. He's a thief," Ixchel says. "He's stolen something from the timeline. A book of lost, ancient knowledge. Without that book in this history . . . I guess things are different."

"A book of ancient knowledge. . .?" Susannah sounds

thrilled, intrigued. "Dearie, I sure-as-shootin' wanna hear about this. . ."

I take up the story. "Martineau . . . he wants to control the ancient knowledge. He wants to fix things so that only he and his people can control the future. You know about the Mayan Long Count ending in December 2012? Well, that's because something is going to happen. Something bad that could destroy civilization."

"And this time-meddler, this Martineau, he wants to see civilization destroyed?"

I shake my head slowly. "I don't think he cares about that. I think he just wants his group to be in control. They think they're special, better than everyone else. Survival of the fittest – and they're more worthy of survival. The event at the end of 2012 will let them take control of everything. That's what they believe."

Susannah considers this while dropping a cube of sugar into her tea. "You think Martineau changed history so that there would be a nuclear war in 1962?"

"It doesn't seem like something that would help his plan," I admit. "But time travel can be tricky. You try to change things, you try to find the 'zero moment' from which everything begins. Then other things change, things you didn't plan." My eyes meet Ixchel's. "He must have done it; Martineau. He told me he'd used the Bracelet more than once. He found out how to go back to the 'zero moment'."

"Sound awful complicated," says Susannah. But her tone has changed suddenly and there's a look in her eye as though something has just occurred to her. Or as if I'd said something alarming.

Ixchel frowns. "It sounds dangerous."

"I don't reckon this history is the result of something planned," I say to Ixchel. "But it *is* something to do with the Ix Codex. To do with the disappearance of Ek Naab, also."

"In our timeline, Ek Naab's citizens were not the only people to know about the ancient technology," Ixchel reminds me. "Remember? Your grandfather's Muwan crashed and the US government took it to Area 51."

"Yeah, the Americans, you're right! You think they secretly used the ancient technology to prevent the nuclear war in our world?"

Ixchel shrugs. "That has to be the connection."

I stare at her. "It could be! But no way can this be how Martineau wants things to turn out! Without Ek Naab, there's no Bakabs. And the Sect of Huracan started from Ek Naab!"

"It's a shame he didn't read Arcadio's warning," remarks Ixchel. "You can't 'swim against the stream of time'."

"My, my. You children are saying some extraordinary things now," Susannah comments.

I manage a chuckle. "I'm sorry, I bet we're weirding you out."

Shrugging, she replies, "Well, it may be that what I'm about to say will have a similar effect on you. . ."

Ixchel and I gaze at her with bated breath.

"I would really like it," Susannah says, "if you would show me the Bracelet of Itzamna."

We're stunned into absolute silence. *She knows about the Bracelet.* But how?

I stare at Susannah for a full minute before saying in an accusing tone, "You've met Arcadio."

But she just shakes her head, smiling mildly.

"You must have," I insist. "Or else how could you even know about the Bracelet of Itzamna?"

"Well, my dears," Susannah says, "that is exactly why I brought you to Mexico City."

If Susannah imagines we'll be able to sleep after telling us something like that, she's crazy. As soon as all the lights go out, I hear the door to my room creaking open. Then Ixchel is perched on the edge of my bed, turning on my night light.

There's about five seconds of awkwardness before we pounce on each other. Within minutes I'm trembling from the intensity of my own impulses. Ixchel notices and gently pushes me away. I'm not upset, though, not like when she went all chilly on me in the Sanborns hotel. Ever since we first got together we don't seem to need to discuss it. Instead we're collecting small moments of understanding. Before, it felt like there was this electric fence between us. I might get a shock if I tried to get close, or I might not. That's gone now. We're going somewhere with this, that's all that matters. The relief is incredible.

"How does Susannah know about the Bracelet?" Ixchel

says, raising the subject with dizzying abruptness. "Do you believe that Arcadio never visited her?"

Carefully I say, "Yeah, I do."

"If Arcadio did visit her, you realize that kind of implies that you *are* Arcadio?"

"Huh? How do you get that?"

"Arcadio is a Bakab – he must be if he can use the Bracelet of Itzamna. There's no Ek Naab in this reality so there are no Bakabs – except you."

I don't like where this conversation is taking Ixchel, so I change the subject. "I just can't believe how different things are without the Ix Codex. Yet . . . this can't be what Martineau wanted."

"I agree. When you saw him in seventh-century Calakmul, did he say what he was planning to do?"

"He did say he was taking the codex out of history. But only the Ix Codex! Ek Naab always had the other three books of Itzamna."

"Have you thought about where Martineau is now?"

I shrug. "He could be anywhere, any time. He's probably used the Bracelet again. If he turned up in *our* Ek Naab, he could have been captured. That would have created a whole different future, but Ek Naab would still be there. I'm guessing if he found himself in Ek Naab, he probably used the Bracelet right away – to take him somewhere else. Unlike me, Martineau actually knows how to change the settings."

"Where would he go? What would he do?"

"Wherever – or whenever it was, it was pretty darn drastic, what he did. To change things so there's no Ek Naab? That means going back way before seventh-century Calakmul. He'd have had to go back to . . . I dunno. To when the Books of Itzamna were written. And somehow stop them being written."

Ixchel chews this over for a moment. "But if that's a better strategy, why wouldn't he try it the first time? Why even bother to go to seventh-century Calakmul?"

"Well, that's easy. Why did *we* go to seventh-century Calakmul? Cos it's the only time and place we know for sure the Ix Codex was at." I shrug. "It's the same for Martineau."

She frowns. "But the completion date of each book of Itzamna is written in the end of every codex. If Montoyo had wanted to send you to Itzamna's time, he could have."

"Yeah, but *Martineau* didn't have that information, did he? The Sect had the beginning of the Ix Codex, not the end. They don't have any of the other three books. Yeah . . . Montoyo sent us to Calakmul because it's the *first* place that Martineau would have gone. And if I just hadn't handed him the Ix Codex, everything would have been fine."

Ixchel murmurs, "If you hadn't rescued me, you mean."

Our eyes meet for several seconds. "I had to," I say, very quietly. "Can't you understand? I'll always choose you."

Her fingers touch mine. She breathes a heavy sigh. "Instead, Martineau's just kept trying, going on and on, changing the timeline."

I agree. "He's crazy, unhinged." For a second I wonder if using the Bracelet makes you lose your mind. The rush you get from knowing you've changed world history could have some dangerous side effects.

"So how come you think he's gone back to Itzamna's time, finally?"

"Because I gave him the Ix Codex." I stall. "Because of me, he knows just when to find Itzamna. Jeez. It's a full-on nightmare."

"If he wants to stop the books being written at all . . . the only sure way is to kill Itzamna."

"Yep." I nod grimly, considering the theory. "Killing Itzamna . . . that would do it for sure. No books, no ancient technology, no Ek Naab, no Muwan to crash in Orizaba and give the Americans all that sophisticated technology." I stifle a yawn, feeling suddenly sleepy.

"And instead, a nuclear war that wipes out hundreds of millions of people."

"Yeah. . ." There's not much else I can say. Every time I think about that, I get a creeping sense of numbness and disbelief.

Certainly kills the romantic mood.

In the morning, Susannah doesn't join us at the breakfast

table until we've eaten our way through plates of fruit, sugar-covered concha rolls and cups of hot chocolate. When she does, she's carrying a cordless phone the size of a brick. It's the first cordless phone I've seen since we arrived. She asks the maid to bring her a black coffee, then takes a muffin from the basket.

"I'm sorry for the delay. I've had so many telephone calls today. I didn't have the heart to tell them their calls were pointless."

It's a strange way to start a conversation. Neither Ixchel nor I know what to say.

"Josh," Susannah says after sipping her coffee. "Do you have the Bracelet?"

I roll up the sleeve of my cotton *guayabera* shirt to expose the Bracelet of Itzamna above my elbow. Susannah gasps slightly, leans forward and touches it lightly with two fingers.

"My goodness, you really do."

There's an awkward silence. Susannah turns to me. "What am I like, in your reality?"

The question takes me by surprise. It hasn't properly sunk in that Susannah actually believes us, that somehow she knows about the Bracelet of Itzamna.

"Um, well, things turn out different. You still live in Mexico, but not like a rich businesswoman. In a little house in Tlacotalpan. A really nice house," I add, reassuringly. "And you paint."

"Am I happy?" she asks in a faraway voice. "Do I seem happy?"

I glance downwards. "I couldn't say for sure. You . . . the Susannah I know . . . she was crazy about this bloke. He disappeared. After that . . . I don't know if you could say she's happy."

"Hmmm." Susannah seems strangely unmoved. "Well. A painter, gee! That's kind of surprising. I haven't painted since I was young."

With a blunt air of finality Ixchel asks, "So how come you know about the Bracelet of Itzamna?"

"I'll tell you all about it when we get there."

"Where are we going?"

"To the National Museum of Anthropology."

Susannah's driver picks us up and drives us through the leafy streets of her neighbourhood before turning on to the main boulevard of Mexico City – Paseo de la Reforma. From there we swing into the shady green lawns and parks of Chapultepec. The driver drops us off.

This part looks exactly as I remember the city, right down to the stalls that line the street selling blue and pink candyfloss, a thousand varieties of brightly packaged sweets, huge sheets of deep-fried pork crackling drizzled with lime juice and chilli sauce, guys blowing up gigantic acrylic bubbles that reek of pear-drop-scented solvent. A little kid with huge eyes approaches me with a transparent plastic bag of Chiclets chewing gum in tiny boxes, all different flavours. I take the Chiclets and give him a few pesos.

As we pass the giant monument of the Aztec rain god, Tlaloc, that stands guard at the museum entrance, Susannah begins by asking us if we've heard of a ruined city known as Izapa. Hearing that, I feel a ripple of excitement. I'd been afraid that Susannah's story would be a red herring, just a rumour. But linking Izapa with the Bracelet of Itzamna makes this feel real. After all, Izapa is where Blanco Vigores told me he found the broken Bracelet, which he then gave to my father, which I then fixed. Izapa is where Itzamna found the super-ancient Temple of Inscriptions of the Erinsi, which he copied down in the Books of Itzamna.

Izapa is at the beginning of everything.

"Part of Izapa was destroyed by a volcanic explosion. Much of it was flooded by water from underground rivers," says Susannah. "A few years ago a scuba diver got lost for an hour in some underground tunnels. He claims to have come across a flooded chamber with a wall full of inscriptions. He took photographs of the inscriptions. Eventually he was able to find his way out of that labyrinth. But he couldn't remember how to reach the chamber with the inscriptions. People have searched since then and failed to find it. All we have are his photographs."

It's obvious to Ixchel and me that diver must have found

288

part of the destroyed Temple of Inscriptions. So not quite every bit of Erinsi knowledge has been lost to this reality. . .

"There's a room in the museum that's dedicated to famous hoaxes or fakes in the world of archaeology. It's an extremely popular exhibition, even though it's very controversial. Many people think it's a mistake to display such objects in a museum, even in a room that's very clearly labelled 'Fakes and Hoaxes'. It has everything you can imagine, that room: images and writings from ancient Atlantis, spaceships visiting Sumeria, cuneiform writing from the alien progenitors of the Anunnaki. People love it, which is why I want us to get there early, before the crowds."

"So the Bracelet of Itzamna is mentioned in these inscriptions that the scuba diver saw?"

"You might say that, dear. Unmistakably mentioned!"

We're strolling through the vast marble lobby of the museum as Susannah says this. Then we enter the courtyard with its wide-open spaces and extensive horizontal lines: concrete, glass, water. Ixchel stops in her tracks, absolutely amazed. I watch her for a few seconds, feeling a rush of pleasure to see her evident joy in something new and totally unknown.

"Josh . . . this is . . . an incredible place!"

"I know," I say, beaming. "I remember my first time here, with my dad. When I was, like, nine. A-mazing."

Susannah leads us across the courtyard, past the Olmec

room and upstairs. For an exhibition that's pretty hidden away it's already quite busy, even by ten in the morning. Right away I see why Susannah brought us.

"I've always been fascinated with this particular 'hoax'. It's unusually elaborate in detail. Why would someone go to all this trouble just to make something so unbelievable as this photograph? Time travel, ancient knowledge of advanced technology – heavens, who would believe that? That's why I've always wondered about the Bracelet of Itzamna."

The photograph of the Erinsi inscriptions has been blown up to an enormous size, presumably the actual size of the wall as reported by the diver. An eerie bluish tinge to the photograph combines with glassy ripples to give a deep underwater feeling. You can even see the detail of the diver's own air bubbles.

"The inscriptions are in some strange language that no one has seen before. It's something like ancient Sumerian," Susannah says, "but not quite. People have tried to decipher it, and that's where the trouble began. That's why it's considered to be a hoax."

"Because it includes technical words than couldn't have existed in ancient times," says Ixchel with an ironic grin. She reaches out to the glass sheet that covers the photo. "The Erinsi inscriptions, Josh! Can you believe what we're seeing?"

Susannah eyes her curiously. "You know what language this is?"

"Even better than that," Ixchel says loftily, "I can read it. . ."

My eyes are scouring the image, which is the size of a wall in an average school classroom. It's obviously been taken by combining dozens of smaller photographs. The more I gaze at it, the more I feel sorry for the photographer – he risked his precious diving air for fame as the discoverer, only to have no one believe him.

Then I find it. Amidst hundreds of lines of inscriptions, each symbol less than a knuckle in length, is a carved image – detail of the control settings on the Bracelet of Itzamna. Right beside it there's a rough inscription. But these few words are not written in Erinsi. They're written in English.

"The Bracelet of Itzamna at the zero moment."

I'm still staring at those words when I feel Susannah's hand on my shoulder. "Do you know what to do? You do, Josh, don't you? Ever since you mentioned the 'zero moment' last night, I knew you would."

Turning, I see her standing with tears in her pale blue eyes. She continues, "I asked you if she's happy, that other Susannah, Susannah St John. But you didn't ask me if I'm happy." She begins to shake her head, tears trickling down her cheeks. "I'm not, Josh. None of us are. A holocaust like ours is a scar that doesn't heal. Remember, for all the millions who were killed by their side, we slaughtered even more. Nations were erased. That doesn't go away. The memory hardly fades, the legacy is like a deep, weeping sore: it bleeds; it rots within you."

"But . . . but everyone here seems so chilled. . ." I say, bewildered at her sudden rush of emotion. Ixchel's looking pretty distressed too.

"Young people ignore it, they pretend it never happened, they shut down any conversation about the war. Mexico, thank the lord, escaped relatively unscathed. But Europe! Russia! The eastern seaboard of the United States. . . Josh. You can barely even begin to imagine horror on that scale. So I'm asking you – *do you know what to do?*"

Susannah's grabbing my hand now, giving me such an imploring look that it breaks my heart.

"The Bracelet at 'zero moment'. . ." I mutter. "That must mean Izapa, in the time of Itzamna. That's when it all started – the Four Books of Itzamna."

"The man you called Martineau – you say he stole the book of lost knowledge. Can you go back, stop him from stealing it, stop him from changing history? Can you make it so that the war never happened?"

"I . . . don't know. . ." I tell her. "It's all a bit unpredictable."

"We could warn Itzamna about Martineau," Ixchel suggests.

She's right. Martineau must be stopped. Yet I'm starting to wonder if there's any way that can happen. That's when it dawns on me that if we ever meet again, Martineau will have the exact same thought about me. He'll realize that I'll never give up, that there's only one way to stop me.

Martineau will have to kill me. Something tells me that if there's a next time, he'll have no problem with that.

Ixchel takes me to one side. "You're really ready to do this?" I frown a bit and nod. "You've thought about what it means? Using the Bracelet again? That would be three times in a few days. Aren't you worried about losing your memory, like Arcadio? Or me losing mine?"

"It could be even worse – the crystal could burn out and we'd get stuck there. Let's face it, we have no idea how long one of the Crystal Key things last. We have to try, though. Don't we? I mean it's like, I dunno, like having a chance to stop Hitler. You have to try, don't you?"

Ixchel only looks at me with immense sadness in her eyes. "You said it yourself, there's no way to predict the outcome of interfering with the past."

"In this case we *can* predict the outcome, sure we can! Because we've been there, *we know*. You and me, we come from a reality where Itzamna wrote the four codices, where Ek Naab existed to guard that knowledge. We just have to put things back the way they were. Martineau is the time-meddler, just like Susannah said. We have to be, like, the *time-fixers*."

"But . . . this world won't be affected by the superwave in 2012. . ." she murmurs. "We . . . could stay here. . ."

"Yeah, but . . . nuclear holocaust! That's got to be worse, hasn't it? And if we put things back the way they were, the Ix Codex goes back to Ek Naab, there's no nuclear war, just like in our own history, and everything is sorted for 2012. Right?"

She nods, biting her lower lip. "OK. OK. You're right. We have to try."

I walk briskly to the enlarged photograph and take a hard look at the symbols on the Bracelet. The disc of metal which holds the Crystal Key in place seems to have rotated by a quarter of a clockwise turn. It's the first time I've noticed the Bracelet in that configuration. It must be how you remove the default setting which returns you to ten minutes before you set out. I get my fingernails around the disc and try to turn it, avoiding the crystal. Suddenly the metal gives way under my fingers, pushes into the Bracelet. Now I can feel it rotating freely. I turn it to the same position as on the inscription. It's a delicate operation.

Immediately the symbols on the edges begin to rotate, like pictures on a fruit machine. I touch one row lightly, and immediately, that row stops moving. I touch it again and it advances one symbol. I keep doing this until the symbol matches the one on the inscription.

"It's like a combination lock!" I whisper to Ixchel, aware of a few curious eyes on me now.

Susannah steps forward. "Are you. . .?" she asks in wonder.

"We're gonna give it a go," I tell her, trying to smile.

If we succeed, Susannah won't remember anything. There won't be a nuclear war in 1962. The past fifty years of her life will be totally different. Only Ixchel and I will have any memory of the other path that Susannah's life might have taken.

The idyllic, Caribbean-beach future I'd started planning with Ixchel – that won't happen either. We'll be right back to our luxury prison of Ek Naab.

If either of us gets hit by the amnesia thing, even the memory of our time on the beach will be gone. We might not even remember how to use the Bracelet. We'll be stranded deep in the Mayan past, lost in time.

Well, I'm hoping that with two of us travelling, at least one of us will remember.

Trembling slightly, I begin the process of matching the second symbol to the one shown on the inscription. Ixchel puts a hand on my arm and I can feel that she's trembling too. There are six symbols in total. When they're all matched up, I look from Ixchel to Susannah.

"That's it. Now I hit the crystal and we're gone."

"Goodbye, Josh. Goodbye, Ixchel. Oh my dears . . . I hope this works." Her eyes glisten with tears. "You're doing a wonderfully brave thing."

Silently, we hug Susannah goodbye. I step back and Ixchel wraps her arms around me tightly.

As I press the crystal I can't help but wonder – will this be the last time Ixchel does that?

The cool marble hall and the museum's glass cases are ripped out of view, Susannah's dazed expression and that of the few bystanders, all torn away.

My field of vision fills with a wide-open space under a sweltering sun – a stone-built terrace surrounding a dusty pitch, as long as a tennis court and about half as wide. Brown-skinned players wearing loincloths and headgear dart around on the pitch, bouncing a hard rubber ball the size of a cricket ball around the court.

The ancient Mayan ball game. My heart flutters. Did it really end in the gruesome sacrifice of the losers? Maybe we'll get to see. . .

We're surrounded by people – Mayan citizens. They're dressed in simpler clothes than the last time, their hair loose or in basic topknots. It takes a few seconds before more than a handful of people notice us. Everyone's looking at the ball court and the players, who are furiously rebounding the ball off the walls of the court, to each other, off their hips and elbows. Finally one sends it whizzing through a small stone hoop fixed high against one of the longer walls of the court. Half the players leap into the air and the crowd erupts. Ixchel and I almost get knocked down.

That's when people really notice us.

The effect spreads like a Mexican wave around the terrace. Within thirty seconds every face in the ball court is looking in our direction. Most of the audience doesn't even know what they're looking for; only that everyone else is looking our way. For a couple of seconds there's silence. A young woman, very thin, gives Ixchel an indignant shove.

She says something in Mayan that sounds like, "You pushed me."

"Sorry," Ixchel replies, speaking Yucatec. Her voice sounds shaky; she can barely talk. "Didn't mean to." She gags, leans over and throws up all over the terrace.

Suddenly everyone in the ball court starts talking at once. It takes me a second to work out what they're all saying.

Itzamna, Itzamna, Itzamna.

Like Chinese whispers, the call is going around for Itzamna.

This time, the Mayans aren't freaked out by our appearance, our clothes. The second they saw us they knew we had something to do with Itzamna.

He must be here. We made it.

I put an arm around Ixchel's shoulders as she wipes her

mouth, groaning slightly. Finally, she looks up at me. "That's it. I'm never going through that time-travel thing again."

"But you have to," I remind her. "When we go home."

The crowd before us parts, letting someone through. Right away I know two things: the man standing before us is indeed Itzamna. And he's not Mayan. He's about forty years old, fair-skinned, shoulder-length dark brown hair, blue eyes, not particularly tall – around my height, in fact. He's slim and lightly built, wearing a simple tunic of unbleached cotton decorated only by a shell-studded hide belt. The guy looks as though he hasn't done a day's heavy work in his life, unlike most of the Mayan men around him – all fierce-looking and armed with black daggers.

"Well, good day to you!" he says in Mayan, with a cheerful beam. One eyebrow goes up. He switches to English, speaking with an accent – could be Aussie, Kiwi or South African. "Or perhaps in English? Good day!"

Hesitantly, I shake the hand he's offered. "Hi . . . I'm Josh. I guess you're Itzamna?"

"So they say! The name's actually Zsolt Bosch. You can call me Bosch. I might even remember to answer to it. Who's the lovely young lady?"

Ixchel shakes his hand too. "I'm Ixchel."

"Ah, we should get married then!" The guy laughs as though he's made a huge joke. "I'm supposed to take a wife called Ixchel, right? To fulfil the legend. Only between you and me," he says, winking, "the wife might have a bit of a problem with that."

The crowd is watching our conversation with huge interest, but they obviously haven't a clue what we're saying. Itzamna – or Bosch, as he wants to be called – he just ignores everyone. "Where are you from?" he asks. "I mean, *when*?"

"The twenty-first century. From 2011."

Itzamna frowns. "Don't say it! Does something go wrong with my plan for 2012?"

We shrug, helplessly. "So far as we know . . . it goes wrong."

All Itzamna's good humour vanishes. He steps closer, pushing away the restraining arm of one of his guards. "If you're here to help me fix things, then you're right on time. Come with me; there's something I need you to do."

With a few words to his men, we're left alone, all the citizens reluctantly shepherded away by Itzamna's warriors.

"You're from the future," I say, staring with deep curiosity at Bosch/Itzamna. He nods curtly and begins to walk, urging us to follow.

"I'm from the twenty-second century. I was an archaeologist, specializing in Pre-Columbian civilizations. And here in Izapa I made some truly incredible finds."

"The Erinsi," I say. "The 'People of Memory'."

"Well, of course," he says, casually. "It figures that you'd know about the Erinsi. Presumably you found one of their time-jump bracelets." He glances at me as he walks. "I can't imagine how. You're just kids! Did you borrow it from your parents? Actually, do you mind me asking where you found it? I must admit I only ever found one Erinsi ruin. Even though I worked out that there must be more. The Revival Chambers, for example. There are five of them, although I didn't get around to finding any of the others."

Bosch's questions have the same energy that he carries in his whole body. I can't imagine this guy sitting still for long enough to translate the inscriptions. Either he's a real live wire or else he's agitated about something.

Instead of answering any of his questions, Ixchel asks one of her own. "Why are there five Revival Chambers?"

"Why?" He shrugs. "Redundancy, I guess. The Erinsi placed a human element into their plan for 2012. Unfortunately, ah, there was a mishap with the chamber in Mexico, and all those people were revived too early. But with four other chambers, I guess there'd still be someone around to be revived in 2012, to operate the moon machine. Even with more mishaps."

"People," I repeat, "to be 'revived'? And did you say 'moon machine'?"

Bosch nods vigorously, but doesn't slow his pace. We're crossing behind some small stone platforms now, low temples, and heading towards a village of straw huts about a hundred metres away. Behind the city are fields of what might be maize. Beyond, the forest rises swiftly towards a range of mist-shrouded volcanic peaks, including Mount Tacana.

It's striking just how similar this city is to seventh-century Calakmul. It's on a smaller scale, definitely. But I can hardly believe that we're more than a thousand years deeper in the past than we were in the Snake Kingdom.

Unlike ancient Calakmul, in Izapa there are no towering pyramids, but many low temples and terraced platforms. But the more I see, the more I realize that it's pretty large. I spot limestone constructions in every direction, dark grey from the recent rain that's made the ground soft and loamy. The sun is blazing, and my skin already feels hot, slick from a thin film of sweat.

"The Erinsi civilization was devastated by a massive burst of electromagnetic radiation that wiped out all their computer technology. This is around seventy-six thousand years ago, mind you. Then a few decades later their main city complex was destroyed by the explosion of the caldera under Lake Toba."

"Caldera. . .?"

"A caldera is a gigantic pool of magma under the earth's crust. When they explode it's called a supervolcano. The explosion throws trillions of tonnes of dust into the atmosphere. It's like a long, dark winter lasting years. Crops won't grow! A major extinction event! Two major disasters

302

like that, well, it's enough to finish off even a complex, advanced society like the Erinsi. But they had a plan." Bosch taps a finger to his nose. "Smart people! The ones who survived, they pooled all their resources. They set things up so that their knowledge wouldn't be lost. They spent their last efforts making a machine that would protect the earth from another massive electromagnetic pulse, like the one caused by the galactic superwave. Then, they left."

I stop walking. "They left?"

"That's right. They put themselves into hibernation. In the Revival Chambers. Those chambers were built to preserve people for up to a hundred thousand years."

"So . . . so all along they planned to stop the 2012 superwave?"

"Yeah." Bosch grimaces. "Like I said, there was a mishap. When I found the Revival Chamber in Mexico, it was empty. I found their lab too. Listen, kids, it's a long story. A really long story – the story of the last fifteen years of my life. But now, I need your help. You've got a functional time-jump bracelet, right?" With vague interest, he glances at the bracelet on my arm.

"Well, yeah."

"Good. So you have a way out of here. I have to stay longer and see some things through. But you two can help me."

"Us help you? How?"

"The seismic readings I've taken lately are not good," he says grimly. "Not good at all. I think Mount Tacana is going to blow her top. So I've been copying down the inscriptions and translating them. . ."

Ixchel interrupts, "Copying from the Erinsi Temple of Inscriptions?"

Bosch looks at her with a faint air of disquiet. "Yes. Odd that you've heard of the inscriptions . . . seeing as how you're from the twenty-first century. Rather thought that I'd discovered them, in the twenty-second."

"The Erinsi are not known in our time," Ixchel tells him with care. "Except by a secret group. A group set up by *you* to guard the ancient knowledge until 2012."

Bosch chuckles, grins widely and winks. "That's one hell of a plan. Sometimes I'm such a genius, I scare myself."

Bosch is striding faster and faster towards the village. Ixchel has to break into a slow jog to keep up. Breezing through the village, Bosch dismisses the questioning looks that are thrown in our direction with a simple, "They're with me, from my country."

Ixchel hangs back slightly and tugs at my arm. "This doesn't seem strange to you?"

"What, Itzamna-I-mean-Bosch? We guessed he might be from the future, didn't we? What with the Books of Itzamna being written in English."

"I know, but don't you think he's behaving strangely?"

"Well, yeah. He's obviously in a hurry. Look at the mist around the volcano. I don't think it's a cloud. And that smell, don't you reckon it could be smoke?"

"From the volcano?"

In the time it takes for this brief exchange, we've passed through the village and into the forest beyond. I call out to Bosch, "Where are we going?"

He slows to let us catch up. "I have my office in a cave nearby. It's dry; all my equipment is there."

"You brought equipment from the twenty-second century?"

"Some. Mostly it's Erinsi stuff, taken from their lab."

"Their lab? Where is that?"

Bosch stops in his tracks and gives me a long, searching look. "Why do you ask?"

Ixchel and I exchange a nervous glance. She begins, "It's just that. . ."

". . .we don't know much about you," I say. "We've read about you, of course, and we know you write those four books of inscriptions."

"Four?" he says, alarmed. "God, it's worse than I thought. I was planning on five! The last part was going to be my history, and about the Oracle."

Ixchel says, "Five? But . . . you can't have planned five. Why else name them after the four Bakabs, who represent the four corners of the Earth?"

Ruefully, he grins. "You like that, hey? I hoped it would seem appropriately mysterious and portentous. The fifth is more of an appendix. It's a real pity if it doesn't survive."

"But . . . you're from the future," I say, puzzled. "You must know if it survives or not."

"I'm from the future," he responds, tight-lipped. "But maybe not yours."

Now we're both bewildered.

"You're from a pre-2012 future, yes?" Bosch explains. "Whereas I'm from a post-2012 future. In my future, the superwave hits the world very hard. A group takes over, a group known as the Sect of Huracan. No one knows how, but they seem to be prepared for the crisis. When it hits, they're the first organization to start offering support to all the countries that are going to pieces. That's how they take over. By the twenty-second century, there isn't a world leader who isn't part of the Sect of Huracan."

Ixchel and I simply gape.

"They found some way to persuade folk to do what they wanted. I was one of a clandestine group investigating the Sect," Bosch continues. "The top members of the Sect claim to be descended from an ancient civilization. That's why I was brought in – to search for traces of the Erinsi. I found them, too. Incredible stuff; you wouldn't believe how incredible. Not just the time-jump bracelet but the Oracle too."

It's the second time he's mentioned the "Oracle". I ask him what he means.

"The Oracle is an Erinsi device for calculating the odds that a single rogue element – say, a time traveller – has interfered with the timestream. They developed the time-jump device to use with the Oracle."

Open-mouthed, I ask, "So . . . you're not meant to use the Bracelet randomly?"

Bosch's expression darkens. I might almost say that he blushes. "Of course not. That would be highly, highly reckless. The Oracle calculates when time travel has *probably* been used to interfere. The difficulty lies in knowing what the intervention is. The Oracle only gives a probability. Well, I ran some calculations, using statistics from recent history; I'm talking about from the twentieth century onwards. Historical data isn't so good before then."

"And. . .?"

"And the single event that most highly correlates with time travel is December 22, 2012. The Oracle showed that what happens in 2012 is almost definitely the result of a time traveller's actions."

"But the superwave is a natural phenomenon," Ixchel says.

"Yes, it is. How the world handles the superwave event, though, that is not. In my reality, the Sect of Huracan takes over. Somehow, they're ready for it. Taking over the governments of the world was all part of their scheme. My group decided to put a spanner in their plan, to see if we couldn't engineer a different turnout."

"So . . . the Sect of Huracan are supposed to win? That's how things are meant to turn out?"

"No," says Bosch very firmly. "We don't believe in 'meant to'. That's fatalistic rubbish. There's always a better way."

I'm starting to get the impression that Bosch hasn't used

the Bracelet very much. If he had, chances are that like Ixchel and me, he might realize that you can't easily interfere with history. When I tried to get my dad out of the prison in Area 51, that's inadvertently what I did. Marius Martineau too – his interference has resulted in at least one reality that wasn't planned – the one with the nuclear holocaust.

How can Bosch be certain that he isn't the very agent that causes the outcome he is trying to prevent? It's beginning to look horribly likely to me that he is. Without the writings of Itzamna, how would the Sect even know about the superwave and 2012?

How does Bosch know that he isn't playing right into the hands of the Sect?

"Have you never met anyone from the Sect?" I ask. "I mean, since you've been in the past."

"I haven't," he says. There's no obvious sign that he's lying. "If you know I'm here then presumably they do too."

"Maybe not. We didn't know exactly where and when to find you."

"Yet here you are."

"Because of the inscription on the temple wall," I say. "The diagram of the Bracelet of Itzamna at the 'zero moment'. We just copied the settings."

"'Zero moment'?" he says. "You mean like, *t* equals zero, in chemistry?"

I shrug. "I guess. In our reality, *this* is the 'zero moment'. It all starts with you."

Bosch shakes his head. "There's no diagram of the Bracelet on the temple wall. The only Bracelet diagrams in the Book of Ix are mine."

"Then maybe you'd better make an inscription," I tell him, wide-eyed. "Or else how will we know when to warn you about Martineau?"

"Martineau? Who's Martineau?"

"Marius Martineau. One of the leaders of the Sect of Huracan. He's been interfering with the 2012 plan. He's stolen the Ix Codex from the group you set up to protect it. But things didn't turn out the way he planned."

"Someone from the Sect is trying to find me. . .?"

"In the reality we've just come from, there's been a nuclear war in the twentieth century. A really big one. Two thousand twelve is the least of their worries. That's why we came to warn you. Martineau started time travelling, changing things. Eventually, he gets rid of the Books of Itzamna completely. When that happens, there's a nuclear war in the twentieth century."

Bosch seems appalled. "A nuclear war? But how?"

I shrug. "We don't know. But there has to be a connection. Martineau takes those four books out of history, and all the technology written in them is lost. Somehow, it leads to nuclear war."

Bosch looks dazed.

"We figured that he could only do that by coming here, by doing something to you."

"What. . .?"

"By killing you," Ixchel says bluntly. "We think Martineau will try to kill you."

There's a deep, low rumble and the weird sensation, for about ten seconds, of the ground shifting under our feet. The tang of smoke in the air gets sharper, with the added smell of bad eggs.

Darkly, Bosch says, "If we stay around here much longer he won't have to kill me. The volcano will take care of that. You say you're here to help, that's good. I'm going to take you to my study in the cave and set you up with writing the Book of Ix. There are only a few more pages to go, but they're essential to the 2012 plan."

"What about the volcano?" I say, unable to take my eyes off the pillar of smoke that has begun to twist out the peak of Mount Tacana.

"I've been warning the Mayans to prepare for evacuation," he murmurs. "I'll go back to the village now and tell the Jaguar Priest that it's time."

"But . . . but what about us?"

Bosch scowls. It's the first time I've detected hostility from him. He plants both hands on his hips. "Listen, you two. If I don't finish writing those books, there'll be no way to save

311

the Erinsi knowledge. In the future, that whole temple is destroyed by lava. I don't know if this is going to be the explosion that destroys the temple or not. It might happen now, it might happen in five hundred years. I can't take the risk, do you see that? Listen, I can't imagine how or why a couple of teenagers have got hold of a powerful ancient relic like the time-jump device. Right now, I don't have time to listen to your story. I only have time to get these people out of here and to finish the Books of Itzamna. With your help, I might just do that. So what do you say? How serious are you about stopping the Sect of Huracan?"

"We're serious," I tell him. "Totally. You might even say it's my destiny."

Bosch manages a smile. "Destiny, eh? Don't let me hear you talking like that again! That's *their* language. The Sect of Huracan, destined to rule for hundreds of years. Ancient overlords restored to their former splendour. *That's* destiny, where I'm from."

Bosch's cave is about two hundred metres into the forest. By the time we get there I'm already scratching at new mosquito bites. He shows us the opening to a narrow *cenote*, then abruptly, he stops, standing very still. Ixchel and I are motionless, listening. Then we hear the sound that's worried him. The crackle of some twigs. Then the unmistakable sound of footsteps in the undergrowth. They grow fainter, heading away.

"I think we've been followed," he murmurs.

"Who might follow you?" Ixchel asks.

"It's no secret that I work here. But I've created enough mystery and intrigue around the place to keep most people away. Sometimes, though, the children get curious."

Bosch seems more worried than his words suggest. He points into the well, at a wooden stake that's been hammered into a gap between the rocks. There are similar hand- and footholds halfway down the well, stopping about fifteen metres above the surface of stagnant water. Where the footholds finish, there's a hole in the wall. The gap is just wide enough for an adult man, but we all have to crawl on hands and knees. Bosch goes first, promising that it isn't far. We crawl for about five minutes, which is long enough that my leg wounds and rib bruises start to ache again. The tunnel widens and becomes high enough to stand in.

"This place is a honeycomb," Bosch says. "But it's all limestone. When the volcano blows, there's no way to know what will happen. Might fill with water, might fill with lava."

"Or both," I suggest, remembering the photographs the diver took of the underwater temple wall. Montoyo had always told me that the Erinsi temple was buried by lava. Bosch seems to think the same. But what if the lava flow swept part of the wall away, to be lost in an underwater cave?

Bosch leads us into an office where there's a wide wooden desk, which takes up about a third of the space in the room. The desk is covered with pieces of Mayan bark paper. He picks up a neat, concertina-folded heap of paper about five centimetres thick.

The Ix Codex.

Amazingly, I realize that it's the first time I've ever seen the whole, actual codex, outside of its protective case.

Except that this one isn't quite complete.

Bosch disappears into a small antechamber and returns

with an extra wooden stool. Without a word he places it next to the other stool under the table. I can't help wondering at his slightly furtive manner. Then he shows us the scraps of pages where he's written the English translation of the Erinsi inscriptions. For a second I wonder if there's a whole translation of the codex that we could see. It's quickly obvious that he reuses the paper, coating each piece with gesso after he's written what he needs and then using it as a palimpsest, a manuscript that's been covered and written over and over. Ixchel and I concentrate as he shows us how to use the cipher key to encode the English words into Mayan hieroglyphs.

We work together then, speaking in low voices and only about our work. It's like when I deciphered those first few pages of the Ix Codex at my house in Oxford, only in reverse. There's hardly even time to reflect on how fully amazing it is that the final few pages of the codex are written by me and Ixchel. I'm badly tempted to scrawl "Josh woz here" in the margins. Without knowing whether that was actually written into the codex in our reality, though, I don't dare.

That's how scary it can be to fiddle around with history. You never know where things will end up.

All sorts of thoughts cross my mind over the next few hours as we work. Some of the stuff I manage to read while I'm transcribing is amazing. I keep looking out for instructions on how to use the "time-jump device" but they don't turn up. I guess that they're in part of the Ix Codex that Bosch has already completed.

"Where are the Bracelet instructions?" I ask him.

"Listen, buddy of mine, you just take care of this job and I'll see you right. They're not in this section. As I'm sure you've worked out."

"Well, at least tell me how it works."

Bosch sighs. "Do you have a degree in ten-dimensional physics?"

"Yeah," I say flatly. "I have two."

"Don't knock it, *tjommie*; where I come from some kids your age can do that stuff. Look, it's like this: the Bracelet is a remote control. It sends a signal to a power source, which opens a vortex in the space-time continuum. Only a tiny one, mind. And any mass up to about a hundred and fifty kilos gets transported through the vortex – to another time, another place. The Bracelet sends the instructions and it acts like a focal point for the vortex. That's why it's so small. The actual power source – now that's huge."

"And where is it?"

"Funny you should ask" is all Bosch will say.

I start looking through the glyphs even more closely, to see if I can find the answer. There's loads of amazing concepts. For example, there's a thing that Bosch/Itzamna has translated as "Large Hadron Collider". I ask Bosch if that's the power source and he sort of grunts, "Might be."

"So the Erinsi built something like the thing that's in Geneva?" I ask. "Where?"

"It's close to their labs," he replies, not without suspicion. I can't help noticing that Bosch doesn't like me asking questions about the exact location of the Erinsi remains.

Another thought I keep returning to is this: if Itzamna/Bosch didn't inscribe the image of the symbols on the Bracelet into the temple wall, then who did? Was it me? If it was, then I need to find that temple wall soon . . . or else there'll be some horrible time paradox. Without that added inscription we wouldn't be here now.

So I ask him again, "Where exactly is the Temple of Inscriptions?"

Bosch is quiet for a minute, scratching an unshaven chin. "Kid, I appreciate the interest, but right now I need you to stay focused on the writing. I can't finish this on my own."

Ixchel looks up from her work. "It won't take long to tell us."

"To what end, though?" Bosch flushes angrily. "You want me to give you coordinates? How will you get there? You want me to take you? There isn't time. All I want is for you to help me finish."

"Where are the other three books?" I ask suddenly. There's been no sign of the other three codices: Muluc, Cuauc and Kan. Nor of the protective cases, embedded with the deadly toxin that can kill at a touch.

Bosch throws an involuntary glance towards the antechamber. "They're safe."

The atmosphere in the room is suddenly tense. Bosch's trying to hide something.

There's another deep rumble, an almost throaty roar that travels through the rock and via the tunnel. Almost as if in response, the room shakes. Ixchel and I stare at each other in terror. I'm suddenly intensely aware of how much rock there is above us. The room carries on quivering for almost a full minute. When it stops we're completely covered with a fine layer of dust.

Pushing the inscribed pages away, I stand up. Taking Ixchel by the hand I say, "We're out of here."

"Don't be infantile," Bosch snaps. "It gets much worse before an actual eruption. Sit down again, we'll be finished in an hour."

"No," I tell him, firmly. "Finish on your own."

Bosch looks baffled. "You can't leave now. What about your man Martineau?"

"We just came here to warn you. You've got your own army back there. Let them take care of Martineau."

He steps forward. Slowly, he reaches behind his back around his belt and draws a stubby blade. In a voice that's suddenly lower and infinitely more menacing than any tone he's used before, he says, "You're going nowhere."

My hand goes for the Bracelet, but Bosch leaps forward,

grabs Ixchel's arm, jabs his dagger against her throat. For a couple of seconds, none of us moves a muscle; we don't even breathe.

"The time-jump device has so many design flaws, don't you agree?" Bosch is nervous, I can tell, breathing through his mouth. He licks his lips. "There's the oh-so-fragile Crystal Key, which didn't last me even two time-jumps. Then there's that countdown. It'd leave just enough time for someone like me to slit this girl's throat before you zap back to the future. Little wonder that the Erinsi never used it for time travel."

"Why did *you* use it?" I say, trying to buy some time.

Bosch laughs. "Why did *I* use it? By mistake, of course, you stupid boy! Here's a lesson for you – don't use a machine without reading the damn manual." His voice rises hysterically. "What an idiot! *Why did I use it?* You think I wanted to be trapped here in the past? You think I *enjoy* being Itzamna, bringer of writing, agriculture and science to the Mayans? You seriously think that *anyone's* got that huge an ego? I'm here because I'm stuck with this useless, burnt-out, hunk-of-junk Bracelet-of-freakin'-Itzamna. Not by choice!"

"But . . . so why are you doing all this stuff to save civilization in 2012?"

He rolls his eyes. "That's quite enough from you. Give me your Bracelet."

"No."

"The Bracelet, or I cut her throat."

In one jerking movement, Bosch switches the blade from her throat to mine. As he takes the step, the cave lurches sideways. There's another angry roar from the volcano, followed by a terrifying rumble. We're all rigidly still with every seismic shift, wondering when the ceiling will crack.

Struggling to keep my voice even, I say, "Can we just get out of here first?"

"You can do what you like once you've given me the Bracelet." Bosch's hand goes to the Bracelet on my arm. His knife hand is still at my throat, pressed against the jugular. I gulp, trying to think.

"We won't help you finish writing the codex."

He gives a sardonic laugh. "These were the final pages. Congratulations, kids, your work will go down in history."

But from the opening to the escape tunnel there's a voice. Even though I can't see who is behind Bosch, there's no mistaking the strident, confident drawl of Marius Martineau.

"Regrettably, *none* of your work will go down in history. This time, I shall make quite sure of that."

Bosch's eyes narrow. Slowly, he looks over his shoulder, keeping the blade pressed to my neck.

"Marius Martineau," says Martineau with a tired smile. "Delighted to make your acquaintance, Itzamna, or whatever your real name is. Now be a good chap and move away from the boy."

Dumbly, Bosch steps aside. That's when I see Martineau. He's dressed in the simple rags of a Mayan peasant, his skin tanned dark and leathery. He looks leaner and older than when I saw him last. His only adornment is the Bracelet of Itzamna, clamped around his right bicep. I wouldn't have taken him for anything but Mayan, from a distance.

The transformation is complete. Only this time, he's pointing a gun.

39

"Drop the knife," Martineau says without expression. When Bosch doesn't obey, he fires the gun, a deafening sound inside the cave. The bullet hits the wall next to Bosch's head, scattering debris and dust over Bosch, Ixchel and me. "Next time it's your head," Martineau tells him.

Bosch drops the blade at arm's length. Martineau retrieves it, his eyes and pistol levelled at Bosch the entire time. "I don't blame you for wanting to kill Joshua Garcia," Martineau admits wearily. He's waving the gun, switching the aim from me to Bosch. "We're alike in that respect, you and I. But I've been waiting a long time to get all of you together. Now, he's going to fetch those four codices for me."

Bosch doesn't turn around. "If you know anything about the Books of Itzamna, then you'll know that he'll die. No one can touch those codices but me."

"You *and* Josh." Martineau gestures with the pistol. "Move away from him, boy. Into that antechamber, where I suspect that you'll find the codices in their cases. Don't touch them, though. It might seem like a convenient way to dispatch me, but don't forget – the girl dies with me. I want you to wait until we're out of range; then count up to one thousand and only then bring them to the surface."

I nod at Bosch. "What about him?"

"He's no concern of yours."

"He'll kill you," Ixchel tells Bosch. "I hope you realize that?"

Bosch turns reluctantly away from me and faces Martineau.

"Yeah," I say. "That's the only way he can be sure that you don't write the books again."

"Then you'll kill Josh," Ixchel says to Martineau. "Won't you? Once he's done your dirty work for you."

"I don't understand how you think the kid will survive touching the codices," Bosch says. "They give off a biotoxin."

"He'll be fine," Martineau replies smoothly. "Like you, the boy has been genetically modified to resist all four types of biotoxin. I imagine it's a rather simple procedure in your own time. When would that be, incidentally? I've been hiding here amongst your people for several weeks. No one knows anything about your other life as a time traveller."

"How is this fella even here?" Bosch asks me, with increasing bewilderment. "You have my Bracelet, yes? You found it, repaired it? What about him? Is there another Bracelet?"

I shrug, saying nothing. I still don't know where Martineau got his Bracelet. Even if I did, why should I do anything to help Bosch? All he wants now is to steal my Bracelet and escape. I move away, towards the antechamber. A plan is beginning to form in my mind.

"I'll get you the books," I tell Martineau. "But if you destroy them, you'll end up causing a nuclear war in the twentieth century. The Sect will never take over."

Martineau hesitates, slightly lowers his gun. "You're bluffing."

I attempt a sneering laugh. "I wish! But me and Ixchel, we've seen the future where he never writes the books, the future you're about to create. It's just what you promised me: a reality where I never existed, my family never existed; a future without Ek Naab, without the Sect of Huracan."

Now Martineau seems really annoyed. The gun is raised again. "Foolish boy, remember who you're dealing with!"

"He's telling the truth!" Ixchel blurts indignantly.

"You're both lying," Martineau says, irritated. "But I'll make you a deal: do as I say, and I promise you can go free. Both of you. I'll set your Bracelet to wherever and whenever you like."

Now who's lying. . .?

"Hold it!" Bosch shouts at Martineau. "I need the kid's

324

Bracelet. It's my only way out of here. If you want those books, you're going to need my help. That's my price."

"I don't need your help."

"The boy can't carry all four books and climb out of the well. Even with two he'll have a problem, climbing with just one hand. It takes two people to carry four books."

Martineau only smirks. "Then he'll make two trips. You'll build me a fire at the top. We'll have a good old-fashioned book-burning."

Bosch visibly pales. He starts to move towards the antechamber, but Martineau aims the gun and stops him with a barked yell.

"I'm only going to show the boy where I keep the boxes," Bosch murmurs, hands raised. Then he pushes me ahead of him, into the antechamber. Inside, he points to a pile of dried palm branches. "The books are under there. Don't touch the boxes until they're well out of range." He passes me the folded pages of the almost-completed Ix Codex. "Put this in the empty box."

Then he grabs me and pulls me close until his mouth is right against my ear. In a voice that's barely audible, he says rapidly, "OK, Josh. You probably don't have a good impression of me right now. After how I threatened you and everything. But listen. You need to trust me. This Martineau is very, very dangerous. Your girlfriend is right – he's going to kill me. I don't think you're safe either. I think I can get us out of this. But I'm going to need your help."

I hesitate. "Why should I trust you?"

Bosch pulls back. His hard blue eyes stare into mine. "I can't think of one good reason. Josh – you gotta go with your gut. I'll make you a promise: help me and I promise that I won't take your Bracelet. I'll take his."

Thoughtfully, I nod and mouth, "OK. What next?"

"I'm going to go for Martineau. Be prepared, that's all. Leave all the books by the entrance to the cenote."

Then he leaves. I stay behind, starting my count to one thousand. Martineau forces Bosch and Ixchel out of the cave and into the escape tunnel. When I've finished my count I pick up two of the codex boxes. I can just about wrap both under one arm. Then I crawl through the tunnel and climb up the *cenote* wall. Bosch is right; it's exhausting to climb up those stakes with only one hand. I reach the top already breathless. My climbing arm tingles with pins and needles.

At the top, Martineau is guarding Ixchel, leaning against a tree with a gun pointed against her head. They're about ten metres away, a safe distance from the effects of the biodefence toxin. Bosch is trying to make a fire under another tree, also about ten metres from Martineau's position. I drop the two volumes on the ground and risk a look at Ixchel. She shrugs and tries to smile, but even at this distance I can see that she's nervous.

The air is thick with the sulphurous smell of the volcano. There's another rumble from the mountain. The tremor buzzes through my feet. Above the treeline there's a steady plume of smoke rising from the peak. Bosch said it gets much worse than this before an explosion. Well, maybe. To me, though, that volcano looks like it might go off at any minute.

With a heavy heart, I crawl back into the *cenote*, climbing down. Is Bosch right? Will Martineau kill us all? If he burns the four books and leaves their author alive, he's risking the chance that Bosch will write them all over again. As for me, I'd already made up my mind that Martineau would probably try to kill me eventually. He's only ever let me live because I was useful to him.

Bosch is a slippery customer, no doubt about it. But Martineau and the Sect are pretty much my sworn enemies.

I have to trust Bosch. Whatever he's got planned, it's our only way out.

The earth starts shaking again. I freeze, hanging tight to the wooden stakes, spreading my weight. It occurs to me that if I get hit with a tremor like that when I'm climbing with the books, I'll have to drop them, or fall. I gaze into the stinking black water at the bottom of the *cenote*. It looks pretty nasty. And it's a pretty safe bet that it's me they'd send.

When the tremor stops I climb down, return to the cave and fetch the last two books. The climb back up takes much longer, with minor earth tremors every few seconds to rattle my nerves. I reach the top drenched with sweat and exhausted.

The two first codices are still where I left them, next to the opening of the *cenote*. Bosch and Martineau seem to be fussing over the fire, arguing in loud voices. Bosch is saying that Martineau is an idiot; if he hadn't interfered the fire would have got going ages ago. Martineau is accusing Bosch of being an incompetent who can't make a decent fire. The entire time, Martineau has his gun pointed right at Ixchel's chest. I add the last two codices to the pile and climb out, sitting by the hole and rubbing my arms to get rid of the pins and needles.

When Martineau sees me he stands up. He switches the gun from Ixchel to me. "All right, boy. Now, on my mark you're going to open up those boxes and throw the books inside on to this fire."

He grabs Ixchel's upper arm and starts to move away from the fire, all the time keeping a safe distance from me.

In that instant I understand Bosch's plan.

For a second or two, Martineau's attention is wholly focused on me and the books. In that time Bosch slips silently behind him, and as quick as lightning he whacks Martineau's arm hard, forcing it upwards with some kind of karate blow. The gun goes off, shattering the quiet of the forest. As if in reply the mountain rumbles in the distance. While Martineau is distracted, Ixchel darts into the forest, disappears into the trees.

But Martineau doesn't drop the gun. Roaring with anger, he swivels, trying to find Bosch. Bosch is fast – he's already manoeuvred around to Martineau's opposite flank and just as Martineau fires again, he ducks, hooks his legs around Martineau's and topples him.

I drop the books and race forward. Bosch is on top of Martineau now, trying to wrestle the pistol from his hand. Martineau twists the pistol and fires again. Bosch's whole body jerks backwards and he screams. I'm just in time to deliver a hard kick to Martineau's gun hand. The gun flies into the undergrowth; Martineau roars in dismay.

Desperately I shout, "Ixchel, find the gun!" But I don't even know if she can hear me by now – if she's smart, she's running to the village for help. Meanwhile Bosch is on the ground writhing in agony. The bloodstain at his shoulder is spreading at an alarming rate. I take up a *ginga* stance at a safe distance from Martineau, bobbing from side to side to block his access to the gun.

Martineau gets on to his feet. Scornfully, he kicks a whimpering Bosch in the ribs. He turns to me, glowering, and reaches for Bosch's knife, now tucked into his own belt. I sense his hatred of me, pure venomous rage. I've just started to pivot, preparing a capoeira attack, when the swift motion of his blade takes me completely by surprise. It flies through

329

the air between us and with a searing thud sinks into my side, just above the hip. The pain rips through me. I collapse, faintly aware of a faraway sound.

It's the sound of my own voice, screaming.

The dagger in my side overrides every impulse in my body.
Lengthy seconds go by before I manage to hear what Bosch's
been yelling at me. *Get close to the codex.*

I squeeze tears out of my eyes to see that he's crawled
back to the hole and is lying with his head near the pile of
volumes. Looking around, I catch sight of Martineau,
wandering among the nearby trees.

He's looking for the gun.

In the next few seconds I look around in panic, weighing up
my chances. With a knife buried in my hip I can hardly walk.
Running isn't an option. I could pull it out, maybe, try to hurl it at
Martineau. But the idea of touching the blade terrifies me. Do you
take knives out of wounds? Or does that make you bleed faster?

Bosch is bleeding pretty badly. He's taken refuge near the
codices, groaning. Martineau can't go within three metres of
the books. The Ix Codex will be OK, but the others are lethal.
He'll have to play it safe. But if he finds his gun. . .

Crawling, I edge close to Bosch and grab one of the books. I turn around and hurl it in Martineau's direction. The movement of throwing is so painful that it makes me retch. Martineau is picking something up off the ground when he sees the volume flying towards him. He leaps away, running in the opposite direction, terrified by the biotoxin that has surely filled the space he's just left.

I've just widened the area that Martineau can't enter. Bosch stares at me for a second, impressed. I grab a second book with two hands and chuck it at Martineau. He darts away again and this time fires the gun blindly as he's running. Bullets thud into soft mulchy ground less than fifty centimetres from my head, throwing up earth and leaves.

Now I'm panicked. I lift the third book, aim and throw. Martineau fires again as the book flies through the air. The bullet ricochets off one tree and slams into another. I can't see Martineau now – he's disappeared behind some trees.

Then there's a whooshing sound. A spear zips through the air, strikes the ground only metres away. There's a yell and then the incredible sight of Martineau hurtling towards us through the trees, spears flying all around him. Just as he comes into view a spear takes him square in the back of the neck. It skewers him. The black spear tip emerges in an eruption of blood and splintered wood just under his throat. He falls to his knees, clutching his throat, eyes bugging out of his head. He gasps almost silently, only managing a desperate wheezing sound. A second later blood gushes out of his mouth.

Then the effects of the biotoxins begin. Martineau's skin starts to blister and crisps up as though it's being cooked. He's trying to scream, but the only sound that emerges is a gurgling, whining sound.

"Don't get any closer!" Bosch yells in Mayan. A group of Mayan spear-throwers lurk in the forest behind Ixchel, watching at a distance. Ixchel repeats the instruction, telling the Izapans that the books are cursed. They murmur in appreciation.

I can't take my eyes off what's happening to Martineau. It takes him at least three minutes to die, choking, writhing in agony, locked in a silent scream.

Bosch doesn't watch. He stumbles unsteadily to his feet and staggers around, picking up the three volumes that I used as weapons. He fetches them and places them back on the pile near the opening of the *cenote*. He goes to Martineau's fresh corpse and pulls the Bracelet of Itzamna from his arm. Then he approaches me, helps me to my feet and supports me as we hobble, soaked with blood, white with shock, towards the Mayans.

Two warriors hold me still as another one jerks the blade out of my hip. I almost pass out from the pain. I'm dimly aware of them bandaging the wound with a tourniquet so tight it bites into my flesh. Through the mist of agony, I can see Ixchel standing by, nervous, anxious. The minute the battlefield surgery is over she rushes to me and hugs me. I make a feeble attempt to hug her back but it's a struggle to stay conscious, to be honest.

The Izapans help us back to the village, take us straight to the medicine hut. They practically force-feed Bosch and me with some potion that tastes fully disgusting, bitter and like partially fermented leaves. Within ten seconds of drinking it I feel as if I'm floating away, off the bed and into the thatched palm of the ceiling.

When I regain consciousness my hip still hurts but the pain is much less severe. My wound is covered with a loose paper-bark bandage. Gingerly, I lift it to see an ugly scar, raw and inflamed, but amazingly, also neat stitches, practically invisible.

"Spider silk," Bosch mumbles. He's lying in the cot next to mine, his head turned towards me, and smiling, exhausted but relieved. "I brought them opium poppies and taught them how to use spider silk for repairing wounds . . . but to be honest, they do pretty well with what the forest provides. How're your pain levels?"

"Not too bad," I say. "I can feel the wound but . . . it doesn't seem to bother me."

Bosch chuckles. "That's the opium. It'll wear off soon. You'd better get back to the twenty-first century and find some tablets. Get some antibiotic shots too. You were very lucky – the knife didn't puncture your guts. That would have needed proper surgery, not just a muscle-layer stitch-up. You'd have bled to death pretty quick."

I stare at him for a moment. "What about you?"

"I'll be OK. Bullet in my shoulder, they dug it out. Hell, I felt everything, even with the opium!"

"So . . . what are you going to do? You've got your time-travel bracelet now – you can leave."

He looks thoughtful. "Oh, me. . . Well, I've been thinking about what you said before. Maybe I'm not finished here yet. Still have to put the final touches on the Ix Codex. And I guess I'd better do that inscription you talked about, the one that led you here, of the Bracelet of Itzamna . . . or else you and Ixchel will probably disappear into thin air. Then there's the missus. Yeah." He rolls his eyes. "That one's going to take some negotiation."

"Take her with you?"

He guffaws. "A hundred and fifty kilos, remember? We'd both need to lose some weight."

"Be worth it, though, wouldn't it? To take a friend."

Bosch pats my arm. "You're right, Joshua. Course it would."

We share a look for a moment. I wonder who Bosch left behind in his own century. Family? Friends? Really, he's given up his life. I can't blame him for wanting an escape route.

"Sort of panicked a bit back there," he admits ruefully. "Hope you and your girl won't hold it against me."

"It's OK," I tell him. "I understand."

Bosch nods. "Knew you would."

335

"What about the Bakabs? You need four guys to look after the codices. Four guys with the protective genes."

A grin of delight spreads across Bosch's face. Then he calls out to the Mayan medicine woman, a middle-aged lady with solemn eyes and a huge long plait. He whispers something into her ear and she nods.

A few minutes later, four young boys, all aged around ten years old, file silently into the medicine hut.

"Joshua, meet the Bakabs," Bosch says, putting his good arm around one of the boys. "This is my own son, Leaf Storm. He's the Bakab Ix. And these are Swift Wind, Sky Son, and Fire Light, the Bakabs of Kan, Muluc and Cauac. I gave them the genetic modification treatment when they were born. They're going to be the guardians of my books." He ruffles the hair of his own boy. "Aren't you, *tjommie*?"

"Your son is the Bakab Ix?" I say, laughing.

"Exactly. Like you, Joshua. I bet I'm right."

I nod, once. "How did you know?"

"Oh yeah! I can tell one of my own. You're a worthy successor, *bru*. Now get back to where you came from and don't come back!"

"What will you do?"

Bosch shrugs. "Time travelling hasn't really worked out for me. On my first trip I messed up and revived a bunch of Erinsi who weren't meant to wake up. On my second trip I got stuck here! If I do it again, I think I'll find a nice spot and retire. Maybe Mexico in the twentieth century. The world was pretty good before the Sect of Huracan took over. Don't think I want to risk going back to anywhere after 2012."

Martineau was right, after all. . . Itzamna himself disrupted the ancient Erinsi plan! No wonder he is so obsessed with fixing things for 2012.

"Don't you want to see if your plan works?"

"I do. . ." He hesitates, then glances at me. "But I'm scared, to tell the truth. What if it doesn't? Don't reckon I could handle that, not after everything. No – I'll leave all that to you and your friends in . . . what did you call it? Ek Naab?"

"And you're just gonna retire? What about the Bracelet?"

Bosch grins. "Kinda wondered if you'd ask. Thought I'd warned you off the time travel."

I stall. "Yeah, but . . . it's not the kind of thing you leave lying around."

His grin widens. "All right, *bru*, no need to ask. I'll leave the Bracelet somewhere for you. You ever hear of a town called San Cristobal de las Casas? If I ever get done here, that's where I'm headed."

I don't hear what he says beyond that because the volcano bursts the silence with an earth-shattering roar and rumble. Seconds later the air fills with a hot smell of rotten eggs mixed with smoke. Bosch frowns, casting a glance through the open door of the hut. Outside, the Izapans are running around, gathering up small children and packing their belongings.

"You have to leave this place," I tell him. "You have to take the Bakabs and go somewhere safe."

He nods. "It's all in hand. We're going today." He points to the Bracelet on my arm. "Now let's fix this up so you can go back." His eyes become deadly serious. "Just use it *once*. I didn't feel too good about trapping you and your girl in the past. Don't you go doing that to yourselves now, OK?"

BLOG ENTRY: REMEMBER THIS

The first thing I did after they stitched me up in hospital was to look up Zsolt Bosch in San Cristobal de las Casas. Turns out he died in the 1990s at a pretty good age. I was glad to know that after all the stress, he finally got his wish. I hope he finally found some peace. His daughter still lives in the house. I took down the address. Who knows if Bosch left me the Bracelet after all. But you never know. . .

Then I called Tyler. He answered the phone with a low whistle. "Heyyy, Mariposa!"

Right then, my capoeira nickname was the best word I could have heard from Tyler.

He knew me. We'd got back!

We talked for a bit. Nothing major, just catching up on normal stuff. I didn't tell Tyler that he'd been my first clue to the fact that the whole of history had been changed. Of course not. You can't lay stuff like that on a mate. At least, not over the phone.

338

Then Montoyo and my mum arrived from Ek Naab.

Montoyo denied tricking me into time travel. "You knew what I was doing," he insisted. "Deep down, you knew only a Bakab could use the Bracelet."

He came to visit me in hospital in Chetumal, after Ixchel and I time-zapped back to the beach there, about a week after we set out. The surgeon was impressed with the "forest surgery" I'd received but he still wanted to check everything was OK inside.

In Montoyo's memory, he had found Blanco Vigores's handwritten instructions about the Bracelet and decided to try a time-travel experiment. But pretty soon he'd realized that it wouldn't work for him, that a Bakab had to use the Bracelet. "It proved impossible to activate the device," he admitted. "It needed to be in contact with something on your skin." Montoyo didn't remember the "other" timeline, the one where Tyler didn't remember me. No one remembered, except Ixchel and me. Using the Bracelet of Itzamna had somehow protected our memories of the parallel realities we'd experienced.

The Bracelet of Itzamna had taken us to some "dark places", that's what Montoyo reckoned. *Tough times call for tough measures*, all that sort of talk.

He told me, "I intended to explain everything to you. Even now, Josh, I believe you'd have chosen to go of your own free will, once you realized what was at stake. Time travel is an intrinsic part of the solution to 2012. It's written in the Ix Codex."

I didn't argue with Montoyo because I'm actually pretty chuffed that he thinks I'd be so daring or brave. Yet, he's wrong. I would *never* have gone into the Mayan past of my own free will. No matter what is written in the Ix Codex. Somewhere along the line, he's mistaken me for a daredevil.

Or else he's playing with my mind, making me believe things that aren't true. Montoyo is too clever for me, too tricky. I doubt whether I'll ever know for sure.

Montoyo is worried about the problems we have right now in Ek Naab.

There's unrest, whispers of dissent with the way things are being handled. Meanwhile Blanco Vigores is still missing.

The Ruling Executive of Ek Naab are so worried that all travel outside Ek Naab will now be forbidden. Even for Montoyo.

"I looked more carefully at the document we found in Blanco Vigores's apartment," he told me, showing me the handwritten instructions for using the Bracelet of Itzamna. "Look what he's written here at the end. About the possibility that there are parallel times, realities. '*Time forks perpetually towards innumerable futures. In one of them, I am your enemy.*'"

But I've heard that before. Susannah said it to me. I guess it must be a quote.

"Blanco was dedicated to Ek Naab," Montoyo said. "To join the Sect goes against his life's work."

I couldn't tell if he was sad to think that Vigores might have switched sides, or worried that he'd been captured. So I said nothing. Martineau must have got the Bracelet of Itzamna from someone. That someone is probably Vigores. Did he give it freely? Or was he forced?

If Vigores had a functional Bracelet then there are only two possible solutions.

Either there are two Bracelets after all. Or else he had the same one I'm wearing . . . but from the future.

Is someone going to travel back in time and give my Bracelet to Blanco Vigores? Will it be me? Arcadio? Itzamna himself? What if Zsolt Bosch changes his mind about settling down in some nice corner of Mexico in the twentieth century? Maybe he'll decide to take up time travel again. Maybe Bosch is both Itzamna *and* Arcadio?

Yet, I feel as though there's something I'm missing, something in plain sight. Arcadio seems to hold the key to my future. The closer I get to his trail, the more it melts away.

It's a horrible idea, that Blanco Vigores might have gone over to the Sect. The alternative is almost worse. If the Sect have captured him, who knows what they've done to him to get information?

He might not even be alive.

Montoyo left me in the hospital room with my mother, who weirded me out a bit by kissing me whilst sobbing. She didn't blame me, though, for going on a risky adventure. What I said about Montoyo bites just a little too close to the bone. Mum doesn't even want to discuss it. She wants to keep believing that Montoyo will protect me, no matter what.

Then in a bizarre change of mood, she asked me what I want for my fifteenth birthday next month.

Mums. They're crazy.

Finally, Ixchel arrived. My heart started thumping. I tried to act calm.

Now that we're back . . . is she ready to finish with Benicio? On the motorbike ride to Becan, I felt sure I'd be ready to force her hand. But it's not that simple. I want her to choose me over him. Being second best isn't good enough.

Eventually, Ixchel and I got around to the inevitable subject.

Ixchel reaches forward tentatively, touches my fringe with her fingers, sweeps it out of my eyes. "Well, I guess your time-travelling days are over."

"Says who?"

"Your mother. And Montoyo. I heard her outside, making him promise to lock away the Bracelet of Itzamna. She's furious, you know that? It's a miracle she's still talking to him. Convinced that her poor son almost died. . ."

"Like that would ever stop him," I mutter.

"So. . ." Ixchel says, not quite looking at me.

"So. . .?"

She blushes, unusual for Ixchel. "So . . . do you still want . . . do you still feel the same way you did that night on the beach?"

"Do I still want . . . what?"

The words are practically torn from her. "You know. The arranged marriage."

343

I stare in astonishment. "Right. OK. We're gonna talk about that, are we?"

"Do you want to. . .?"

Now I'm as embarrassed as her. "What, get married?"

She looks surprised. "No! Talk about it. Do you want to talk about it?"

"Oh! Well, um, honestly. . ."

We both shrug.

"You don't," Ixchel says, a little hesitant. It's impossible to read her. I get the feeling that one wrong word and I'm in trouble.

"I just want us to be together," I say after what seems like way too long.

Ixchel frowns a bit, but there's a hint of a wry grin, enough to give me hope that I haven't totally messed up.

"Yeah," I continue. "Can I be your boyfriend? After you've had a chance to break it off with Benicio, I mean."

Heck, why even bother? Let Benicio concentrate on healing his bones.

The hint of a grin is bigger. "Well," she begins. I catch a glimpse of a cute and very rare dimple. "It's just that you said some things on the beach. . ." Then it's my turn to redden. "Maybe you got carried away," she adds. There's a definite teasing tone. "I'd understand. It was a very romantic situation."

"Oh . . . I get it," I say, nodding. "This is you having a

laugh with me."

She chuckles. "Maybe a little. But you said other things too. About how we'd spend our lives by the sea." She gazes into my eyes. "If you really meant it . . . I think maybe I'd like that."

"Yeah," I reply quietly. "I meant it."

When I think back to that night, my heart could break. It was so great to be that happy; I felt like it would last for ever. That night, I thought Ixchel and I had it made. We were going to be together, rich and free. Now I don't know if we'll ever get that future back.

The outcome of 2012 is still totally uncertain. In Bosch's future, the Sect will win. Maybe Bosch's intervention in our past will change things. But maybe, like when I tried to break my dad out of the Area 51 prison, Bosch changes nothing at all.

Just the same, it's a future worth aiming for. So I take Ixchel's hand in mine. "We'll get back to that beach one day. You and me. That's a promise."

Ixchel gives this sad smile and hugs me tight. For a second I wonder if she's going to cry. If she does, for once I'll know exactly what to say.

Being so close to her I get this deep, quiet kind of feeling, like being in a bubble suspended in time. It's not that I don't want to grow up, even with all the dangers we face. But right now, I wish that time itself would stand perfectly still.

Acknowledgements

Massive thanks to Polly Nolan for wonderful editorial suggestions and ongoing support for Joshua's missions. To Jessica White, whose scrutiny of continuity issues becomes more crucial with each instalment. To fellow kids' author Susie Day, for reliably enthusiastic company in our "office" (i.e., Summertown Starbucks). To Alex Richardson, Steven Salisbury and Catherine Alport, the brilliant publicity team at Scholastic Children's Books UK. To my Twitter friends (hello tweeps) for minute-by-minute, 24/7 support, including @Redwoods1 and @AlyxP1 (the inimitable Lisa Edwards and Alyx Price of Scholastic Children's Books UK), @NosyCrow (Kate Wilson) and Joshua superfans @LyanaMiranda, @nyall97 and @beccachaplin's son Josh. To my wonderful agent, the charming yet formidable Peter Cox of Redhammer. To my gorgeous girls for being adorable. To my lovely husband, David, who reads every book I write before anyone else – if it keeps him awake at night I know we're on to something good.

The Joshua Files

Will Josh and Ixchel end up together?

Can Josh really trust Montoyo again?

Who IS Arcadio?

Can Josh prevent the superwave in 2012 – or is it really going to destroy the world as we know it?

Desperate to know more? Turn the page to read an extract from the final pulse-pounding book in the *Joshua Files* sequence.

Read a thrilling blog entry from Josh's final adventure

Blog Entry: Crazy Benicio

My cousin Benicio pulled a gun on me. A real one. And he screamed like a psycho.

I was flying a Muwan Mark II. My ninth lesson. They're amazing aircraft – they practically fly themselves. The only reason for so many lessons is in case you get into trouble.

I'd just turned off the autopilot, about a hundred klicks out of Becan. I'd taken the controls, popped a holographic projection of a satellite map in front of my eyes, and started to fly to the contours of a mountain ridge about a hundred metres below.

Then I heard Benicio say, very coldly, "Land. Now. Quick."

"What...?"

He snapped in fury, "Land! Are you deaf? Land, now, or I'll blow a hole through your neck!"

I was so startled that I could only laugh. "Mate ... what are you like?"

"Land this craft or I'll KILL YOU!" he screamed.

At that point I turned to see that Benicio was pointing a gun at me. He eyes were round, wide and livid.

My nervous laugh came back: "You sound like that Achmed the Dead terrorist guy from YouTube ... I KILL YOU!"

That did it, he lost his rag. "Land this plane, you lousy pinche gringo, or God help me I'll..."

"OK, OK, OK!"

I began to lower the craft.

"Faster, *cabron*, like you mean it!"

My heart was thudding by then. So I did what he asked. And said, just to relieve the tension, "Jeez LOUISE, what is your problem? Put the bloody gun away!"

Benicio leaned back, visibly shaking. "*Hijo de...*"

"Watch your mouth," I warned. "Say what you like about me, but don't diss my mum."

The craft bounced to a standstill a couple of metres above the ground. I popped out the undercarriage and felt it thud to the stony ground beneath. I lifted my visor to find Benicio had once again raised the gun.

"What's going on?"

"Spies in Ek Naab?" He smiled nastily. "About time you found out."

My mouth dropped open. "What ... you?"

Benicio nodded. He leaned forward and hit the control panel, opening the cockpit. He stood up, towering over me, then leaned back, making space for me to pass.

"Get out."

"After you..."

He screamed again. "Get out! *Caray*, Josh, don't you know when you're in trouble?"

I held up both hands and stumbled past him on the way out of the craft. "All right, all right, don't have a cow."

When I was on the ground, he followed me, keeping the gun aimed straight at my chest.

"OK, Benicio," I began. I felt a firm yank at my waist. In the next second I was pulled off my feet, dangling. A surge of panic hit me; I twisted around in the air to see the Muwan rising slowly off the ground. It took me another second to realize that I was connected to the open cockpit by an almost invisible thread, a thin cord that had somehow been attached to my belt. I swivelled back to look at Benicio, grinning and waving at me from the ground. I spotted the Muwan's remote control in his right hand.

"Ha ha, Josh. How do you like Crazy Benicio so far?"

I opened my mouth to reply. But the air rushed out of my body. An unseen force flung me against the side of the Muwan. I barely had time to protect my face before I slammed against it.

Benicio called out, "Hold on tight."

Then the aircraft took off. It hurtled along, about fifteen metres off the ground, for about twenty seconds. It came to a juddering halt, and I could hear the gravity dampeners engage. My fingers had clamped on to the edge of the cockpit, knuckles locked so hard that it took a second or two to get them to relax. I heard myself breathing loudly. The craft had stopped in the middle of nowhere, high enough off the ground that a fall might kill me.

From inside the cockpit, I heard Benicio's disembodied voice.

"Climb aboard..."

FACT FILE

Everything you need to know about what's happened in

The Joshua Files

FACT FILE

The Mystery: What really happened to Josh Garcia's father?

Ancient Artefacts: The Ix Codex, a book of Mayan inscriptions lost for over a thousand years.

Key Locations: Jericho (Oxford, UK); the Mayan ruins of Becan (Campeche, Mexico); and Catemaco, a lakeside town of witches in Veracruz, Mexico

Mysteriously Stolen: A copy of Incidents of Travel in Chiapas, Central America and Yucatan by John Lloyd Stephens

Mysticism: Dream-talking, the witches of Catemaco

Action: Car chase; escape into the Caribbean sea; hunted in the misty crater-lake of Catemaco

FACT FILE

Ice Shock

The Mystery: Who is behind the strange coded postcards from Mexico and what do they mean?

Ancient Artefacts: The Adaptor, the Bracelet of Itzamna

Key Locations: The ruins of Godstow nunnery (Oxford, UK); the underground rivers and caves of Yucatan, Mexico; a mysterious riverside town of Old Mexico; the snow-capped volcano Mount Orizaba (Veracruz, Mexico)

Cheekily Stolen: The Adaptor, inscribed with fifteen symbols in ancient Mayan and Sumerian

Mysticism: The spirit-dream of two long-dead young lovers

Action: Midnight chase and fight around Port Meadow, Oxford; lost in the caves; deadly crisis on glacier of a volcano

FACT FILE

ZeRo MoMeNT

The Mystery: Who is Arcadio?

Ancient Artefacts: The Bracelet of Itzamna, the Crystal Key

Key Locations: The giant sand dunes of Natal, Brazil; the tropical jungle of Brazil; the lakes and mountains of Switzerland

Bravely Stolen: The Crystal Key

Mysticism: A message from beyond the grave, a disturbing spirit world

Action: Dune buggy chase; capoeira fighting; time travel; car chase across a mountain pass

FACT FILE

DaRK PaRaLLeL

The Mystery: What's happened to Josh's memory? Why is the Ix Codex suddenly "mostly blank"?

Ancient Artefacts: The Bracelet of Itzamna, the Books of Itzamna

Key Locations: Ancient Calakmul; the Mayan Riviera; the National Museum of Anthropology in Mexico City

Mysteriously Stolen: The Ix Codex

Mysticism: Time travel, alternate realities

Action: Motorbike race; knife vs capoeira fights; shootouts and chases with Mayan warriors

Science of The Joshua Files

Is the world is going to end in 2012?

The Mayan calendar does indeed have an end date of 21-23 December 2012. But there's no real evidence that even Mayans believed the world would end. And MG Harris certainly doesn't believe the world will end then!
Find out more about this on Mayan Mysteries of 2012 – A Guide For Young Readers: **www.mayan2012kids.com**

Calakmul, Snake Kingdom

The ruined city now known as "Calakmul" rose to be a great power in the Mayan world. It was involved in battles with rival Mayan "superpower", the city-state of Tikal. Yuknoom Ch'een II was part of the Ka'an (Snake) Dynasty, He was its longest-serving ruler, reigning from A.D. 636-686.
The "Traitor Bakab" is based on a historical person named K'inich K'ane Ajk, whose name appears in an inscription in

Cancuen. He first appeared in A.D. 653 and is known to be related to the king of Calakmul.

Mayan human sacrifice

Like many early civilizations, the Mayans worshipped gods based on nature and agriculture. They believed that rains were sent by the god Chac only when he was pleased. The Mayans had a variety of methods of human sacrifice – some were extremely bloodthirsty. Drowning in the *cenote* – a fate which almost befalls Ixchel in this story – was the normal method of sacrificing women and children. They would be ritually purified by steam beforehand. The ruins of a steam room were found on the summit of the largest temple at Calakmul, known as Structure II.

Visiting Calakmul and other sites from The Joshua Files.

Like Becan, the ruined city under which the fictional city of Ek Naab is hidden, Calakmul is located in the Campeche region of Mexico. You can visit these amazing sites from Chetumal, which is on the Caribbean coast of Mexico. For more information, see: **www.mgharris.net/travel-mexico**

Time travel and the "multiverse" theory

Physicists can't agree whether time travel is theoretically possible at all, and if so, whether you could travel backwards as well as forwards in time. If it were possible, some have proposed that an attempt to travel backwards in time might take one to a parallel universe, where history diverged from the traveller's original history after the moment the traveller arrived in the past. When Josh first debates the possibility of time travel with Montoyo in *Ice Shock*, he makes the argument of mathematician Stephen Hawking: the lack of tourists from the future argues against the existence of time travel. But if the "multiverse" theory were also true, each time traveller might unwittingly create a new reality...

The Bracelet of Itzamna

One thing is certain – time travel would require massive amounts of power. In *The Joshua Files*, the Bracelet of Itzamna acts merely as a remote control device which communicates instructions to a fictional machine buried somewhere near Mount Tacana. This is the source of the tremendous power which folds space-time around the Bracelet-wearer and transports him or her through time.

Erinsi molecular security

In biochemistry, molecules bind to each other with incredible precision. It is possible to couple the energy of the binding reaction to an electrical current. In theory, you could use that current to open an electronic lock. Therefore, you could have objects activated only in contact with the molecules on a certain person's skin.

The Erinsi bio-defences

The lost, super-ancient Erinsi civilization of *The Joshua Files* also used molecular security to protect objects by releasing deadly toxins. These toxins act in horrible ways, blistering the skin, paralysing the nervous system, or in the case of the Ix toxin, causing all internal tissues to haemorrhage, in a way similar to the Ebola virus.

In the real world, there is an appropriate horror of weapons that have such effects. Biological and chemical weapons are restricted by the Geneva Protocol.

www.thejoshuafiles.com